JOHN EVERSON

THE HOUSE BY THE CEMETERY

This is a **FLAME TREE PRESS** book

Text copyright © 2018 John Everson

FLAME TREE PRESS
6 Melbray Mews, London, SW6 3NS, UK
flametreepress.com

Distribution and warehouse:
Marston Book Services Ltd
160 Eastern Avenue, Milton Park, Abingdon, Oxon, OX14 4SB
www.marston.co.uk

Publisher's Note: This is a work of fiction. Names, characters, places, and
incidents are a product of the author's imagination. Locales and public names
are sometimes used for atmospheric purposes. Any resemblance to actual people,
living or dead, or to businesses, companies, events, institutions, or locales is
completely coincidental.

Thanks to the Flame Tree Press team, including:
Taylor Bentley, Frances Bodiam, Federica Ciaravella, Don D'Auria,
Chris Herbert, Matteo Middlemiss, Josie Mitchell, Mike Spender,
Cat Taylor, Maria Tissot, Nick Wells, Gillian Whitaker.

The cover is created by Flame Tree Studio with
thanks to Nik Keevil and Shutterstock.com.
The font families in this book are Avenir and Bembo.

Flame Tree Press is an imprint of Flame Tree Publishing Ltd
flametreepublishing.com

A copy of the CIP data for this book is available from the British Library.

HB ISBN: 978-1-78758-002-2
PB ISBN: 978-1-78758-001-5
ebook ISBN: 978-1-78758-003-9
Also available in FLAME TREE AUDIO

Printed in the UK at Clays, Suffolk

JOHN EVERSON

THE HOUSE BY THE CEMETERY

FLAME TREE PRESS
London & New York

PROLOGUE

One Night in October

The floorboards creaked as Candace crossed the room.

Ominous.

She caught and held her breath, then kept walking slowly, one careful foot at a time. Tentatively. Just like the rest of the house, this room was mostly dark. She worried with every step that something would run across her bare toes. Why had she worn sandals? A muffled red light warmed the far wall near the baseboard. Maybe *warmed* was the wrong word. The light from the hidden lamp didn't warm, it *bled* up the wall from the floor. Nearby, just barely illuminated by the lamp, a woman lay prone, unmoving on a crimson velvet duvet. She wore a frilly white nightgown, which was spotted in dark splats. The reason was obvious.

Someone had slit the woman's throat. The murder weapon lay nearby on the floor, the knife's silver blade coated in dark red. A spray of blood bled down the wall beside her in visual opposition to the light that bled up the wall. It was a study in opposites...the only constant was the colour.

Red.

She could see it everywhere. Pools on the floor. Spots on the walls. The room was dripping in red.

Candace shivered. What had happened here?

The house was disturbing as hell. They'd gotten that part right.

Something tapped her shoulder. Candace jumped.

"Boo!"

Sara and Briana stood behind her grinning.

"What the hell!" Candace said. "Don't *do* that."

"Isn't this place awesome?" Sara asked.

"There's so much blood," Candace whispered.

"That's what makes it awesome," Briana said. "And they got the colour right too; it doesn't just look like red paint."

Candace shivered. "It's horrible," she said.

Sara laughed. "Scaredy cat. Don't you want to reach out and touch someone? Like the witch?" She pointed at the bloody body lying by the door.

"No," Candace said. "It looks too real."

"Maybe it *is* real," Briana said. Her hands gestured dramatically. "You've heard the stories. Maybe this really *is* a slaughterhouse, and the whole haunted house thing is just a cover. Can you guess what's *really* going on down those creepy stairs in the basement?"

"You guys are mean," Candace said.

"You think so?" Briana said. A wicked smile stole across her face. "How about if we let you finish the house on your own? That way you'll get the full effect!"

"No," Candace said. Her voice took on a note of panic. "You wouldn't do that to me."

Sara grabbed Briana's hand and pulled her past the dead body and through the door into whatever horrors the next room held. "Sure, we would," her voice echoed.

Candace raced after, but they were already gone from the next room when she passed through the threshold...and she didn't know which way they'd gone. This room offered two choices of exit. A sign rested crookedly on the wall with an arrow pointing at the stairs leading down and out of sight. 'Don't Go In The Basement,' it read. The words looked as if they'd been painted freehand, in blood, with a very wet brush. A figure dressed in a black cape and holding a long scythe detached itself from the wall near the basement stairs and began moving towards her.

A second staircase was on the other side of the room, but this set of steps led up. It too was flanked by a sign with drippy red letters, this one reading simply 'Exit'.

Candace debated between the two. But only for a moment, as the reaper was between her and the stairs leading down. She began climbing the stairs leading up. 'Exit' was exactly what she wanted at this point.

The room at the top was strangely bare. The first thing she saw was the raw plank ceiling, with the beam crossing the room to form the centre of the peak's A frame. The next thing she saw was the rope tied to that beam. It ended in a hangman's noose just a few feet from the floor. The loop at the end was swaying slightly.

Candace shivered. At least there wasn't a body hanging from it. But why was it moving?

Something creaked to her left. The hair stood up on the back of her neck. Candace turned to look, but saw nothing. There was an old bureau there, with an oval mirror attached above it. The mirror was cracked. And it blocked her view of whatever was in the narrow end of the room beyond. Probably someone in costume waiting to jump out at her. In a rare moment of bravery, Candace decided to beat the haunted house people at their own game. She stepped around the dresser, prepared to confront someone in a gory ghoul mask.

There was nobody there.

The hair on the back of her neck began to tingle. The small space behind the dresser was a dead zone. A shuttered window marked the wall, but otherwise…the space was empty.

Candace walked to the window, and lifted the wooden shutter slats by an inch. The window looked out on the cemetery. Even in the dark, she could see the tombstones of Bachelor's Grove in silent rows below.

Something creaked again.

She dropped the shutter and started to turn.

But someone grabbed her shoulders and gripped them tight. She struggled, but couldn't turn.

"Wha—?" she began to cry.

And then a hand covered her mouth and yanked her whole body backwards.

Candace slapped and punched at her captor, but her hands couldn't make contact. The arms only tightened around her and dragged her off her feet.

Her upper body suddenly lowered. Her feet thumped down a few inches, and then her head was below the level of her toes.

She stopped struggling then and finally understood what was going on. There was a hole in the floor.

Or rather…a trapdoor.

That had been the creaking sound she'd heard. Someone coming up and through the door.

She had figured out one piece of this puzzle, but it was too late to matter.

Candace tried to scream as her head dropped down another stair below the level of the floor. A moment later, her feet dragged afterward, cracking painfully down the steps to follow her.

Her heels bounced off wood at least eight or ten times, and then the thumping stopped, and she was dragged across a floor.

She should not have walked around the bureau. Because now she had literally disappeared behind it. Maybe forever. This couldn't be part of the haunted house attraction gimmick.

Something cold touched her wrist, and then clicked. The hands abandoned her for a moment, and Candace twisted her body until she could see the chain that now locked her to an old steel bedframe. A few feet away, she heard the creaking sound again.

The trapdoor had lowered once again.

Nobody above would have any idea where she'd gone. If Briana and Sara came back to look for her, they wouldn't find a clue.

Candace opened her mouth to scream, but almost as soon as she made a sound, a hand closed solidly over her lips. The hand was cool and firm.

Her captor whispered softly.

"Shhhhhhhh."

PART ONE
THE HOUSE

CHAPTER ONE

June 23rd

"But the place is already haunted," Mike Kostner said. He shook his head and gave Perry the eye. "You want to haunt a *haunted* house?"

"That's the beauty of it," Perry said. "Half the work has already been done. We just need you to go in and put down some planks. Shore up some walls. Make sure nobody's going to fall through the floor."

Mike lifted a pint and downed a couple gulps. Stalling. Then he looked at Perry. "You don't really believe that, do you? That place hasn't had anyone living in it for fifty years. Probably more. You'd be better off knocking it down and building a new place from scratch. Actually, you'd be better off renting the space of the old Dominick's grocery store on Cicero and just setting up your haunted house there."

Perry shook his head. "We don't want to be like the Jaycees! A dead Dominick's ain't no Bachelor's Grove. You know that. C'mon. We've got access to an old cemetery in the woods, with an old spooky house behind it. And stories…lots of stories. Everyone in Cook County knows the place is supposedly haunted. Hell, everyone in Illinois who has ever heard of the place knows it. That's the beauty of this – most of the marketing is already done. People have heard ghost stories about Bachelor's Grove since they were kids. When word gets out that we're letting people into that old locked-up shack hidden back in those woods? That the police have kept under guard with chains? People will flock to this on Halloween! The place has been under lock-and-key for decades."

Mike nodded. "There's a reason for that."

"Rumours," Perry said.

Mike shook his head. "People died there. People are buried there. It's next to a cemetery!"

Perry shrugged. "People are buried everywhere. They don't come back. I don't care what the ghost stories say. They've had chains on that place because of a bunch of drug-smoking Satan worshippers who vandalised the place. That's all."

"It just seems wrong, man," Mike said. He picked up his beer, and moved the level down another inch. When he set it down, he looked at Perry. The other man had been his friend for more than ten years, since they'd met at Mike's ex-wife's sister's wedding. But Perry wore a suit, while, at his best, Mike wore jeans and a t-shirt. Even now, sitting at a sticky black round table at The Edge, a shithole shot-and-a-beer bar frequented by Zeppelin and Journey cover bands on the weekends, Perry was wearing a white shirt and tie. And Perry talked to Mia, Mike's ex, a lot more than Mike did.

"It's not wrong," Perry said. "It's business." The other man ran a hand across his balding dome, reminding Mike that when they'd first met, Perry had had a full head of blond hair. Now…he had a dome and a paunch. Things change. Kind of like Mike's marriage. Mike had kept building houses, and while he did, Mia had kept checking out other houses. In particular, the beds in those houses. That had been the sticking point for Mike.

"Look," Mike said, "I don't know what you did to bankroll this, but it just seems like a bad idea. I mean…Bachelor's Grove…they've talked about that place since I was a kid. People see ghosts out on the boulevard. I just don't think—"

Perry held up his hand. "Mike, seriously. When was the last time you had a gig? Three weeks? Four?"

Mike shook his head. "I had a roofing job last week."

"For a day?"

Mike shrugged. "Two."

Perry levelled two iron-grey eyebrows. "And what do you have lined up for this week?"

"It's Thursday."

"Okay, next week?"

Mike deflated. He said nothing. What could he say? He was a carpenter in prime season, and he'd only worked a handful of days in the past three weeks. His bank account was currently looking a lot smaller than the rent on his apartment.

Perry nodded. "That's what I'm talking about." He put his hand over the opening at the top of Mike's pint just as Mike was about to lift it.

"Look," Perry said. "You've had some bad luck. I get it. But not everybody does. You do this, and things could turn around. This is a good gig. We sold the county on a sweet deal here. They spend thousands every year trying to keep people out of that cemetery in October. Now instead of bleeding money, they can make a profit on the place. We'll fix it up, open it as a haunted house, and they get a percentage of the ticket price. If you're a part of this…there are a lot of jobs that the county could reference you on. This could put you back on the five days a week circuit instead of five days a month. I'm telling you."

Mike pulled his glass out from under Perry's hand. "I don't know," he said.

"All we need you to do is reinforce the floors and the staircases," Perry explained. "Some of it needs to be torn out, but we've already had it inspected and I think we can save a lot of the surface stuff that looks old and creepy. You'll be building a lot of new support underneath. Redo the entry, and probably build a couple room dividers once the decorators have a traffic plan."

"It's going to be a black hole," Mike said. "That place is probably ready to sink into the earth just like the coffins around it."

"What else do you have lined up this month?" Perry countered.

A tall lanky guy got up on stage at that moment and plugged in his guitar. A moment later his fingers were walking across the strings and the half-empty bar filled with steel arpeggios. The guy wasn't bad. But he was clearly a wannabe Eddie Van Halen.

Mike could sympathise. He felt like a wannabe carpenter lately.

Perry was looking at him expectantly. Mike shrugged. Noncommittal.

"This is your ticket back," Perry said. He grabbed Mike's shoulder and squeezed. "You do this, and the county makes money this fall…and you will be working again. All the time. I promise you."

Mike rolled his eyes.

"Again, what else do you have lined up this month?"

"When would I start?" Mike asked.

"Monday," Perry said. "We need the structural work done by the end of August so there's time for the artists to come in and decorate the place."

"Decorate how?"

The guitar player behind them held one note – and the guitar – high in the air. Mike put one hand over his left ear.

"Like a haunted house?" Perry said. He reached across the table and cuffed Mike. "What do you think?"

"Why don't they just leave it exactly the way it is?" Mike said. "Like you say, it's creepy and haunted now. You don't need me to do anything."

"One word: lawsuits." Perry shook his head. "You go in there and make sure people don't fall through the rotten floors. I'll make sure this thing becomes the best haunted house attraction in the state this fall. It will all be good."

"Two words back atcha," Mike said. "*Haunted* house. As in...already!"

Perry shrugged. "Two more words: Ticket sales." He paused, and looked hard at Mike. "And you pay your rent."

Mike bowed his head and stared at the half-empty glass.

"What time on Monday?"

CHAPTER TWO

Monday morning came fast. And when it did...Mike wasn't ready. He wanted to be. He'd *tried* to be. He'd loaded the truck over the weekend, putting anything onboard he could think that he might need. But the reality was, until he got into the place and really scoped it out...who could say?

Plus, Sunday had run wrong...lonely. And consequently, he'd had one too many beers again. The truth was, his head hurt, his lower back ached, and he really didn't want to be here.

The sun was still low in the sky and there was a fuzzy haze along the top of the grass when he followed the gravel path that led from Midlothian Turnpike down and into the cemetery grounds. His shoulders shivered slightly with the chill in the morning fog as he walked past the stand of silent gravestones. There honestly weren't many at this point...the place had only been a small community cemetery from the last century, after all, and some of the stones had fallen over, while others had been vandalised or removed. There was a reason the police had put chains up across the forest preserve fencing to protect what remained of this place.

It was somewhat hidden. And largely abandoned. A sad place.

And thus...ripe for abuse. Mike had heard that Satan worshippers had been run out of here on more than one occasion. There were all sorts of stories about black masses and witchcraft.

Whatever had happened before, on this particular July morning, it was just an empty and kind of forlorn clearing that he saw on an otherwise quiet morning. Behind him the echo of cars whizzed by on the asphalt. But step by step as he approached the old house...that sound receded. Ahead, there were wisps of fog rolling off the ground. And as he rounded a bend in the path, the roof of the old, abandoned cemetery farmhouse edged into view.

His summer project.

Mike walked until the full face of the old place was visible. And then he sighed. The arch of the roof lifted halfway into the tree line, and the black of the shingles was almost completely obscured in green moss. The place was sided in what was probably cedar, but whatever rustic allure it had once had, today it just looked grey, rotted and warped. There were obvious dark holes in the wood, and one of the window frames hung down in a twisted L in front of the dirty glass.

He didn't want to look inside.

But not only was he going to look inside…over the next few weeks he was going to gut the place.

His head hurt at the thought.

The porch sank, its wood spongy, as he walked up its two steps, and he mentally made a note of it. *Replace porch.* Probably the easiest repair he'd be doing here over the next couple months. He turned the key in the padlock that held the warped door closed, and took a deep breath as it creaked open ahead of him.

The sun didn't want to enter there.

He didn't want to either.

"I never wanted it to come to this," Mike said, as he stood in the door of the old house.

Thankfully, nobody answered. For a heartbeat, he'd worried someone might. But then he took a breath and stepped inside.

The front foyer was half-covered in yellowed linoleum. But there was a hole in the middle of it, where some animal had gnawed its way through the floor. Whether it had been digging into the basement below or digging its way out, he couldn't tell.

Either way, it was just one of many repairs he'd have to add to his list. First thing, was to make the list.

Perry had said that structurally the place was solid, and just needed a month or so of touch-up work, but Mike wasn't going to be responsible for people falling through the floor. Or a floor collapsing. He had his list from Perry of things their structural engineer had noted, but Mike was going to do his own assessment. And the first way to begin was 'the stomp test'.

Mike walked past the hole in the linoleum and stamped his foot down on the dusty, colourless wood that he assumed was probably maple or oak. It was impossible to tell with the grime, but that would have made sense in this area. That's what grew in the forest; that's what people had worked with a hundred years ago when the first settlement had populated this area and started to bury their dead around the small pond now known as Bachelor's Grove.

He stepped around the hole in the foyer and walked slowly into the front room. It was quiet here…eerily quiet, with the occasional hum of the road and the buzz of insects suddenly blotted out. The morning sun fought through dirty windows layered by years and years of spiderwebs and bug carcasses. He was in a different space here.

A sacred space, his mind suggested.

"A dusty place," he whispered aloud. As he walked, the dirt moved from the floor to the air in lazy currents of filth.

Mike walked around the corner. Once there had probably been a formal table and chairs in the shadowed space beyond. He could still see the dark shadows and holes where sconces had been mounted to the walls. But now…all that remained were holes…. And yellowed, faded wallpaper that had curled back from the seams at some points.

The dark plank floors might once have been varnished and shiny. Now…they were simply dark. And stained. Any beauty they once held lost in dust and neglect.

Mike retraced his steps to the hallway. The wood had creaked beneath his weight, but had not sagged. Surprising, but good.

Then he stepped through the door across the hall and into the kitchen.

"Oh shit," he said.

The wood floor suddenly turned to tile, and the tile, stained and yellowed…eventually gave way to a ragged hole in the middle of the room. There was a dark trail from the cabinets near the sink to a low spot in the centre of the room that had apparently rotted through. He guessed that the water lines had been left on long after the last occupants had moved away. Or been buried out back.

"Well," Mike said. "There's one week."

He knelt down at the edge of the rotten wood and looked through the floor into the basement below.

"And there's another," he said.

The basement was a mud pit, with furrows and troughs in the bare earth where puddles of stagnant water gathered. The thick smell of rot and mildew rose up through the hole.

"Remember, you don't need to make it livable," Perry had said. "Just give us some floors, shore up the staircases and reinforce the beams in the basement. We want to make that into a crypt."

Mike stood up and shook his head. The crypt part was going to be easy.

"Well...first things first," he said. "We need to air this place out. It reeks."

He walked over to the window above the sink and after mopping away six inches of grey web with the back of his work glove, tried to lift it. A dozen spiders scurried out of the heavily webbed upper corners as the old wood creaked. But the window didn't budge upwards.

"That figures," he murmured. He tried the front room window, which looked out on the porch. It shifted up a few centimetres at his push, and then stuck fast.

"No, sorry, that's not acceptable," Mike said, and reached into his portable tool bag for a small crowbar. "I'm not working in this stink all day."

The wood at the base splintered...but a minute later the window slid up the warped track and the morning air rushed over the sill.

"Better," he pronounced.

He walked around the rest of the main floor, and jimmied a handful of other windows open. The stale, mildewed stench of the house began to give way to the scent of the summer breeze.

Then he put his foot on the first step of the stairwell leading upstairs. Perry had mentioned that there was an attic suite that they had plans to use. Mike was apprehensive that the flooring would be dry-rotted...if not wet-rotted from holes in the roof. But he'd seen no signs on the first floor of black spots on the ceilings, so maybe the roof had somehow maintained integrity.

He put his weight down on the first dark-stained step, and when it didn't give, he gave it a good stomp. When nothing bad happened, he did the same to the next. And the next. There were 13 in all. When he stomped past the last one, he let out a sigh of relief. Then he looked around.

The attic room was long – it was a single open space that extended across the whole length of the house. The sun shone in through one dirty window at the far end, and dust motes swam in the murky light that filtered through. The ceiling wasn't finished; instead, when you looked up you saw the support beams and the actual upside-down V arch of the roof itself.

The room still held the remnants of its last occupant; a yellowed mattress rotted atop a bedspring to his right. Grey chunks of the bed's stuffing lay in clumps all around the bed frame, hanging from holes in the side of the mattress fabric; obviously humans hadn't been the last creatures to sleep in this bed. A night table with an old wooden lamp on top flanked the bed. On the other side, a stack of old brown boxes leaned away from the wall; the topmost box had long ago given way and toppled to the floor; its contents – a mix of books and papers – lay spread across the wood plank floor.

A tall bureau stood to Mike's left, blocking part of the light from one of the attic's two windows. But the light from that window was still enough to expose how long it had been since anyone had lived in this room. The dust on top of the dresser was so thick that if he hadn't been able to see the side, he couldn't have told the colour of the wood.

Mike looked up at the wood arch of the ceiling and followed the beams to the edges. There were some dark areas in spots near the edges, especially in the northeast corner, but otherwise, the roof appeared sound. Hard to believe, but that would explain why the rest of the place hadn't rotted into the dirt. He walked back and forth across the planks, testing the give. While there were some creaks, nothing felt soft. He shrugged. Maybe Perry and his engineer were right after all. If he just had to shore up the main floor, add support to the basement beams and drop some planks across the mud down there...that would be all right with him.

Speaking of which...while he'd seen the basement through the hole in the kitchen floor, he realised he hadn't actually seen the stairs to get down there. Mike walked back down the stairs and circled the walkway on the main floor. He poked his head into two empty bedrooms there, and a bath between them with a yellowed tub and black and white granny-tile floor that looked like a power wash with bleach was in order. He opened two hallway doors and found a couple musty closets, but did not find the stairway down.

What the hell?

Mike walked outside. Maybe the only entry to the basement was exterior? Odd, but this *was* a really old house.

The sun had risen higher since he'd first stepped inside the place, and the fog had already burned away from the clearing. It was going to be hot today; the air smelled fresh, but pregnant with summer humidity. Great. He had a headache, he was going to be working in a stinking wreck of a rot-heap, and it was going to be 90 degrees. And he couldn't find the damn basement.

This week was starting out great.

He took a walk around the perimeter of the place. Once you passed the old rotten wood of the porch and turned the corner, the lower five feet of the house was obscured by scrub bushes and grass. He waded through the tall grass, sticking as close to the stone base of the old house as possible. When he hit the back, the grass began to thin as the tree cover took over. The entire rear section of the house was shaded by the tree line of the forest. He saw the entry he was looking for almost immediately. Stone steps that led down below the ground.

Mike stepped down the old stairway half hidden by a thick cover of leaves.

"The door is not going to open," he said aloud. But he reached a hand out to the old rusty knob anyway.

And damned if the thing didn't turn.

"How about that?" Mike said, and pushed the thing open. It gave a stubborn creak as it dragged along the sandy earth floor.

Inside, the place smelled dank and dead. The ceiling was barely above the top of his head, and Mike ducked beneath beams that dropped lower to support pipes from above. Everything in front of him was black as night, no windows. He pulled a flashlight from his pocket and shone it around.

The earth dipped in places where water obviously sat sometimes after a storm. And as he moved inside, he could see the one spot of light on the mud, streaming in where the floor had given way above in the kitchen.

"All right...so there's a bearing," he said, orienting himself.

Mike scoped the whole basement out. Perry said he wanted to put down a plank floor and lead people through here...but if they were going to do that, Mike needed to drop a stairway down; it had to be part of the walk through the house – you couldn't send people outside to find the basement!

But then, in the far corner, he finally saw it.

A set of plank stairs leading up. He walked over and stepped on the first stair.

And with a spongy snap, the stair broke in half.

The second one sagged when he put weight on it, and he stepped back down before it gave way. There was a wooden doorway perched at the top of the greying, rotting steps.

"Okay," he said to himself. "These go up somewhere...but where?"

He used the pipes beneath the kitchen and bathroom as a guide, and tried to figure out where the stairs had to open, based on his brief survey of the house above.

He shook his head. It seemed like the door should come out right where the den had been.

Mike made his way back out of the dark pit that was the basement, and breathed an unconscious sigh of relief when he made it back up the steps outside.

He stood at the top of the stairwell, studying the century-old stone and wood facade that stretched up and away into the tree-hidden sky.

Something tapped him on the shoulder.

"So, what do you think?" a voice asked from behind him.

Mike nearly jumped out of his skin.

"Perry?" he said, turning to face his friend. "Don't ever fuckin' do that to me again!"

Perry stood there in the grass, incongruous in his standard grey suit and blue-striped tie, grinning from ear to ear.

"Scared of an old haunted house?" Perry asked. "We ain't even decorated it yet!"

"Bastard," Mike said, and shook his head.

"Listen, I can't stay," Perry said, still grinning. "But I wanted to stop by and see what you thought of the place."

"It's a pit," Mike said.

"But you can fix it?"

He shrugged. "Yeah, enough for what you want, sure. I don't think anyone's going to want to live here again, though."

Perry nodded. "That's what I wanted to hear. Let me know if you need anything. Besides wood." Perry laughed.

Mike rolled his eyes. "I'll need plenty of that."

"I thought you had plenty of that," his friend said. "That's what you always tell me when you're drunk."

"Go to work, Perry," Mike said.

"Not before we talk through the job," Perry said. He pointed at the front of the old house. "Take a walk with me?"

Mike nodded, and a minute later, they were inside, stepping through the debris as Perry pointed out the repairs he wanted to make sure Mike made. His head swam as Perry pointed out walls to be re-drywalled, and floors to be re-surfaced. At the end of the day, his friend/boss really wanted him to re-face the whole place. The Halloween decorators would be making it look creepy, not the naturally decrepit vibe of the old, ageing materials that were here. Mike would really be building a 'pathway' through the decay. A frame amid the ruin to hold their pretend decay.

After Perry had finished going on about how amazing this place was going to be and returned to his car, Mike walked back inside the old place.

He'd almost forgotten his foray into the basement until he stepped into the den at the back of the house. And then...he walked the perimeter of the empty room. Where the hell was that stairway door? It had to be here somewhere. Perry had talked so fast and furious, he'd never even brought up the question of the 'crypt'.

Mike returned to the hallway and tried the closet doors there, following it back to the family room.

He shook his head. Nope. The stairway just did not exist. Never mind that he'd seen it, along with a door...but still, it didn't exist.

"All an illusion," he murmured.

But he'd seen the evidence. And it all pointed...

Mike walked back into the den and looked harder. The room was empty, sure, but that was empty of furniture. It was not, however, simply four blank walls and a floor. There was a closet and chair rail trim and a fireplace built into one wall. He walked across the long room and opened the creaking closet door...that led to nowhere. And then turned and looked at the old wooden bookcases built into the walls next to the fireplace.

With his fist he knocked on the back wall of one of the bookcases. The echo that came back was empty, and Mike nodded.

The case might look solid, but it wasn't a permanent part of the wall.

With his hands, he began to take down the old shelves to search for the creases he knew had to be there. He was going to have to find a way to pull at least one of these cases away from the wall they guarded.

The basement was hidden from the main part of the house...and the entry had to be hidden here. He was convinced.

He traced the outline of the bookcase carefully, finding both loose shelves and solid, immovable ones. When the second shelf on the far right segment shifted at his touch, Mike didn't hesitate to lift it.

That's when things got interesting.

The back wood of the case suddenly moved away from his hand with a creak. The shelf was actually a latch, and the back of the bookcase was really a hidden door, which now hung open.

"Seriously?" he whispered. "The fucking haunted house has a hidden door?"

He punched the thing open and lifted the lower shelf so he could step through into the small hidden room beyond. He still had his flashlight from walking the basement, and he flicked it on. The space was windowless and small, and the décor didn't help make it feel any more expansive. The walls were all painted jet black, and the harsh white of what looked like bones littered the dark floor.

He reached down and picked one up. There were three teeth sticking out of it. A jawbone! He dropped it back to the floor.

"Holy shit," he whispered.

In the centre of the floor was a symbol he recognised from horror movies. A circle painted in white on the dark wood...a five-point star traced in the middle. More white bones were stacked in the dead centre of the circle. Dark smears of something old and previously wet marred the floor.

Blood.

And bones. In the middle of....

A witch's sign.

What kind of demonic rituals had gone on here?

"Damnit," Mike whispered. "I asked him, why haunt a place that's already haunted? Seriously."

He walked across the circle, and found the thing he'd been looking for on the other side.

A wooden frame.

A door. He turned the handle, and confirmed his suspicion almost instantly. It opened onto the rotted stairs that led down to the basement.

But why was this room hidden from the interior by a bookcase?

And who had been performing rituals there in the witch's circle?

CHAPTER THREE

Bong-Soon Mon walked up the broken sidewalk in front of Jeanie's house lost in thought. The day had not gone quite as planned; he'd been working overtime all week to try to finish a coding project and he'd hoped to have it completed by the weekend. But now he was going to be spending the next two days wondering why the Quality Assurance test failed. On any other night, he would have stayed until he'd figured a way to address the critiques, whether it took 'til eight p.m. or two a.m. But tonight, he and Jeanie had a date.

He rang the yellowed doorbell next to her beat-up old screen door and waited. She had told him in the past to just walk right in if the door was open, but he still felt funny about barging into someone else's place. So, he waited. And then rang the bell again. He knew that she was in there or the inner wooden door wouldn't be open.

Something crashed inside. It sounded like glass breaking.

"Jeanie?" he called through the screen.

He was answered a second later by a blood-curdling scream.

Bong no longer worried about being invited to enter. He threw the screen door open and charged inside. "Jeanie?" he called once more as he crossed the rug in the foyer.

The scream came again, and this time he knew for sure that the anguished sound came from his girlfriend. But before he could do anything, a second later she appeared, running around the corner from the hallway to the back bedrooms. Her face was covered in blood – she looked badly cut – as if someone had slashed her with a knife. A slab of her cheek dangled away from her head near her chin. The whole right side of her face was glistening and wet, and he could see the white of her teeth through the hole where there had been perfectly smooth flesh when he'd seen her last night.

"Bong!" she shrieked, and ran to his arms.

"Oh my God," he cried as she grabbed him. "What happened? Who did this to you? Is there someone else here?" He had a vision of a knife-wielding maniac turning the corner and coming at them any second now.

She sobbed in his arms and he hugged her tighter. Her back hitched up and down frantically and he wasn't sure if he should get her out of the house or call 911 first. Was somebody here? He needed to know what had happened.

"Jeanie," he said. "Please. Try to tell me what happened."

He could feel her sobs changing. Her back was vibrating faster, in fast panicked hitches and he gently pushed her away from his chest to see…

…that she wasn't sobbing at all.

"Gotcha," Jeanie cried. She threw her head back and let out a spurt of laughter that stopped her from speaking for a minute. When she finally regained control, she said, "Who did this to me? I did!" She fingered the flesh hanging from her face and with both hands pulled on it. It stretched like taffy.

"What do you think?" she said. "Pretty sick, huh?"

Bong pushed her away. "*You* are pretty sick," he said. "I can't believe you did that to me." His voice rose louder than he ever spoke. His words trembled with emotion. "I thought you were really hurt. You had me scared to death for a second."

"Then it worked," Jeanie said. "That's the best thing anyone has ever said to me!"

"That was mean," Bong said, shaking his head. He could feel his legs still trembling. "Really uncool."

Jeanie took his hand and pulled him closer to her again. "Oh, c'mon, don't be mad. I needed to see if I could pull this off before I apply."

Bong's brow wrinkled. "Apply for what?"

Jeanie grinned. "They're opening a haunted house this fall near Midlothian and they're auditioning for makeup people. I want to do it. You know I've always wanted to do horror makeup." She hung her head and made puppy-dog eyes at him.

They were disconcerting when she had a slab of flesh still hanging off her face. The juxtaposition of cuteness and gore almost made him laugh, and Bong couldn't help but grin. "You could totally get the makeup gig," he said. "But don't ever do that to me again."

"Cross my heart and hope to die," Jeanie said. She reached up and yanked on the fake slab of flesh. It separated from her cheek with a rubber-band effect, slapping against the back of her hand.

"I won't ever do that again," she promised. "But…could you do one thing for me?"

Bong raised an eyebrow. "Maybe. It depends."

"C'mon," she said. "I said I'd be good."

"Yeah, but you didn't say what you wanted me to do."

"I need someone to practise on. It's hard to do good zombie effects on yourself. This took forever."

"I don't know," he said. "What do I get in return?"

Jeanie pressed her hips hard to his and licked the tip of his lips. "I can think of a few things."

"Hmmm…." he said. His voice betrayed his interest. Jeanie didn't waste the moment.

"I signed up for an audition on Thursday," she said. "So, I really do need to practise. Could we stay in tonight?"

Bong thought of the potential payoff at the end of the night, and decided that a couple hours in the makeup chair would probably be worth it. Jeanie could be on fire when she was in the mood.

"Okay," he sighed. "Whatever you want."

She smiled. Kind of a weird smile, since she had painted teeth on her cheek. It was like he could see her whole jaw through half her face.

"But you have to wipe that makeup off first," he said. "It's too creepy to look at you that way."

"I can do that," she agreed. "By the way, what are you doing on Thursday?"

"Why?" he asked.

"I need to show off my work so I get the job, silly. That means you get to come with me to the audition."

Jeanie grabbed his hand and dragged him down the hallway towards the bathroom.

Bong kept up a smile, anticipating the 'payoff' to come later. But inside…he was groaning.

CHAPTER FOUR

There were now piles of 2x4s, fresh pine flooring planks and some crossbeams next to the abandoned house near the cemetery, which wasn't looking quite so abandoned anymore. Mike's friend Aaron had helped him lug the wood down here after filling up the back of a pickup truck at Home Depot, and now Mike would be spending the next few weeks installing it all. With what Perry was paying, he couldn't afford to pay for help to put it in, but he couldn't have gotten it all down here from the turnpike on his own.

For a little while, during the load-in, this gig had felt great. He was working again. Something was happening. He'd make rent again this month.

But now, as he stood in the overgrown clearing, in front of a dilapidated old house, half-obscured by trees…he felt lost. Lonely. Isolated.

Mike was completely on his own, both here and at home. It wasn't a feeling he enjoyed. Though it was one that he'd been forced to get used to since Mia had walked out last Christmas.

He started to whistle, some new pop song he'd heard on the radio just now on the drive over. But that whistle died out, quickly. It sounded false here. He felt as if he was intruding. This place had stood as it was for decades without anyone living here. And now he was changing it.

Part of him felt as if the trees themselves were watching him. And disapproving.

Mike shook it away and took his hammer to the rotted boards that comprised the porch of the old house. He'd be going in and out of this place all summer, so he might as well make sure he was not going to break a leg while doing it. So rebuilding the entryway came first.

It was also somehow comforting to be working for a while outside the house, rather than in, where every sound echoed. Where the air smelled of age. And forgotten history. Unseen death. Hidden witchcraft.

When he'd called Perry to tell him about the hidden room, his friend had assured him that whatever witchcraft or devil worship had gone on in the house had happened and stopped long ago. "No worries," Perry had said. "That shit's from like, the '60s and '70s when the teenagers and weirdos got in there. That's when all those gravestones were knocked over, and that's why the police have protected the place all these years. Keep that riff raff out."

And then Perry had laughed. "Now we're going to invite the riff raff in! Hey, make sure you open that back wall to the hidden room in the hallway, so that we can have easy access to the stairs to the basement. I don't know that we'll want people going through the bookcase in the den to get there…though you never know."

Mike wedged a crowbar between a sagging grey plank and the post that supported it, and with one long creak, the board separated and popped. Perry's story of devil worshippers hanging out in the cemetery and the house kept coming back to him. He imagined women with black capes and long silver blades walking in and out across these boards, with God knows what victims waiting in fear in the secret room inside….

He shook the thoughts away, and pulled the board free. It was just the first of many boards quickly lifted and thrown aside. In just over an hour, he'd stripped all of the surface wood, and piled it up in the long grass nearby. Most of the surface planks had come off easily; some crumbled to pieces instantly at the first prod of the crowbar. The side posts, amazingly, still seemed solid enough. He decided to simply reinforce them with new inner boards and use them, rather than replace, which would save a couple days. He pushed against a couple and they didn't move much.

Mike shrugged. A couple crossbeams on those, and the new deck would easily support throngs of people stomping up his new stairs and walking into the house of horrors that was about to be constructed. He couldn't rationalise spending any more time out here. He began to measure and mark and cut. Board by board, the new entryway to the house was born. When Mike was 'on', he was good. By four o'clock, he was done with the new deck to the old house. He could have improved its footprint and built a longer deck, but that wasn't the mission. People only needed to line up and get in the front door. And now it was time to get past that. Because the easy work was done. Mike had to go inside the house. Where the bugs lived.

Where the rot awaited.

Where, according to the stories, a witch once lived.

Mike stepped across the new porch and nodded. It felt good.

Solid.

Then he opened the door and stepped into the foyer. The sunlight slipped away and the temperature dropped about ten degrees. Part of him whispered that this wasn't simply because the house was holding the cool air still from overnight. He remembered the things in the room behind the bookcase. Bad shit had happened here. Of that, he had no doubt.

He walked down the hall and looked again at the hole in the kitchen floor. He frowned. He should probably start on this room next. Cure the obvious structural problems and stop any critters from climbing up from the basement.

Something creaked upstairs. Almost like a door opening.

The hairs on the back of his neck stood up. He swore he heard footsteps above his head.

Mike cocked his head to listen closer. They couldn't be footsteps. But...it could be an animal. Maybe a raccoon had come through the roof. "Shit," he whispered. Something creaked up there again, and his vision of a raccoon sniffing around evaporated. That didn't sound like an animal.

He took a deep breath and then quietly stepped out on the new deck to grab his crowbar. He wasn't going upstairs without something to swing. No matter what it was. Mike took the stairs slowly, one at a time. He tried not to make them creak and give away his presence. Of course, the steady pounding outside for the last few hours should have done that handily anyway.

Still.

Mike reached the seventh and then eighth step. He realised he was holding his breath. His head poked above the floor of the attic, and he raised the crowbar, ready to strike, not sure what to expect. He stepped quickly through the threshold.

The room was empty.

He looked across from the dusty bureau to the boxes stacked on the other side, and watched the dust motes lazily cascade through the air in the beam of sunlight that streamed in through the small attic window.

He let go of his breath, slowly. Then he stepped onto the old plank floor. The wood creaked, and he looked back and forth across the expanse of the attic. He couldn't see anything but old boxes and chests. He walked down the centre of the space, holding the crowbar at the ready, in case something jumped out from behind a box. Something fast. With teeth.

Nothing did.

He walked back and forth twice, to convince himself that there was nothing here.

He returned to the stairwell, and then passed it to walk just beyond the old bureau. There was just a small space behind it, but he looked.

Nothing.

Mike shrugged. Maybe there was an animal in the eaves somewhere. He could push Perry to have someone deal with that. All he needed to worry about was carpentry on the inside of the old house. Not pest removal.

He returned to the stairs, and was just about to step down them when a glimmer on the floor caught his eye. He must have stepped right over it on the way up.

He bent down and picked up a silver chain with a small locket in the shape of a heart attached.

Weird that he hadn't seen it before.

He opened the clasp on the locket and saw a black and white photo of a young woman's face, faded almost beyond recognition. Mike shrugged and thumbed it closed before slipping it into his jeans pocket. Then he descended the stairs, looking frequently over his shoulder.

Something just didn't feel right.

When he turned away from the last step at the bottom of the stairs, someone spoke.

"Hi there," a cool, girlish voice said.

Mike nearly jumped out of his skin. She stood just to the left of the old stairway. A slim young woman with dark black hair, deep brown eyes and an obvious spark of energy that could melt the shield of a blizzard. Her smile made his lips shift.

"Um…hey," he answered.

There was another woman, he belatedly realised, standing behind her. This one could have been a case study in opposites; she was heavyset, with long, tangled brown hair. Her face looked lifeless. No energy. Even her eyes were dull. She was the epitome of a wallflower; she seemed to literally blend into the background.

"What are you doing here?" Mike asked the first girl, stumbling over his tongue. She might be cute…but she didn't belong here. This was a construction site. He wanted to be firm, but his voice didn't carry the stick.

She didn't seem to notice his discomfort. "I just wanted to see what it was like," she said. "I heard you were going to turn this into a haunted house for Halloween."

Mike nodded. "That's the plan."

"So…where will you put the dead bodies?" she asked. She put a hand up to her face to stifle the snort.

"They won't really be dead," Mike said.

"Ahh," she answered. "They won't?"

"No one ever really dies," he said.

"Well," she said. "I don't know about *that*."

She pulled a long silver blade from the back of her shorts. "When something like this goes in…it doesn't usually come out the same way."

Mike grinned…but it was a nervous grin. His grip on the crowbar tightened.

She laughed and tossed the blade at his feet. "Don't wet yourself," she said. "It's fake."

He picked it up and realised that yes, it was just a plastic toy.

"Isn't that the kind of thing you'll be using in here when the haunted house opens?" she asked. "Toy knives? I just picked it up on the side of the turnpike."

He dropped the knife back on the floor and looked at her with his sternest expression. "You shouldn't be here."

She laughed.

"No, *you* shouldn't be here," she said. "But we can work around that. I won't tell anyone."

Mike shrugged. "Um, I was hired to be here, so yes, I absolutely *should* be here," he said. "You, on the other hand, are definitely trespassing. But I guess it doesn't matter anyway – nobody cares much about this place outside of Halloween."

"Well, then it all works out," she said.

"I suppose it does," he said. "Who's your friend?"

"This is Emery," the girl said. "And I'm Katie."

He held out his hand. "I'm Mike," he said. "Glad to know you."

Katie nodded and squeezed his palm tight. Her touch gave him a shiver.

"You will be," she said. She sounded confident. It made him nervous.

He held out his hand to Emery, but she did not reciprocate. After a moment, he dropped his arm back to his side.

"You really shouldn't be in here," Mike said again. "It's dangerous."

She shrugged. "I wanted to see what the place was all about," she said. "I heard it's haunted."

Mike nodded. "It has a bad reputation," he said. "And I guess, this Halloween, we're only going to make it worse."

Katie grinned. "I like the sound of that."

Her friend didn't say anything.

Mike pointed towards the front door. "Sorry, but you guys really have got to go now."

Katie pouted and crossed her arms. She didn't budge.

"Seriously," Mike said. "I've got work to do here. I'm afraid you're going to have to wait until Halloween if you want to see this place."

"Do I have to wait until Halloween to have a beer with you?" Katie asked.

"Are you asking me out?" he said. His voice couldn't hide his incredulity.

Katie shrugged. "I don't know about *out*," she said. "But we could sit on that nice new porch you built."

"We could," he admitted. "But there are no tables or chairs. Or bartenders."

"All we need is beer," she said. "What've you got in there?" she pointed at the red cooler sitting at the entrance to the kitchen. Mike had honestly gotten so wrapped up in the porch, he'd forgotten he'd even brought it.

He nodded, walked over to it, and popped the lid. The thought of having a beer with this intriguing (and damned cute) woman made him suddenly reconsider doing any further work today. "Don't know how lowbrow your taste buds are," he said. He held up a can of Pabst Blue Ribbon.

Five minutes later the three of them were sitting on the new planks of the deck, staring at the dark grey wood of the ancient house. Mike emptied half of his first can in about three gulps. Emery followed his example, but Katie only seemed to toy with hers.

"What do you normally like to drink?" he asked.

She grinned, looking at him with those wide brown eyes. They melted him, instantly. "Whatever's handy," she said. As if to prove a point, she took a slug of PBR.

"Do you live around here?" he asked.

Katie shrugged. "Not far. You?"

He nodded. "I've got a place in Oak Forest."

"Girlfriend?" she asked.

He shook his head.

"Hey, we have something in common," Katie said. "Blissfully single!" She tapped her can to his. "Cheers!"

He drank. And quickly popped another. He didn't even look at the can. He couldn't take his eyes off the girl.

Katie said she was 23 and liked baseball. Emery answered a few questions, eventually admitting to being 26 and also single, but really didn't say much of anything, though he tried to politely draw her out now and then. When he mentioned movies or music or other potential interests, she just smiled and answered in monosyllabic shy yeses and nos. He eventually gave up trying to pull her into the conversation and just focused on Katie, who at some point popped him yet another beer, and sat with her hand on his thigh as the sun began to set. Eventually, when the words grew slurry and the belly painfully full, he excused himself to take a leak at the side of the house.

"What are you doing?" he chided himself, once he was alone again. "These girls can't be interested in you, but you're acting like a college kid."

He shook his head and zipped up, then took a deep breath before stepping back around the corner. He needed to wrap this up and head home. It was weird to realise, but he had to work again in the morning.

The girls were gone. The deck was empty, except for a bunch of empty beer cans that lay strewn about.

"Well, there ya go," he whispered, and then picked up the empties. He grabbed one that still felt full, from the spot where Katie had been sitting. He drained a few gulps into his mouth, and then upended the rest, throwing that and the other empty cans into his now-empty cooler.

The air felt like his head…warm and buzzy, with the hum of summer locusts.

It was getting dark, and time to get out of the cemetery. His eyes were swimming, and he already knew that there was a headache in store for the morning.

"Damnit," he mumbled, and looked once more inside the old house, before closing the place up, and walking back to his truck.

"I bet she wasn't twenty-three," he mumbled to himself, as he walked down the dark trail towards the turnpike. "Lucky if she was over eighteen. Probably just wanted free beer."

He shook his head and tossed the cooler in the back of the truck bed. "Gullible," he accused himself. "With a capital G."

He started the truck and signalled to pull out onto Midlothian Turnpike. There was almost no traffic, and a moment later, the truck lurched onto the road. But even as it did, he couldn't shake the feeling that someone was watching him.

Someone from the old house.

Maybe through that attic window.

He shivered and refused to look in the rearview mirror, focusing on the yellow lines in the centre of the road.

CHAPTER FIVE

"Seems like a strange place to hunt for ghosts," Ted said, slipping into the chair across from Jillie Melton.

"That's because I'm not hunting," Jillie said. She raised a paper cup with a large M on it and took a sip. "I do have a life when I'm not out with you at midnight, you know."

"Uh-huh," he said. "And that's why you're having breakfast in a McDonald's across from a cemetery."

"The cemetery has nothing to do with it," she said. "It's all about the hash browns." Jillie wrinkled one pale blond eyebrow and shook her head. "I am only here for fat."

"I hope you mean in the food," Ted said. "Because I don't think you're ever going to actually put on any. You're too twitchy to gain weight."

She laughed. "And you're too fond of burritos to lose any."

"Ouch," Ted said. "I'd be offended except…."

He reached into his bag and pulled out two breakfast burritos. And a hash brown.

"I'll take that if you're not eating it," she offered.

The idea that he wasn't eating it was somewhat ludicrous. Ted weighed in at over 220 pounds, while she might have just been able to nudge the scale over 130…if she rocked up and down on it.

"Listen," he said. "Are you doing anything right now?"

She shrugged. "Other than eating?"

"I have something I want to show you."

"You didn't just stumble on me here, did you?" she said.

He shook his head. "I saw your Facebook."

Jillie frowned. If he was stalking her to run her down….

"Okay," she said. "Care to tell me what?"

"It's at Bachelor's Grove," he said. Ted's eyebrows raised precipitously.

"Yeah…what about it?" she said. "We've recorded there a half dozen times."

He nodded so fast, the flesh of his jowls seemed to flap like wings. "I know," he said. "But I think.... Listen, I just think you need to see this."

"What?" she asked again, but he only shook his head.

"I'll take you there."

Jillie shoved a hash brown in her mouth and chewed, considering the expression on Ted's face. They'd worked together for a long time, both out of respect and love for what they did. They *believed*. Which was a lot more than could be said for most of the people who filed into buildings with crosses on top of them on Sundays.

Ted believed, just as she did. And he looked about ready to burst with whatever it was he had to say. But she knew he wasn't just going to give it up. She respected that he had a reason, and stuffed the rest of the hash brown into her mouth all at once. Before she finished chewing, she stood and mumbled, "Let's go then!"

Ted looked surprised, still working on his burrito, but he didn't hesitate. Two minutes later, they were driving in his car north on Harlem Avenue.

"You're kind of creeping me out now," Jillie said, as they sat at the stoplight of 143rd Street, waiting to turn left onto Midlothian Turnpike. The Bachelor's Grove Cemetery was just a few blocks away. She'd been there dozens of times over the years. It was one of the most celebrated 'haunted places' in Illinois, and so she'd taken her cameras and equipment there in daytime, at dusk, and at night. Ted had been there for most of those outings.

The light changed, and they finally moved down the turnpike, following an old rusted red Ford pickup. Jillie found herself leaning forward, mentally pushing the old vehicle down the road. And then finally Ted pulled over at the familiar bridge that presaged the entry to the old cemetery.

"I didn't want to just tell you this," he said, pulling the keys from the ignition. "You had to see it for yourself."

Jillie opened her door and stepped out onto the gravel. She heard the sounds of a saw echoing through the forest. And then the repetitive pound of a hammer.

"What's going on?" she said as Ted stepped around the bumper.

"Take a look," he said, and led the way down the gravel path past the cemetery. When they passed the stones and reached the clearing, she began to shake her head.

"No, no, no!" she said. "What are they doing?"

Ted made a face. "They're building a haunted house."

Jillie's eyes nearly popped out of her head. "They're doing *what*?"

"They are rehabbing the old Bremen House, and turning it into a haunted house for Halloween."

"But…they can't do that," she breathed. "This is county property. It's protected."

"Apparently the county felt otherwise," Ted said. "They've decided to sell tickets to the cemetery…and the house. I read about it in the *Daily Southtown* this morning. They're turning Bachelor's Grove into an attraction."

Jillie's face turned grim. "They can't," she said. "They mustn't. The souls that rest here…don't rest easy. You know…you've seen them."

He nodded.

"There is already too much anger here," she whispered. "You know what happened to those kids that broke into the house and woke the spirit of the witch. If they do this…."

"Something bad is going to happen, isn't it?" Ted asked.

She nodded. And then took a breath and steeled her jaw.

She began to march towards the house. "We have to stop it," she said, "before someone else dies."

CHAPTER SIX

Mike stopped swinging the hammer for a minute and just listened. The calls of forest birds filled the resulting silence. He waited a moment, then shrugged, and swung the tool again.

And again he heard the sound that had stopped him before.

A scuttling. He pressed his ear to the wall and listened.

And this time he heard it. Feet moving. It had to be feet, right? Something inside the wall was shuffling across the boards.

Mike shook his head. Just what he needed. He had visions of punching through a wall to find a raccoon family enraged and ready to pounce.

"I'm a carpenter, not an exterminator, Jim," he murmured.

Something in the wall thumped, right near his face.

Mike jumped back, shaking his head. "Not what I signed up for," he complained.

He moved a few feet to the right. Maybe if he put the braces up elsewhere, whatever was in the walls would move away. Maybe he'd trapped it in the space he had been working in.

He raised the hammer to start a new anchor 2x4. Before he could hit the wood, something slammed against it from the other side. Right where he was about to hammer. As if it knew.

He jumped backwards, holding the hammer out above his head. Ready to brain anything that came through the wall.

And what, exactly, was really going to come through a wall?

He didn't want to find out. Mike decided that this would be a good time for a scene change. He needed to shore up a couple pilings in the basement. Maybe whatever it was in the wall would find an exit while he went below.

Mike picked up his thermos and walked through the house to the now unhidden room that led to the basement. He'd already fixed the rotten stairway down, and installed guardrails so that a parade of people could safely walk down them come fall. Now he needed to make sure the ceiling wouldn't cave in on them if they did.

The atmosphere changed as soon as he stepped down the first two steps. It went from musty, mouldy to cool, wet, and rank.

Mike wrinkled his mouth and shook his head. They would have to do something to air this place out before people came in. Creepy was one thing, stinky was another.

He picked up a board from the stack he'd brought down earlier, turned on the string of bare-bulb lights he'd strung across the centre span of the basement and went to work on one of the wooden joists. Some of the wood was solid, but he'd felt spongy patches in parts. Best to double any of the support wood and just make sure nothing was going to start sagging once a parade of people started putting weight on the floors upstairs. If this was going to be a house people lived in for the next thirty years, he would have taken a different course. But for a short-term haunted house? Reinforcement, not reconstruction.

He started nailing in one board, and wrinkled his nose. The mix of mould and...decay...was palpable. It smelled like something had died in here. He tried to block it out and focused on setting the board. He should be using his electric gun for this but sometimes he just felt like being old school. His shoulders would thank him later. Not.

He followed the beam down into the dark reaches of the basement. With every foot, the smell grew more rank. Then he stepped on something that squished.

"What the...."

The mud beneath his foot was a darker shade of black. Because a coil of something reddish black twisted out from beneath his shoe. He pulled the flashlight from his belt and shone it at the ground.

His first thought was that he'd stepped on a large dead snake.

But then he realised that there were no scales. And the flesh had ridges. It wasn't a snake.

It lay in a loose circle, and at the centre was a fist-sized lump of blackened flesh. It glistened on one side in the light of the flash.

"Holy Jesus," Mike said.

It looked like a heart, surrounded by a halo of intestines.

The flies that suddenly swarmed at his face when he spoke forced him to back away.

He choked and moved quickly towards the exit, trying not to vomit.

Once outside, he pulled out his phone and dialled his friend's number through bleary eyes.

Perry laughed at him.

"It's a raccoon or something that brought a tasty little dinner down there last night," he said. "Roadkill takeout. Get a shovel. You can even expense it. Look, I gotta go. We have actual problems here."

The line went dead.

Mike considered his options. He could shovel entrails out of the basement, or fight with a raccoon or opossum or whatever the hell creature was in the upstairs wall.

After a minute, he went to his truck to find a shovel and a plastic garbage bag.

Guts didn't bite.

*　　*　　*

But no sooner did he step outside than he was faced with another problem.

A witchy-looking woman was marching across the grass towards the house. She was all pointy – bony elbows and legs, and a long beak of a nose. Blond hair sprayed away from her face like a shower of kinks and curls. She looked birdlike and fierce. And driven.

A man who couldn't have been more her opposite strode along behind her, clearly struggling to match her pace. He carried a camera in his hands, the strap hung loose around his neck. Mike stepped back on the porch.

"You have to leave this place," she announced when she put a foot on the stair to his new porch.

Mike frowned, then shook his head.

"No, I don't think so," he said. "I work here."

"Is it true then, that you're turning this place into a haunted house attraction? Something that will bring gawkers instead of reverence?"

He shrugged. "If you mean that I'm rehabbing it so they can use it as a haunted house this fall, then yeah."

"You have to stop it," she said. "Don't you understand that this whole place is a graveyard? People who come here need to do so with the proper respect that the dead deserve. This isn't the place for a carnival. There are spirits here that are better left undisturbed and unprovoked. You can't turn this place into a parade of people."

"Look," Mike said. "I'm just the carpenter. If you have a problem with the business aspect of the house, you should call the county. I can't help you."

"Well, *I* can help *you*," she said. "I can help you understand that what you're doing is akin to grave robbing."

Mike laughed. "I'm not digging up graves," he said.

"No," she said. "But you're disturbing the dead. They are everywhere here. I know you've seen the stones over there," she pointed. "But this whole clearing is an old graveyard. It should be left in peace. This is not the place for a party. The spirits get angry."

"Good thing the spirits can't throw stones then," Mike said. "Because there are going to be plenty of people here this October."

"They can do much worse than throwing stones," she said. Then she stopped talking for a moment, as if she was reassessing the situation and realising that she was not going to get anywhere with him. Which was the truth. "Please, you have to listen to me. Stop what you're doing here. It will only lead to something…horrible."

She started to step up onto the porch and Mike put his hand up.

"Look, lady, I don't know what you're talking about, and I really don't care. I've got a job to do here, and you're trespassing. If you don't leave now, I'm calling the police."

The fat guy behind her put his hand on her shoulder, clearly trying to convince her to hold back.

"I want to see the inside of this house first," she said. "I want to see what sacrilege you've already committed."

She pulled away from the man's hand and stepped towards Mike on the porch.

He only shook his head and pulled out his phone.

"Two more steps, and I call the police, lady."

"Just a look inside?" she begged.

He shook his head. "I don't care about you, or your spirits or ghosts or whatever. I've got a job to do, and you're stopping it. If you want to complain, call the people who can answer you. They're at the Cook County Forest Preserve offices. And they're going to get on my ass if I don't get back to work."

She stopped, and the big guy put a hand on her shoulder again. Mike could see him squeezing his fingers, giving her a silent message.

She considered, and then nodded.

"All right," she said. "But I'll be back. And I know it sounds all dramatic and everything, but seriously, if you value your soul, you won't keep doing this. The dead aren't going to call the county. They're going to come to you."

She looked at him with a raised eyebrow. "Do you understand what I'm saying to you?"

"Sure," Mike said.

She turned and began to walk away, when he couldn't restrain himself.

"But ghosts don't pay my paycheck and my rent."

She looked back over her shoulder and her gaze was deadly serious.

"They don't now," she said. "But if you continue this...you might find that things turn out differently."

The big guy turned and shot a photo of the house, and then quickly put a hand back on her shoulder to push her away. This time, she left without protesting.

* * *

The afternoon went better.

After disposing of the entrails of...whatever it was...behind the cemetery pond, Mike used up a good stack of 2x4s and completed his reinforcement project. At the end, he stood with hands on hips and reviewed the work. The dark grey wood ceiling of the basement was now striped with blond fresh wood. It was a jarring juxtaposition, but they were probably going to spray a coat of industrial black or dark grey paint over the whole thing anyway. Nobody would see the difference between new and old wood.

He walked over to the spot where he'd found the intestines, and was greeted with a buzz of flies. Mike swatted them away from his face and shook his head. This was not going to do. He needed to get rid of the remnants of the blood that had soaked into the earth, or he was going to be plagued with flies. And probably, in a couple days, maggots. He grimaced and his whole body shivered.

He hated maggots.

"Nope, nope, nope," he said, and walked out of the basement to retrieve the shovel. He would just have to turn over some of the earth and nip this one in the bud.

When he returned, he used the shovel to dig a shallow hole near the place where the ground was still streaked with glistening…blood? Pus? Gut slime? Whatever it was, the flies were loving it. He piled a small mound of earth to one side and then used the shovel to skim off the top of the ground where the intestines had lain. He dropped it into the hole, shovelful by shovelful, until it appeared that the area was clear of anything but dry sandy earth. Satisfied, he slammed the shovel into the ground in the centre of the area, right about where the heart had been.

Instead of the shovel lodging in the earth and standing upright on its own, there was an odd cracking sound beneath the spade, and the shovel suddenly dropped a couple feet down below the surface.

"What the hell?" Mike said. The shovel lolled loosely to one side, the spade lost beneath the earth. He pushed the handle one way and then the other. It moved easily. There was apparently an empty space below his feet.

Mike pulled the shovel back up, at first gently, then with a bit more force and began to stomp his foot down on the ground around it. How far did the hollow spot extend? he wondered.

Without warning, his foot fell through the ground.

Mike yelled, and quickly jerked his leg back up. He was more careful then, and began to pile the earth from where his shovel and leg had broken through in a pile to the side of the area.

He didn't have to dig very long before his shovel kept hitting something hard. Something that scraped. It sounded like hollow wood.

Five minutes later, he was brushing the dirt off the top of an old weathered piece of wood. He cleared off more than two feet of earth before he found the edges on either side. The wood angled and grew narrower near the top. It continued beneath the earth and Mike kept digging more and more out until he was sure. The shape seemed hexagonal, flat on top, with sides sloping wider before slimming back again after a point. There was no doubt in Mike's mind as to what he had stepped in to.

"Fuckin' A," he breathed, and looked at his foot, as if to make sure that there were no bones still clinging to it.

He'd punched his shovel, and foot, into the rotted face of a coffin.

It occurred to him that there was likely a worm-eaten skeleton lying just inches below where his hand was clearing away earth. Hell, maybe the intestines and heart that hand lain on the dirt just above the coffin had been from the body buried inside it?

He jerked his hand back.

"Okay, no," he said. "No, no, no. I did not sign on for this."

Mike stepped back from the hole and shook his head. "Fuck this," he said, and turned away. He marched to the exit with the shovel, intending to go to the truck, pack up, and never come back. Let Perry find some other sucker to work on this heap.

He marched across the newly cut 'lawn' in front of the porch to where the pickup was parked in a narrow lane that entered the forest. It was a little farther to walk from the worksite, but it kept the truck cooler than parking it in the direct sun in the clearing. He stopped just before launching the shovel into the back of his pickup.

Katie was sitting on the bumper of the back of his truck.

"Going somewhere?" she said. Her eyes met his, unblinking.

"Yeah," he said. "I'm going anywhere but here."

She pursed her lips in a spoiled pout. "You can't just abandon me here. I thought you were going to build me a haunted house?"

"I don't need to build it," he said. "It already exists." He pointed at the old house behind them. "There are skeletons in the basement and monsters in the walls. My work is done here. I'm going home."

Katie stood up from the bumper and put a hand on his shoulder.

"Please don't say that," she said. "My friends and I are looking forward to coming to the haunted house when it's finished this fall. And...." She looked shy suddenly and her eyes moved to the ground, as she murmured, "I was hoping you'd show me how to build things."

"What are you talking about?" he asked, looking back at the old house.

"My dad used to be pretty handy," she said. "I loved watching him build stuff. I always wanted to learn how. I was hoping to watch you this summer."

"So ask your dad to teach you," Mike suggested.

"I can't," she answered, hanging her head. "He's dead."

"Oh." Mike felt like a shit then. He always seemed to be able to say just the wrong thing at just the wrong time. "Sorry."

He laid the shovel in the bed next to her and then walked to the driver's side of the truck. He'd left his cooler inside and needed water. And then discovered he'd automatically locked the door when he'd gotten out this morning. Mike reached into his pocket to grab his keys, and a shiny strand of metal pulled out with them and fell to the ground. He bent over to pick it up; it was the locket he'd found in the house and shoved in his jeans the other day.

"You should put that on so you don't lose it," Katie said behind him.

He turned and she was holding out a chain around her own neck. "I have one just like it."

Mike hesitated a minute and then followed her advice, slipping the chain around his neck. The locket slipped beneath his damp t-shirt and quickly warmed to his flesh.

"Since you're going to be building stuff here all summer, I thought maybe I could kind of come by and help out," Katie said. "Plus, I could keep you company. It gets lonely out here."

Mike found himself nodding. It would make it a lot easier to work in that dump if there was a friendly voice nearby. Then he reminded himself of why he was outside. He shook his head.

"There's a coffin in there."

"Where?" she asked.

"The basement. I put my foot right through it."

She shrugged. "We are standing next to a cemetery. Maybe whoever lived here just buried one of their own close. Or...maybe they built the house over part of the cemetery. Maybe that was here first and there are a bunch of people buried down there."

She stopped and gave him an evil smile. "Think of all the ghosts there might be in your haunted house!"

Mike shook his head. "That's exactly what I'm afraid of."

She tilted her head and made a sad face. In a slightly mocking voice she asked, "Ahh, are you afraid of the scary ghosts?"

"Yes," he said. "I mean no, I'm not afraid of ghosts, but I don't want to be working around a bunch of dead bodies."

She shrugged. "I don't think they come out much during the day when you're here."

He couldn't help but laugh at that.

"So what do you say?" she asked.

"About what?"

She fingered her necklace and asked, "Will you show me the ropes?"

He hesitated, and then thought of his rent bill. Maybe he could handle this place if someone was with him. And he had to admit, he welcomed the opportunity to have the chance to spend time with her.

"I guess so," he said. "But that depends what they decide to do, now that I found this coffin. That may stop the whole project."

"Why?" she asked.

"If they decide to excavate the whole basement to look for other coffins...."

She shook her head. "Why would they do that? The bodies are buried, if there are any. And you're probably going to put in a floor down there anyway, right?"

He shrugged. "Part of it."

"There you go," she said. "Better to build right over the coffins than disturb them, right?"

"I'll have to check," he said. "That's not my decision to make."

"Can I see it?" she asked.

"The coffin?"

She nodded.

"Yeah, I guess so." He led the way back to the house. Katie followed a step behind.

"I didn't think girls were into coffins," he said.

She didn't answer.

When they reached the short staircase down, he turned and said, "It's down here."

But she wasn't behind him.

"Katie?" he called. The clearing between him and the truck was empty.

"Right here," she said. He jumped. She had slipped ahead of him and was standing on the first stair down. "What are you waiting for?"

Her head disappeared down the cellar entrance. Mike shook his head and followed her down.

The damp stink of the place got to him instantly and he grimaced. "This place reeks," he complained.

"You just need some candles," she said. "Or incense. That'd fix it right up. Where's the body?"

"Over here," he said, and led her across the sandy floor.

When they reached the spot, she bent over and looked down at the hole in the ground. "You can't really see anything," she complained. "I thought you'd dug the whole thing out."

He shook his head. "Were you hoping to see a skeleton?"

"Kinda." She grinned. "Do you have a flashlight?"

"Are you serious?" He laughed.

She met his eyes but didn't say anything. She *wasn't* kidding.

"Hang on," he said.

Mike walked to the end of the basement and lifted the work light from the nail he'd pounded into the ceiling joist. He lifted the next lamp as well and dragged the extension cord and lamps over to the hole his foot had broken through. The jagged splinters of wood suddenly shone in sharp relief to the dark space beneath. Katie got down on her knees and peered into the hole.

"All I see is dirt," she said.

"What did you expect?"

"Well, it's a coffin," she said. "There ought to be…bones."

"Maybe it was a small body?" he suggested.

Mike crouched next to her and looked into the space as well. He could see the bottom of the coffin, and a scattering of dirt where the cave-in had occurred. But she was right. He couldn't see anything else in the space, even if he angled the light right or left.

"Hang on," he said, "I'll be right back."

Mike returned from the truck a minute later with the shovel he'd just put away. Then he began to clear more of the dirt from the top of the coffin. It only took a few moments to fully clear the upper third of the coffin. Most of it appeared to be buried less than a foot or so below the surface of the earth. Mike's foot had plunged through the old wood right about where the ribcage of a normal-sized body should have been.

He turned the shovel upside down then and used the grip of the handle to punch through the coffin lid next to the original hole he'd stomped. A couple of plunges cracked off another foot of rotted wood and the whole upper part of the casket was soon visible in the harsh light of his lamps.

He stopped after a couple more stomps and stared into the hole.

"Huh," he said.

The coffin was clearly empty.

"Well, that's disappointing," Katie said.

"And weird," he said.

She nodded agreement. "That should make you feel better about digging up bodies down here, though."

"Yeah," he said. And then he put the spade into the earth and began digging around the outside of the coffin.

"What are you doing?"

"What are *we* doing," he corrected. "I'm not going to leave a big hollow spot under my basement floor. This thing's coming out of here. And since you're my new apprentice, you're going to help me move it."

★   ★   ★

Once Mike trenched around the old coffin, they lifted and walked the rotting thing to the far side of the basement and set it down against the wall. "I'll let Perry decide what he wants to do about it," he said.

Then he filled in the hole in the earth, scooping soil from all around the area to even out the surface.

"I signed on to this project as a carpenter, not a gravedigger," he complained.

Katie smiled from where she sat nearby. "You do what you gotta do," she said.

"Well, what I gotta do is get a shitload of work done," he said.

"I'm here to help," she offered.

"That's great," he said, as he tried to quickly do some math in his head. "But I can't really pay you much. This contract is a one-man job. And they got me cheap."

She shook her head. "I don't want money. I just want to watch what you do. And I might not be able to be here every day or anything. But I'll help when I can."

He nodded. "Fair enough. But I'm going to tire you out while you're here. It's a lot easier to carry wood with two people than one."

"Most things are easier with two people," she said.

Mike thought of his recent history with Mia and frowned. "I wouldn't know about that."

"Maybe I can show you then," she suggested.

"We'll see," he said and looked at his watch. Somehow the afternoon had moved on, and it was already past four-thirty. "Right now, I'd like to get some things ready for tomorrow. Because it's quitting time."

"What do we need to do?" she asked.

"While you're here, I'd like to move some boards inside so I can start right in tomorrow morning."

She agreed, and together they carried stacks of 2x4s and some 2x6s into both the basement and the first floor. At some point, Emery had shown up and helped with the carting. When they were finished, Mike's forehead was dripping with sweat and Emery's normally pale face looked flushed, but Katie looked none the worse for wear. She smiled as he put his hands on his thighs after moving the last load and took a deep breath.

"You look like you could use a drink," she said.

He nodded, too hot and tired to speak.

"Did you bring a cooler today?"

He nodded again. "Yeah, in the bed of the truck," he said.

"Meet you on the deck?" she said, and disappeared out of the room.

★   ★   ★

"They say that the woman who lived in this house was a witch," Katie said.

Mike tilted back a Pabst Blue Ribbon and shook his head. "Yeah, I've heard that," he said. "Not surprised. I don't know who else would choose to live out here in the woods."

"Oh, come on," she said. "Back then, this whole area was woods. But the woman who lived here, they say she killed her husband in a ritual to gain power over life and death."

"She sounds lovely," he said.

Katie shrugged. "He was an asshole anyway."

"Why, did you know him?" Mike asked with a smile.

Katie's face looked odd for a moment. Then she laughed. "No, of course not. That was like, fifty years ago or something. But they say she had his baby and he treated her bad and then killed her baby in a fit of rage. So…she took his energy for her own."

Mike emptied the last drops of the can before crumpling it in his hand. He tossed it to the side, and after a moment of consideration, pulled another from the cooler and popped the tab. He offered it to her, but she put out a hand and raised her can in the air. "Still working on it," she said.

He leaned back against the grey wooden siding of the old house. Katie shifted her position and a moment later, rested her head on his shoulder.

Mike tensed a little, but then went with it. He slid his back down a hair against the house and slowly moved his arm until his hand gripped her shoulder, pulling her closer. She sighed and took a sip of her beer.

"It's so peaceful here, isn't it?" she asked after a minute.

The sun had disappeared behind the house and the upper leaves of the forest before them glowed with the rays of the setting sun. Bird noise coloured the breeze that shivered through the trees, making the leaves shimmer with light and shadow.

"Yeah," he said. "You almost can't hear the turnpike back here."

"It's like a secret place," she said. "Hidden from the world."

Mike nodded. "It won't be hidden for long. This fall there will be lines of people from the turnpike to this house."

She pulled closer to him. "Well, for now, we can enjoy it like it's our own secret place."

Mike felt the buzz of his second beer beginning and looked down into the girl's face in the crook of his arm. She didn't look away.

Part of him wondered exactly what was happening here. The other part was an opportunist. Mike bent down and kissed her.

Katie's lips were cool and moist and he felt his entire body relax as her tongue slipped into his mouth.

What the hell? a voice in his head asked.

Another voice countered. *Shut up and kiss her.*

Soon he was lost in her mouth and her touch. His beer can rolled across the deck, nearly empty, and he used the freed arm to slip around her, drawing her closer. Never mind that he was sweaty and probably smelled like shit. She didn't seem to mind and he wasn't going to miss the opportunity for the first real taste of a woman since his wife had left him months ago.

Maybe she was too young. Maybe it was wrong. He didn't care about anything but the soft touch of her lips against his, and the feel of her skin as his hand slipped inside her shirt and rose up towards her....

"No!" she said suddenly, and broke the kiss, moving away from him across the deck.

"Not here," she said. "Not now. I'm sorry."

She got up and ran down the steps to disappear into the trees.

Mike picked up her beer, with beads of sweat running down the can, and downed a slug. It was still mostly full, and cold.

The forest was silent, except for the evening hum of crickets. Once again, he was alone. Just when it had felt good to be near someone again, he'd fucked it up.

He guzzled the rest of the can and closed his eyes before the tears came.

CHAPTER SEVEN

"You are my favourite Asian zombie ever!" Jeanie said as Bong walked into the living room of her small apartment. She threw her arms around him and kissed him as if she hadn't seen him in weeks. Never mind that they'd gone out to Teehan's just last night for drinks.

"Wha—" he said, between her frantic kisses.

"I got it!" she said. "I got the haunted house job!"

Bong smiled. "Ah. And here I thought you were just happy to see me."

She slapped him on the shoulder. "Well, I *am*, silly. It was the makeup I did on you that got me the job. Plus – and here's the coolest thing – they said that they wanted you to work as one of the actors who scare people at the house. Can you believe it? We can be together all of October and you can get paid too!"

She took in his look of dismay and put a finger to his scowling lips before he could say a word. "Say that you'll do it? Please?"

"Why would I want to be a spook in a haunted house?" Bong asked. "I already have a job, I don't need another one."

"Because we'll get to do it together!" she said. "They want me to do makeup, but they also want me to be a spook too. So, we can haunt the house together. How awesome will that be?"

He looked up at the ceiling, and then back at her. He couldn't complain too much. He enjoyed being with Jeanie. And to be with her while she was in her element, having fun....

Bong nodded in a hesitant yes.

"Oh, I love you!" Jeanie said, bouncing up and down on her toes and planting kisses on his lips with every move.

"I'll cross off every free minute in October," he said. "But as for today...."

"Oh, that's what I wanted to tell you," Jeanie said. "There's a meeting today for everyone who's going to work in the house. I thought since you were coming over anyway, maybe we could go."

"But we had a date...."

"It'll still be a date, silly," she said. "Only we'll be with a bunch of other people who love haunted houses as much as we do."

She looked at his face and quickly corrected herself. "Okay, as much as *I* do. But we'll be together?"

"Okay," he said.

"Good," she said, and walked across the room to pick up her makeup kit. "Can you drive? Because the meeting is in fifteen minutes."

*　　*　　*

They pulled up in front of a tan duplex house in Oak Forest as dusk was setting in, and clearly, they were not the first to arrive. The street was filled with cars on both sides of the street.

"How many people are coming to this?" Bong asked.

Jeanie shrugged. "I dunno. But I know that anyone who works on haunted houses on the south side wants to be part of this, since it's at Bachelor's Grove. So, I'm not surprised if it's crowded. This is so cool. It's a total honour to be part of this."

Bong couldn't hide the fact that he didn't put the experience on quite the same level she did. But she grabbed his hand and dragged him forward down the sidewalk to the doorway of the host house. There was a picture of Jack Skellington from the movie *The Nightmare Before Christmas* on the window.

"This is it," she enthused. She lifted her hand to knock on the door, and a face appeared in the window. A black man with almost no hair, and a t-shirt that featured the steel claws of Freddy from *A Nightmare on Elm Street,* opened the door.

"Do you know the password?" he asked. "I have just one clue for you: Haunted."

Jeanie grinned. "House?"

"You're in," he said, and pushed the screen door open wider.

"Hi, I'm Lenny," he said, extending a long thin hand once they were inside.

Jeanie took his hand and introduced herself and Bong. "Is this your house?" she asked.

Lenny laughed. "Oh no," he said. "I don't play that way. I live in an apartment down on Harlem Avenue. This is my pal June's place. She's got the big corporate job and mortgage and all, but I don't rib her about it too much. Because, well, she likes haunted houses and shit still."

"That and the fact that I let you sleep here most of the time," a woman's voice said from behind him.

A thin girl with pale features and long auburn hair walked up behind him and smacked him in the back of the head before smiling and ducking left down a hall.

Jeanie and Bong followed Lenny into a crowded kitchen that connected to an equally crowded living room. There were at least thirty people in the house, and half of them seemed to be wearing shirts from horror movies.

Jeanie squeezed Bong on the arm and gestured at the group with a grin. "I feel like I just came home," she said. "And I don't know any of these people."

Bong smiled. "So…what are we supposed to do here exactly?" he asked.

Jeanie shrugged. "I don't know. But I guess we'll find out."

At that moment, a guy in a shirt dominated by a decayed face with gnarled teeth and maggots crawling from a rotted eyeball (the text beneath the photo said *Zombi*) stood up in front of a widescreen TV that was playing *Halloween III: Season of the Witch* with the sound turned off. Jeanie could hear the 'Silver Shamrock' theme from the movie instantly play in her head. The thing was so obnoxiously addictive.

"Hey everyone!" he said, calling out to still the room. "Some of you know me and some don't, but we're going to be working together a lot over the next few weeks. My name is Lon, and I'm the production manager for Bremen House, the Bachelor's Grove Haunted House attraction. I've done a lot of work on stage design, and worked for a couple seasons on the Stateville Prison haunted house. Plus I've always put together a haunted house in my garage for the kids, so I'm really psyched to be working with you on this. It's going to be awesome."

He looked around the room for a minute and then grinned. "There you are. June, come on up here."

The auburn-haired girl slipped between a couple guys in Metallica and Anthrax t-shirts, and joined him at the front of the room. She hung her head a little, clearly uncomfortable with being the centre of attention.

"This is June," Lon said. "For any of you who haven't met her, she's the best monster makeup artist you're ever going to meet, and she'll be leading all of you who are here to work on makeup and costume design. She's really amazing, and if she didn't hang out so much with Lenny, I'd ask her to marry me and turn me into a zombie."

June looked up at Lon, clearly mortified.

"I'm kidding," he said. "But she is really good. And in a couple minutes, I'm going to ask all of you who are here for makeup to follow her for direction. But some housekeeping first. I'm your official 'stage manager' for the next few weeks, so if you have any problems or questions on anything, I want you to let me know. We'll figure out how to fix it. Or kill it. Whatever it takes."

He motioned for a thin guy in a *Suspiria* t-shirt to step forward. "This guy calls himself Argento. You'll always be able to find him – just look for the *Suspiria* or *Opera* or *Four Flies on Grey Velvet* or *Deep Red* or *Phenomena* t-shirt. I don't think he owns a shirt that isn't a Dario Argento movie. Don't ask me what his real name is; I don't know and I don't care."

He pointed at another wiry guy with brown hair standing nearby. "And where you find Argento, you'll also find Lucio. I'm guessing that's not his real name either. All I know is they make amazing sets – if you went to the Rob Zombie Great American Nightmare house in Villa Park last year, you know what I mean. Argento's going to be in charge of designing all of the rooms in the house. Anyone who's doing painting and set stuff, you'll be working with him. And please feed him some ideas – because we can't have every room in this place end up looking like a set from *Suspiria*."

"I don't see why not," the guy who called himself Argento said, but Lon just shook his head. "No. But I don't want to see a *Sharknado*-themed room either."

"This is a twister...*with teeth*," someone yelled.

Lon held up his hands and smiled. "So, here's the way it's going to go down. For the next month or so, there's a guy out at the house fixing it up. Don't go out there; you can't get in. He's putting down new floors and shit and fixing it up so the place is useable for us. While he's doing that, we're going to be planning out the room themes. We want every room to reference a really cool horror movie. I know the people who walk through in October probably won't always get half the references, but if the rooms are good – really good – then they'll have an awesome time anyway. And for those who are really big horror movie fans...they're going to be in heaven. So once we have the themes all mapped out, the set folks are going to work with Argento to figure out how to make the rooms look real. And the makeup peeps are going to plan out their spooks based on the room themes. We'll have a couple big group meetings between now and September, but mostly we'll be working in smaller groups and we'll communicate what's going on with everything in a private Facebook group. Before you leave here tonight, make sure you write down your Facebook ID on the signup sheet in the kitchen so we can add you."

"Are those knives on your fingers?" Jeanie whispered. Lenny had ended up next to them. He raised his hands and flexed his fingers with a smile. His fingers were the colour of milk chocolate, but the blue blades of the tattoos looked dangerous. He nodded.

"Are you a *Nightmare* fan?" he asked.

Jeanie grinned. "Freddy forever."

"Then you have to see this." He nodded his head towards the back of the room, and then turned and walked.

Jeanie and Bong followed.

Lenny led them up a short flight of stairs to a bedroom. He grinned as he pushed a door open and gestured for them to enter.

"What do you think?" he asked as they stepped inside.

"Holy shit, what happened in here?" Bong gasped.

The pale lavender walls were splattered with spots of what looked like blood. It dripped down the walls in dark, dried trails but the real disturbing part was on the ceiling. A life-size female manikin hung from the centre of it, just above the bed. Her nightgown hung in tatters and her mouth was open in a silent scream.

"June let me decorate the bedroom," he explained. "So, I chose the film that started it all."

"*A Nightmare on Elm Street*," Jeanie said.

"Reel One!" he grinned.

Jeanie smiled in appreciation, and noted that one wall appeared to have a phrase on it finger-painted in what looked like more blood. It read, 'To Sleep, Perchance To Dream…'

"It's really cool, but I don't know how you sleep in here," Jeanie said.

"Nah," he said. "It's comforting. A refuge. The world of *Nightmare* is way more safe than the world out there." He pointed out the bedroom window. "Human beings, those are the monsters that you've gotta fear."

Jeanie nodded. "Can't argue with you there."

He walked to a closet and opened the door. A moment later he turned around, a latex mask of Freddy Krueger covering his face.

"Do you think you can make me look like this with makeup instead of a mask?"

She frowned. "I dunno," she said, hesitating. "Your skin is already pretty dark."

"See, that's what I'm always talking about," he said. "Black guys never get the good parts in horror movies. We're always just bums or zombies or shit like that. And just look at this cast for the haunted house. I'm the only black guy in the group."

"I'd guess that's just because no other guys came out for this," Jeanie suggested. "Or...if this is like a horror movie, maybe it means you're the only one of us who is going to survive the entire month of haunting the house."

Lenny shook his head. "More likely, it means I'll end up dying in some ridiculous way on Halloween night when this thing is open to the public...and everyone will just think I'm a prop."

At that moment, June walked into the room, shaking her head.

"Are we back to the poor black man bit again?" she said. "Just get over it. There are plenty of black guys in horror and they have great roles, not just victims. What about Tony Todd in *Candyman*? What about Duane Jones in *Night of the Living Dead*? If horror discriminates against anyone, it's women. Always whiny screaming victims who can't run more than five feet without falling down."

"Not true," Lenny said, quickly warming up to what was obviously a continuing argument. "How about one of the strongest characters in a horror movie ever – Sigourney Weaver in *Alien*. Or even Heather Langenkamp as Nancy in *Nightmare*? She's a kid but she goes up against Freddy. She doesn't just run away and whine."

"Exceptions," June said. Then she turned to Jeanie and asked, "What do you think? Who gets the short stick more in horror films, girls or black guys?"

"I think you can make a generalisation about pretty much anything to support whatever argument you want to support," Jeanie said. "If you're a black guy, you're the victim of racial prejudice. If you're a woman, there's the glass ceiling of The Man keeping you down. If you're a white guy...all of the minorities – and women – are out to get you. Everybody can point to some one or some group that is 'keeping them down'. So...I just don't go there."

June grinned and clapped Jeanie on the shoulder. "Well said! I think I'm going to like you...um...."

"Jeanie," she answered.

June grinned. "June and Jeanie. Let's make some monsters," she said, leading them back into the hall. Jeanie saw Bong waiting for her at the foot of the stairs and waved.

"Black or white or Korean," June continued, noticing Bong. "They're all going to be scary as hell."

CHAPTER EIGHT

The field grass around the cemetery was wet with dew as Mike pulled the truck down the slim gravel road bordering the old stones. It was going to be a hot one; while the air was heavy with the fresh smells of summer and a gentle morning breeze, he could taste the coming heat of the day in the air. The moisture beading on the tips of the grass right now would be burned off in an hour.

He parked and pulled his cooler and toolbox from the back bed of the truck. He had a feeling he was going to need the former more than the latter in a couple more hours.

Despite the outdoor weather, the basement of the house was cool and dank as he went down the steps and turned on his utility lights. As long as he had to work down here, the day might not be too bad.

All the lights on the far end of the basement were off, and then Mike remembered that he had unplugged part of the strand yesterday when he'd been digging, because the hanging lamps kept hitting him in the head. He'd ended up laying the problem lights on the ground out of the way, and using a camping lantern he had in the truck to light the area of the dig.

As he walked a few steps from the door, the basement turned pitch black almost immediately. Mike reached down and grabbed the extension cord that fed power across the room and used it as a guide to trace his way across the floor until its end, walking slowly step by step into the darkness. When he found the end, he felt around on the damp earth until he located the disconnected cord that fed the lights in the back half of the basement. He plugged it in, and the dark disappeared in a wash of yellowish light, though some was beaming directly into the earth, where he'd laid the lights down yesterday.

When he stood up with the cord in hand, something *thunked* against the back of his head. He jumped, and then turned around.

A dark object swayed from the joist above.

"What the hell is that?" he whispered, and grabbed for the nearest light lying nearby on the ground. It was encased in a metal hood with a protective lattice across the open portion so you could drop it without breaking the bulb. The casing had a hook and typically hung from a nail in one of the joists; the open end of the case where the light came out was currently beaming into the ground. He lifted it up by the hook and turned it around to point the light at exactly what he'd bumped into. Mike felt his jaw drop as he took in what the bulbs illuminated. He slowly aimed the light from left to right, noting one carcass after the other hanging from the beam.

They all looked like bloody lumps of fur. Three raccoons. A couple of squirrels; small striped things that he guessed were chipmunks; a rabbit. One pale grey thing with a long snout that boasted a row of sharp yellowed teeth. An opossum.

The animals were strung from the beams in a circle all around the old coffin area that Mike had dug up and then immediately re-buried yesterday. Beneath each body, the ground was dark with drained animal blood. And in the centre, above where the coffin was buried, a symbol was drawn in the earth. It was faint, but Mike could see it still. He guessed that someone had made it using the animal blood, and while it might be dry, the earth would hold that darker colour for a long time to come. The symbol looked like something he'd seen in a horror movie dealing with witches and the devil. A circle, with a star inside it.

"Okay, that's really it," he whispered and backed away from the scene, step by step. He could feel his heart beating, harder and harder with every second that passed.

What the hell was going on in this place?

* * *

Once he got outside and could take a couple of deep breaths in the dappled sunlight that came through the trees, he dialled Perry's number with shaking fingers.

"Hello, Bremen Enterprises," his friend's voice answered.

"Your devil worshippers are still here," Mike growled. "The work site is full of dead bodies."

"Bodies, what? Is this Mike? What are you talking about?"

Mike quickly explained what he'd seen, as he walked around the outside of the house and back up the porch steps to return to the main level. He could feel his emotions growing with every word that described the scene with the blooded animals.

"That's it, I'm done," he said. "This place is rotting, stinking and creepy. It should be left alone to rot into the earth and disappear. That's what it was in the middle of doing when we started trying to save it. There are animals in the walls and fucking devil worshippers apparently hanging out here at night. I don't want any more part in it."

"Whoa, calm down, man," Perry said. "We'll work this out. I need you to finish this now, I really do. We've got the set builders and decorators ready to come out in two or three weeks to start working on the rooms. I can't lose even a day now."

"I'm not working in a place where people are killing things," Mike said. "For all I know, they're just waiting around in the trees and I'm going to be their next human sacrifice."

Perry laughed on the other end of the line. "It's just kids screwing around. You're overreacting. But I get it, I do. You're kind of remote out there. How about this? We'll put a night watchman on the place from now on, so nobody can get in there when you're not around."

"I don't want to work in this craphole," Mike complained.

"Nobody does," Perry said. "Trust me, I asked around."

"I thought I was your first choice?"

"You're my friend," Perry said. "But originally I tried to get a couple of bigger contractors in to do this job faster."

"Well, I suggest you give them a call again," Mike said.

"Time and a half," Perry said. His voice sounded panicked. "We'll give you a watchman and time and a half for the rest of the month." His voice calmed then, and he said softer, "I need you to finish this, Mike. Please."

At that moment, Katie walked into the room, and leaned against the doorway. Her eyebrows lifted in askance, as if to say, 'what are we gonna do today?'

His fear of devil worshippers suddenly dissipated, and Mike thought of the opportunity to work with Katie at his side all day.

"Okay," Mike said into the phone. "But only because it's you."

And only because Katie is here…his mind added.

Perry said something that he only half heard. And then Mike was mumbling goodbye and thumbing the end call button. He dropped the phone into his pocket and took a step towards the doorway.

"Hi," he said. "I thought I'd scared you off for good."

Katie smiled and shook her head. "Can't scare me," she said. "What's the project for today?"

It was Mike's turn to smile. "Well, after I bury a bunch of dead animals, we're going to put down a wood plank floor and make sure that nobody can stumble on any other hidden coffins or blood puddles from sacrificed animals. Basically, we're going to make the scary basement not scary so that they can come in with a bunch of paint and props and make it scary again."

"Seems like a waste of time," Katie said.

"Yep," he agreed. "But you know, it pays the rent."

*   *   *

Katie held a plastic sheet as one by one, Mike clipped the strings that held the animals suspended from the beams. When all of the bloody balls of fur were lying on the sheet, he grabbed the opposite side of the plastic and walked it to her. When his hands brushed hers, he felt a spark shoot down his spine. His skin grew strangely warm. He was sure he saw a glint in her eyes as he took the plastic from her hand and pulled the ends together so that he could drag the plastic out of the cellar without losing any bodies. Or blood.

"Thanks," he said.

"Whatever you need," she answered. Her voice was soft. Like rose petals.

He dug a hole on the edge of the cemetery, away from the house, and dropped the animals in. Katie moved boards into the basement as he piled dirt back in the hole and retrieved his saw from the truck.

"How's this?" she asked, as he came down the steps to find a neatly stacked pile of 5/4x6 boards on one side of the door, and 2x4s on the other. Emery stood nearby, leaning against one shadowed basement wall. He nodded at her but she didn't move.

"Um, perfect," he said to Katie. "We'll frame it out with the 2x4s today and depending how far we get, slap down the wide boards tomorrow."

With Katie's help, the rest of the day passed quickly. And at the end, she brought him his cooler as they sat on the edge of the deck near the entry door. He popped the top on a PBR and almost couldn't wait for the telltale sound of the hiss of carbonation to down the first gulp. He hadn't eaten or drunk anything in hours, he realised. But he'd been more productive than he'd been on a job in months. Maybe years.

"Thanks for your help today," he said to Katie. "I couldn't have done it without you."

"Whatever you need," she said again with a slight smile. "I just want to help you get it done. My friends and I are looking forward to a haunted house this Halloween."

"Well, they will have you to thank for it," he said.

Katie smiled, but said nothing.

★   ★   ★

Over the next three days, Katie turned up shortly after Mike arrived, usually with Emery in tow, and they helped him carry, cut and measure wood as he framed out and ultimately hid the dirt floor of the basement. Mike had covered the earth beneath the wood with a heavy plastic sheet to help keep the dampness and mildew odours contained.

"Why do you always use that?" she asked at one point, as he slapped a square on the board he was measuring. "My dad used to just mark wood really fast using another board."

"Maybe I'm not as good as your dad," he said. "This helps me make sure my cuts are always ninety degrees."

"Does it even really matter down here?" she said. "I mean, it's a basement floor that is just to give people something dry to walk on. It doesn't have to be perfect."

"Maybe not," he said. "But I don't work sloppy. Every cut you make says something about the carpenter. Whether I'm building a treehouse or a mansion, I make my cuts true. It's just how I roll."

She shrugged. "Just was curious. That's good, I guess."

Once they finished the floor, Katie helped him place plywood sheets over the frames he'd put from floor to ceiling on two sides of the basement. Perry had asked him to divide the basement into three rooms since they were taking the time to floor it. The division gave them two additional rooms to 'haunt' come fall.

He didn't bother to put full doorways on the carve-outs, since people would just be filing in and out anyway. The decorators would probably hang plastic or beads or something to screen them off.

"Just hold it right there," he said, as Katie held the last piece of plywood square to the ceiling. Her arms were outstretched, crucifixion style, to press the board in place, and he came up behind her with the nail gun to reach over her head, press the trigger and shoot the top nails in. His chest pressed the back of her head as he bent forward to hold the gun in place. When he'd set the last nail, he dropped a hand to her shoulders. He knew he shouldn't touch her that way, but he couldn't resist. Every hour she was near he found himself more and more drawn to her. He said things to her as they worked just to hear her talk. When he got in his truck at night to go home, he found the silence without her voice almost deafening.

He craved her company, almost as much as he craved a cold one.

You're fucked, a voice in his head noted.

"All right," he said, looking at the plywood that sat snug to the beam. "We are officially done down here. They can paint these walls or put spiderwebs on them or whatever...but the walls and floor are in. Now it's time to move upstairs."

"What room is next?" she asked, not moving from beneath the press of his hand.

"I thought we'd start in the attic and work our way down," he said.

"Sounds like a plan," she agreed.

She moved away from him, but not without a knowing look in his direction, and the faint hint of a 'I kinda liked you touching me' smile.

He led the way back up out of the basement, which now smelled like clean fresh-cut lumber instead of mould and blood and rot. Maybe not the best prerequisite for 'haunting'. But that wasn't his problem.

They passed into the house through the kitchen and walked up the creaking steps to the attic.

"If we find any dead deer or raccoons hanging from nooses from the rafters, I'm leaving," Mike said.

"I'll be right behind you," Katie said. "That's gross."

There were no dead animals in the attic. But there was a lot of dust. And a dry smell of age. The heat was palpable; the air felt thick enough to cut with a knife.

"We need to get these windows open," Mike said. He walked to the right side of the long room and pulled with all his might on the handle of a window. It didn't move.

"Shit," he said. Crowbar time again.

"I got this one," Katie said at the other end of the attic.

The window squeaked, but seemed to rise easily under her hands.

"How did you do that?" he said, walking across the attic to join her. "The other window is dry-rotted shut."

"Magic," she said with an eyeroll.

He ran his hand over the edge of the window sill and shook his head. "Magic is what we're going to need to keep this place from falling down once hundreds of people start walking through it."

"I thought you fixed all that," she said. "I mean, all of the stuff you did in the basement made it more sturdy, right?"

He shrugged. "Well, I don't think the first floor is going to fall into the basement," he said. "But that doesn't mean this place is sturdy. Look at this wood. It turns to sawdust under your fingers."

As he said it, a chunk of the window frame snapped under his fingers, and an inch-long piece fell to the attic floor.

"See what I mean?"

She grinned. "Well, I guess that just means you can show me the best way to fix a rotted-out window."

"I'll tell you how," he said. "In this place? Just board it up."

He ran a hand around the window frame, and then pounded a fist against the wall. He repeated the motion a foot or so out from the window, and then stepped down the wall and did it again, cocking his head to listen at each spot.

"What are you doing?" she asked.

"Just trying to get a feel for what shape the walls are in up here."

He stomped a foot on the floor, close to the wall. His face filled with worry lines as he did it. He stepped a couple feet away from the wall and tried again, looking as if he expected to punch one boot through the floor. After several stomps, his face lost its look of trepidation.

"I'm shocked, but happy," he said. "Amazingly, it sounds pretty solid up here."

Then he put his foot down again and frowned. "That will teach me to open my mouth."

"What is it?" she asked.

"*That* sounded hollow."

He stomped again, a few inches away, and then dropped to the floor. With one finger, he followed a line in the wood. A gap.

"I think there's a trapdoor here," he said. "You almost can't see it, because the handle is fashioned to drop down into the wood and basically disappear."

Mike slipped his fingernails between two indentations a few inches apart and lifted. A slim wooden handle rose from the floor.

"Now that's craftsmanship," he said. "Nicely done."

He began to raise the door, but Katie put a hand on his shoulder. "That's probably just an old laundry chute," she said. "I don't think we want to go down there."

He raised it a foot, and could only see blackness below. A cloud of stale, foul air filled the corner of the room as he peered below. "It looks wide for laundry."

She shook her head. "All these old places had them. And there would be a small ladder, in case something got stuck on the way down and you had to go chase it."

Mike sneezed then, the cloud of dust and mould from below hitting his sinuses like a sledgehammer. He dropped the door and fumbled in his pocket to look for a tissue.

"Maybe you should build, like, a wall or platform or something here to block this corner off, so you don't have a bunch of people stepping on the door?" she suggested.

Mike stood up and sneezed again and again. When the fit passed, he nodded. "Probably not a bad idea. First thing is to make sure the rest of the floor is solid I suppose. I think I'll need to come back with a dust mask and a flashlight to check the chute out."

He blinked his eyes to clear the tears, and went back to stomping on the floorboards, slowly moving away from the trapdoor. His thumps got harder and faster as he felt more and more confident that the floor was still solid.

Just before he reached the other end, a bell chimed from his pocket. Mike pulled his phone out and shook his head. "Damn, it's four-thirty already," he said. "I don't think we're going to start up here tonight. I should start packing things up."

Katie shrugged and looked at him with wide eyes designed to ensure a positive response. "Do you have time for a beer before you go?"

"If you have time to drink one with me," he said.

"Only one?"

"Bad girl," Mike said. But he couldn't help grinning as he said it. "I am pretty sure there are a few still in the cooler."

CHAPTER NINE

"We have to go back there tonight," Jillie said. She punctuated that statement by pointing at him with a long, fresh-cut French fry. They were having lunch at Nicky's Carryout, arguably the best greasy spoon in the south suburbs. It had been there on the corner of 143rd Street, just a couple miles down the road from Bachelor's Grove, for decades. There was history in that grease stuck to the old tile walls.

Ted shook his head. "What's that going to accomplish? You've already lodged a complaint with the county, and you know what that got us. Exactly what you expected. This state has just about the biggest debt in the nation; there's no way they're going to turn down some easy money on a broken-down old house because somebody thinks there might be angry ghosts."

"I just need to know," Jillie said. "I want to feel what the state of the place is. Are the spirits dangerously angry? Are they quiet?"

"And if they're pissed off and grinding skull teeth, what are you going to do about it?" Ted said. "Do you think the county board is going to act differently if you go in to their board meeting in August and say, 'You can't open that haunted house, the dead are really teed off about it'?"

Jillie shot him a just-shut-the-hell-up glance, but said nothing.

"This isn't your fight," Ted said. "Don't go to war on something you can't win."

"Is that what you would have told Washington and Jefferson and the rest?" she asked. "Don't bother, you can't win?"

Now it was Ted's turn to roll his eyes. "What, you're the daughter of the Revolution now? Look, all I'm trying to say is—"

"I get it," she interrupted. "But that doesn't change things. I understand Bachelor's Grove. I know what could happen there if things really get tilted. I have to at least try my best to not let that happen. It's my responsibility."

"So, we go there tonight and...what?" Ted asked.

"You bring the EMF meter and full spectrum camera, and I'll just listen. I want to see what kind of activity there is now that this guy is in the house all the time."

"You think we're going to pick up a lot of stuff?"

"I would make sure your battery is charged and you have plenty of memory," she said. "Yes."

"Okay," he said. "Pick you up at eleven-thirty?"

"Perfect," she said. Then she looked at his plate. "Are you going to eat your pickle?"

*　　*　　*

The Midlothian Turnpike was dark and empty when they edged over to the side and parked Ted's car on a gravel shoulder close to the small bridge near Bachelor's Grove. Fleetwood Mac was singing 'Go Your Own Way' on the radio and the reflection of the radio LED tinted Jillie's face a strange electric blue.

"This is it," Ted said.

She nodded. "Kill the lights before anyone else sees us."

He did, and then got out and pulled the sensing and recording equipment from the trunk. Most of it was stuffed in a backpack, which he shrugged with a grunt over his shoulders. A minute later, they were trudging down the weedy gravel path that led past the old fence beneath the heavy tree cover and into the cemetery grounds.

"Did you bring the flashlight?" Jillie asked as they moved down the darkening path away from the turnpike.

A second later, a light flicked on, and Ted pointed it ahead of them at the path.

"I can always count on you," she said.

"Remember, I have a digital recorder," he said.

"Anything recorded can be erased," she countered.

He snorted. "Not if it's saved to the cloud."

"Trust me," she said. "Everything on the cloud is going to get wiped out one of these days by a thunderstorm."

"Always so negative about progress," he said.

"I didn't tell you to carry cassette tapes, did I?" she asked.

"Touché. Shhh," he said, pointing ahead. "There's a car here."

"Interesting," Jillie whispered. They approached the dark shape carefully, but once they arrived at it and peered into the windows, she pronounced it safe.

"Maybe someone drove it off the road and abandoned it here," she suggested.

"Or someone's in the house," he said.

"I guess we'll see," she said. "But I don't think so. Nobody that we can see with our own eyes, anyway."

They walked silently across the grass to the old house at the end of the clearing. Jillie stepped up the two stairs of the porch and walked quickly across the deck to the door.

"Do you think it's actually unlocked?" Ted whispered.

She put her hand on the doorknob. "Only one way to find out."

The knob turned.

"Check this out," she hissed, and pushed the wooden door inward.

It opened with a slow creak.

Jillie didn't hesitate, but stepped inside.

Ted followed her through the foyer, flashing the light ahead of them. She walked into the front room, and pointed to a spot not far from a dark hole in the floor.

"Set up right here," she said. "We should get started at the front of the house."

He nodded and pulled out a small tripod and camera from the backpack, along with another oblong shape. It glowed with thin blue LEDs when he pressed a button on the side.

"Any focal point?" he asked.

"Your guess is as good as mine," she said. "Maybe the hole in the floor? Maybe there's activity transgressing the basement? I don't know."

"Done," he said, slapping a lock on the tripod base to hold it steady. "Now what?"

Jillie plopped down on the floor with a wall behind her, and crossed her legs Indian style. "Now we wait."

"No. Now you go," a gruff voice said from behind them.

Jillie jumped to her feet. Ted, who had been in the process of easing himself to the floor, fell backwards on his ass before scrambling clumsily to his feet. A short but solid-looking man in a blue button-up shirt and dark pants stood in the doorway.

"What do you think you're doing here?" he asked.

Jillie recovered herself quickly.

"We're looking for EMF activity. Who are you?"

"I'm the guy who's supposed to keep people like you out," the man said. He pointed at the guard badge he had pinned to his shirt. "You're trespassing."

"We're not doing any harm," Jillie said. "We're just trying to see if there is paranormal activity in this place since it's been put under construction. That could cause a surge in—"

"Get out now or I call the police," he interrupted.

"As you like," she said. "But you'll be sorry when people start dying in here."

"Actually, I'm here to make sure that doesn't happen," he said.

She snorted. "Good luck with that." Then she motioned to Ted, who was already fumbling with the latches and trying to collapse and pick up all of their equipment.

"Come on," she said. "We'll have to do this another time."

CHAPTER TEN

Mist still hung in the air just above the long grass as Mike drove down the gravel path and into Bachelor's Grove. It was an eerie blanket across the earth that looked like a special effect for a movie…but it was just the natural state of a cool August morning in the forest. When he pulled to a stop at the clearing in front of the house, Mike saw someone sitting in a canvas chair on the small deck. It looked as if he was sitting in front of a house in a cloud. The guy was sipping from a thermos and wearing a black pullover Blackhawks hat – an odd thing to see in August, but it had been dipping into the cooler temperatures overnight this past week.

Seeing someone at the house momentarily startled him, but when Mike got out of the truck he nodded at the man on the deck. Because the man wasn't a stranger. He was the night watchman, Gonz, who'd been there the past few mornings when he'd arrived. It was still disconcerting to see someone at the house, but it also made Mike feel better. He knew if Gonz was here, then nobody had turned up overnight to perform animal sacrifices in the basement…or God knew what else.

"Quiet night?" Mike asked as he walked up the two stairs to the deck.

Gonz shook his head. He was a short, thickset man with the darker complexion of a Mexican farmhand. Mike had worked with several guys like him on construction crews and maybe because of that, he'd quickly warmed to Gonz when the man had shown up on the site. He trusted him instantly.

When the watchman shook his head, Mike's chest clenched. Damned if this place didn't have him on edge.

"What happened?" he asked.

Gonz rolled his eyes and pushed himself up and out of the canvas chair.

"I took care of it," he said. His brown eyes met Mike's, and the carpenter could see how tired the watchman was. But there was a hint of amusement in that tired gaze as well.

"Couple of ghost hunters showed up and set up their cameras in the front room. Like they owned the place. I told them to take a hike."

The watchman shrugged and took another swig of his thermos. Coffee? Mike wondered. But the guy had been out here all night. Part of him wondered if it was a beer. That same part of him got excited when he thought of that possibility.

"Did they give you any problem?" he asked.

"Not once I threatened to call the police."

Mike nodded. "That can scare people off."

"That and a switchblade," Gonz said.

Mike raised an eyebrow. "Did you really pull a knife on them?"

Gonz laughed and shook his head. "No, no…just sayin'."

Mike let out a sigh of relief. "Good, I wouldn't want you to have to… though, you know, the closer we get to Halloween…."

Gonz nodded. "I know. They told me all about this place. And how the crazies would be coming out in droves."

"Do they let you carry a gun?" Mike asked.

The watchman nodded. "Yeah, but I don't like to have to bring it out. People see that and everything just goes south, you know?"

Mike nodded. "Sure. But good to know you're protected."

Gonz grinned, showing a mouth full of yellowed teeth. "Don't you worry about me," he said. "I can take very good care of myself. And your house."

He turned around and folded up his chair with one quick snap. "And now I hand it over to you," he said. "Go get some work done."

Gonz grinned and slapped Mike's shoulder as he walked past and down the steps. "Maybe I'll see you tonight," he said. "If you survive the daylight."

"No worry about that," Mike said. "You keep surviving the night and we'll both be all right."

But the watchman was already loading his chair into the back of his old rust-ridden red Toyota pickup truck and didn't give any indication that he heard.

Mike got to work and in a few minutes the clearing was filled with the whir of a circular saw. His first mission was to stack up a large reserve of boards… and once he was done with that, spend hours pounding them into position.

The day went quickly, and for once, without any instances of stumbling upon coffins or dead and bled animals. Katie was absent too, and Mike found himself missing her. When he packed up his tools at the end of the afternoon, he took his time, hoping she would turn up. But when five-thirty had come and gone, he had to admit to himself that she wasn't coming. He tried to find the silver lining; at least he'd get home for once before dark.

CHAPTER ELEVEN

Another day had disappeared like a summer breeze. Once again, Gonz Torrenz was back on the job as dusk fell. Considering he slept through the daylight hours, his life sometimes felt like one long string of silent nights. He pulled down the gravel path and parked the car just a few yards from the front door of the old house. The carpenter seemed to have already left for the day; the clearing was empty.

Gonz had worked a lot of oddball locations as a night watchman. But guarding a broken-down haunted house behind a cemetery in the middle of a forest preserve had to be the strangest. Who would *want* to get into this crap heap? Who even knew it was here? From the road, you couldn't see the old cemetery stones, let alone the old house.

He shrugged and took a chug from his thermos. Didn't matter in the end. It paid the bills. He just had to try to stay awake. It may have looked like a cush job, but he'd learned the hard way not to take those for granted. Every now and then the agency would send someone around to check on their watchmen, and you did not want to be sucking Zs when that guy came walking up to your vehicle.

Gonz knew. He'd been written up once for just that thing. On one easy night watch job, he'd leaned back in the truck after downing some cookies and a couple cups of coffee, and suddenly the low buzz of Zeppelin on the local classic rock station had been lulling rather than energising. The next thing he knew, there was something tapping at his window. And then… he'd been written up. If it happened again, he might have to look for real work. And Gonz didn't have the education or resume to nab himself a desk job somewhere. He'd have to go back to using his hands and his back to clear a cheque. He'd worked for a bricklayer once; he didn't ever intend to go back.

No, he liked watchman work a lot more than busting his back. He needed to stay awake tonight. He had his phone set to go off every half hour, to make sure he got out of the truck and walked around – and walked around inside the house. It was an annoying ritual for the first couple hours…but he'd found on watch gigs at remote locations like this, it became necessary by two a.m.

So, Gonz was completely alert at twelve-thirty when his watch announced that it was time to head into the house. He'd changed it up so that he sat for an hour or so in the house, and then listened to the radio for an hour or so in the truck. Or sat on the back of the truck bed. The change of venue helped keep him alert (along with the coffee and phone alarms).

He stepped outside the cab and stretched. It was a warm night, with just the faintest of breezes to tickle the nose. The moon was low in the sky still, but it gave the clearing in front of the house an almost magical glow.

Gonz walked past the tombstones of the cemetery and stepped onto the new front porch of the house. He took a deep breath of the night air, before unlocking the door. The air inside was not nearly as fresh or pure. He wrinkled his nose and turned on a flashlight to illuminate the dark foyer. The light of the moon did not reach far through the dirty windows, and Gonz didn't want to trip over anything. He walked down the hall to the kitchen. Now and then, a floorboard creaked as he passed.

"Who's there?" he called, as he saw a white shadow pass in the hall.

The watchman stood still and just listened. You couldn't move in this house without making some noise. If he really had seen someone, there would be audible evidence that they were here. There were no rugs or draperies to deaden the sound. No matter where someone was in the house, you'd hear them.

Gonz held his breath and listened.

Something in the depths of the house creaked.

"God damn it," he mumbled under his breath. Someone had managed to get into the place while he was sitting right outside watching it. So now it was up to him to shoo them away.

He walked down the hallway and shone the spot into two of the bedrooms on the first floor. They were empty, stripped of any furnishings. There was no place for an intruder to hide. He moved on.

"I know you're here," he called. "Nobody's allowed in this place. Come out now and I won't get the police involved."

He stood still and listened then, hoping for some telltale movement indicating the person was going to leave quietly. Instead, there was a creak over his head. And another. Slow and repetitive and steady.

Like footsteps.

Gonz walked over to the attic stairs. He'd been up there once, on the day he'd started, just to get the full layout of the place in his head. He didn't have any desire to go back. It was creepy up there, full of dusty boxes and spiderwebs.

He put his foot on the first step and shone the light upwards. It caught the rough beam of the attic ceiling. He called again. There still was no answer, but something above creaked.

Gonz shook his head and stepped slowly up the stairs. He debated going back to the car to get the gun he kept in his glovebox, but then shook his head. There was no reason for any intruder in this place to be armed. It had to be a kid, checking out the 'haunted house' after midnight. They were probably scared shitless right now that someone was on to them.

When he reached the top of the steps, he was careful as he put his head above the floor and into the attic itself. He quickly shone the light 360 degrees, and then did it again, moving slower. The flash didn't pick up anything but dusty boxes and bare walls.

Gonz frowned and stepped the rest of the way up until he stood in the room. He shone the flashlight to the right, letting it linger on an old rope coiled atop a wooden crate.

Something creaked again behind him, and then came a wooden snap, almost like a door closing. He turned quickly and moved towards the source of the sound. Or at least where it sounded like the noise had come from.

The carpenter had framed out a wall in the corner near the window. It looked as if he planned to barricade off a small finger of the room, but hadn't put up the plywood to wall it in yet. Gonz stepped through the frame and looked around, shining the flash into every corner. There was a screwdriver lying on the ground; the watchman bent down to retrieve it. As he did, he noticed the gap line in the floor. He followed it with his eyes until it turned in a 90-degree angle and cut across the floorboards. He saw the inset handle, and fingered at it until the handle lifted upwards. Then he pulled. The floor door opened with the same kind of creak he'd just heard a moment before, and he grinned.

So. *You can run, but you can't hide from the watchman,* he thought.

He lifted the door all the way back, and aimed the light downward. He could see the plank ladder, and dusty floor below. There were footstep tracks all over at the base. Someone had been down here a lot.

He stepped down, and after just three steps, jumped easily to the bottom, anxious to catch whoever was down here by surprise...or if not by surprise, at least catch them before they expected him to make it down.

He saw her as soon as his head ducked below the surface of the attic floor.

She didn't look surprised by his entrance.

The woman stood just three feet away, in front of a small bed covered in a tan and green afghan. Was she a squatter? They had told him this place was empty, but that sometimes kids came and trashed it. But this bed was about the only piece of furniture he'd seen in the house. And it was in something of a hidden room. Maybe she'd managed to escape detection until now. She stood in front of him barefoot, in a stained blue t-shirt and ragged jeans. Her face appeared starkly pale in the light of the flash, her hair long and wispy and pale brown. It reminded him of the mane of a horse his mom used to ride, back when their family could afford to go to the stable and ride horses. She didn't move or speak. Her eyes didn't blink.

She simply stared at him. It was a little creepy.

"This is private property, ma'am," he said. "You'll have to leave."

She didn't answer.

"What's your name?" he asked. "What are you doing here?"

The dark of her eyes remained unblinking. She almost seemed a statue. But she was clearly human. He could see the slow rise of her chest.

"Look, you don't want to talk, that's fine. But you can't stay here." He gestured at the ladder with the flashlight, pointing up.

"If you would...?"

Then she moved.

Slowly.

He tensed involuntarily, but she walked past him and in almost slow motion mounted the steps of the ladder. She never said a word. Her dirt-smeared feet were at the level of his face when he let out a breath. She was leaving without any trouble. Thank God.

But then the door above snapped shut. Only, she was still on the ladder. She had simply pulled the trapdoor closed.

Step by step, her feet descended, moving a little faster now.

When she turned from the ladder to stare at him again, her eyes looked black as the void.

"You have to leave," he said.

She shook her head, no.

Then she jabbed out and slapped the flashlight from his hand. Caught by surprise, he dropped it, and the light rolled across the floor to rest, with the light trained on one wall.

A weight hit him then, as the girl's full body piled into his.

Gonz fell backwards, landing with his ass on the floor. She was upon him in a heartbeat, pinning him to the floor with her weight.

That's when he saw the other one stepping out of the dark shadows. She was pale and comely and grinning. But that grin did not hold any humour.

Gonz opened his mouth to scream.

But only the gravestones heard his cry for help.

CHAPTER TWELVE

When Mike arrived the next day, he found Gonz's old red pickup – with the bed door still hanging down – but no night watchman. Which was unusual. Although he had missed seeing him last night because he'd actually headed home on time, for the most part they had 'handed off' the house over the past few days, Gonz arriving to work just as Mike was getting ready to leave, and vice versa. Mike was 'day shift' and Gonz was 'night shift'. That way the place was always under someone's eye. And, not surprisingly, there had been no further evidence of ritual sacrifices discovered, which had helped Mike's work go faster.

Mike unloaded his own truck and trudged his box of tools up to the attic. He needed to finish roughing in the corner where the laundry chute was so nobody ended up falling down a hole during their walk through the haunted house. Then he was going to finish another wall that he'd framed to divide the space – it would serve as both structural support and allow the decorators another room to haunt.

He'd left the circular saw upstairs and so, after taking his tools up, he stayed there and measured and trimmed a couple pieces of wood right away, nailing them quickly into place. Since there was already a pile of lumber there, he measured and marked a couple more and did the same. Quickly the upstairs spaces filled in.

By lunchtime, his face and back were completely drenched in sweat, but he had finished the attic area – he'd shored up the side walls and added new walls to barricade off sections of what had previously been one long room. He wiped his face with his sleeve for the fiftieth time, and surveyed the work.

Mike nodded. It was good.

So. Now he'd taken care of the attic and the basement. It was already August, and finally time to power through the main floor. The haunted house people would need to get in here soon to start decorating the place. Perry had hired a deep-cleaning crew to go through the place so at least

Mike wouldn't be running into piles of dirt and dust on every surface. But he would be replacing the floor in the kitchen and patching several walls where animals and leakage had taken their toll.

He picked up the saw and some wood and moved them downstairs. It took a couple more trips before he'd carted all of his equipment to the front room of the old house. He realised that he hadn't seen Katie yet today and frowned. She'd been turning up every day by late morning, and here it was afternoon, with no sign of her. He hoped she wasn't mad at him; last night, he'd put his arm around her and kissed her, and she hadn't resisted...but when he'd slipped a hand up the back of her shirt and started moving his fingers to trace the line of her bra, she'd suddenly pushed him away and said no. He'd gotten frustrated and walked away to take a piss, and when he returned...no Katie.

Mixed signals. Always the story of his life, it seemed.

Mike shrugged, feeling defeated as always by women in general, and attacked the old yellow linoleum with a crowbar, peeling the stuff off the wood beneath a chunk at a time. By the time he had a sizeable pile stacked up, and was nearly done with the removal project, he heard a familiar voice.

"Looks like fun," Katie said from behind him.

Mike straightened up with a groan. "Not so much," he answered. "Where ya been?"

"Aw, did you miss me?" she asked.

"Could have used a hand, yeah," he said.

She pouted. "So, I'm just an extra hand to you?"

Mike tilted his head and rolled his eyes. Then he reached out and slipped a hand around her thin waist. With a tug, he pulled her close to him.

"Not just an extra hand," he said.

"Hmm," she answered, and took his free hand and pressed it to her breast. "Just an extra chest?"

"Not just that either," he said, but there was a catch in his voice. He could feel his jeans growing tighter.

"Tell me you missed me," she said, and pressed her lips to his for just a second. Then she pulled away. "Tell me."

"I missed you," Mike said. "A lot." In his head, he was thinking that she didn't have any problems bailing out on him last night, but he held his tongue.

Katie smiled. "Good. I work for love."

"Sounds like a Ministry song," he said.

Katie only looked confused. Probably too young to catch the reference.

She shrugged. "I hope you don't mind Emery helping out today. We were hanging out so I brought her along."

"Sure," he said, while inside he groaned. So...today she brought reinforcements. Why? To fend him off?

"Does she like tearing things apart?" He hefted the crowbar with one arm before holding it out.

Katie shrugged. "She'll do okay."

At that, a floorboard creaked in the hall outside. A moment later, Emery's dour face peered around the corner. Mike thought she looked as if someone had kicked her dog. She did not look like she wanted to be here. *Well*, he thought, *the feeling is mutual. I don't want you here, either.*

"Here she is," Katie announced. "C'mon, Em. Mike wants you to help dig up the floor. You're good at digging things up, right?"

The other girl said nothing, but moved forward to take the crowbar from her friend. Then she stood still, waiting for instructions.

"Do you have another one for me?" Katie asked.

Mike picked up a hammer and pointed to the teeth at the back. "You can use this. We're just trying to peel up all the old flooring, so that I can get at the boards beneath. Most of this material needs to be replaced if we're going to have hundreds of people walking back and forth through this room."

He demonstrated swinging the hammer to catch at the old linoleum and pulling it up by the back of the hammer. After cracking off a couple squares, he handed Katie the tool. "I'll be right back," he said. "I should have something else we can use in the trunk."

When he returned a couple minutes later, the two girls were both leaning over the hole in the floor, looking down into the basement.

"Not exactly where we need a window," he said.

"What about a door?" Katie asked.

He shook his head. "Not that either."

Mike got down on his knees and pulled up the old flooring with a second hammer. Emery stared at him blankly for a minute, and then gouged at the floor on the other side of the hole from him.

Katie's lips pursed in a faint smile, and then she began working between them.

With three of them working on it in tandem, the ten or twelve feet of old flooring quickly turned into piles of scrap.

"All right," he announced finally, wiping the sweat off his face with the bottom of his shirt. "That was the easy part. Now we need to pull out the old wood. You might want to let me take care of this part."

He swung the hammer at a blackened part of the plywood near the rotted-out hole, but instead of going through, the tool only bounced back, as if it had hit a springboard.

Emery stepped closer and held the crowbar out in front of her. But before he could take it, Mike realised she wasn't holding it out for him. She was getting ready to swing.

And then the heavy iron hit the board and something cracked. A moment later, she pulled back on the tool, and a two-foot chunk of old flooring popped up and out. It landed next to his feet, and Emery looked up at him. She didn't smile.

He did. "Well, I guess I was wrong," he said. "Looks like you can take care of this part just as well as I can."

Katie raised an eyebrow and he quickly amended. "Okay, maybe better than I can."

He picked another spot, and began working on removing the old wood a few feet away from Emery, who worked like a piledriver, jamming the crowbar down and then bringing it back up only to slam it back again.

The room was filled with the sounds of crashing tools and splintering wood for over an hour, until Mike called a time out.

"All right," he said, standing straight up with a groan. "I think that's enough for one day. It's after five."

Katie rose from where she'd been kneeling on the far end of the room from him. Emery simply stopped moving. She watched Katie expectantly.

"Do you have any beer?" Katie asked.

"I thought you worked for love?" he answered. With the back of his hand, he wiped a river of sweat from his forehead.

"And beer," she said. "Plus, I was really thinking of you. Because you look really hot."

"Thanks," he said. "Nobody's told me that in ages."

"Never let them see you sweat," she said.

"Come on," he said. "The cooler should still be full."

*   *   *

"You know they killed people here," Katie said.

Mike crumpled an empty PBR in his hand and tossed it to the side of the porch. "What are you talking about?"

"I'm talking about human sacrifice," she said matter-of-factly. "They hung them upside down from the rafters and bled them like cattle. And as the victims died, the coven lay on the floor naked beneath them. The blood of the innocent rained on their chests and privates, and they moaned in ecstasy as the hanging ones screamed."

"You're making this shit up," Mike said.

Katie shook her head. "I'm not. Haven't you heard people talk about Bachelor's Grove?"

Mike nodded. "Of course. I've heard all the stories. People have picked up hitchhikers along the turnpike for years. But before they ever get the hitchhikers home, they disappear into thin air. Ghosts."

"Ghosts of the hanging ones," she said. "Ghosts trying to find their way home when their homes have disappeared with their lives, and time."

"Why would anyone have done such a thing?" he asked.

"Anger," she said. "Revenge."

She held a can to her lips, but then didn't drink. She set it back down on the fresh wood of the deck. "You've never heard people talk about the sacrifices here then?"

He shook his head and popped the tab on a new can.

"They talk about ghosts, and strange lights bobbing between the cemetery stones. And they talk about the ghost of a woman, who's often seen crying as she cradles the ghost of a baby. That's probably the thing people talk about the most when it comes to Bachelor's Grove. The woman with the lost child."

Katie nodded. "Well, they have that part right then, at least. Everything that happened here happened because of her. The jealousy, the murder, the rituals and revenge."

"What did she do to cause all of that?" he asked, still not understanding.

Katie handed her can to Emery and stood up.

"She did what every woman does, only she refused to do it the way most women do."

Katie met Mike's eyes with a sad, long gaze before she said simply, "She loved."

Then she walked to the door of the house and went inside.

Mike felt a chill suddenly, as the sounds of the forest birds and bugs hummed unbroken all around him. He looked up, and found Emery staring at him. She said nothing, but raised the PBR to her lips and took a long swig. He sat there with her in silence for several minutes waiting for Katie to come back, feeling increasingly uncomfortable.

Finally, he shook his head and stood up. "I really need to get going," he announced.

When she didn't answer, he picked up his empty cans and the cooler and walked it to the truck.

When he came back, Emery was gone. He picked up another empty beer can, and then emptied another that still was mostly full over the banister. Then he called into the house.

"Hey girls, I've gotta get going."

When he received no reply, he walked inside and checked the kitchen and back bedroom and upstairs.

There was nobody there. They had vanished again. He didn't know where they'd gone; apparently they'd disappeared into the woods surrounding the old house, because they hadn't walked out the main gravel path that led to the turnpike. They'd have passed him.

"So long and thanks for all the beer," he murmured. He locked the front door and went back to the truck. He noticed Gonz's vehicle still remained where it had been this morning. He'd have to call Perry if the guy wasn't back tomorrow.

"People," he said, pulling with a crunch of gravel onto the turnpike and gunning the engine.

"Can't live with 'em, can't gut them with a knife and leave them to bleed out over a coven of devil worshippers."

He looked back at the entry road to the cemetery in the rearview mirror.

"Usually."

CHAPTER THIRTEEN

Sweat trickled down Mike's back in multiple mini-rivers. It was supposed to hit ninety degrees outside today, but the house felt like a hundred and ten, especially in the back bedroom, where he couldn't budge the window. He was going to have to fix that, or the fire marshal wouldn't approve the place for opening. But he'd skipped working on it this morning when he'd started on the outer wall. Animals or an old leak, maybe both, had led to a large rotten section that he had to repair. When he'd first come into the house, he'd found that one corner of this room had a pile of drywall chunks and wood and mud. You could see a small glimmer of outdoor light if you looked into the blackened hole in the wall. Luckily, this was the only full breach he'd found between the house and the outside, and it was small. But it needed to be sealed and patched.

He stood up from gouging out the soft drywall and groaned. His back got stiff way too easily these days. Thanks to his efforts, the hole in the wall had grown from something a mouse or chipmunk could have fit through to a three-foot-wide explosion in the wall. But he'd finally found solid drywall. The outer structure was solid except for a small area where the original breach had begun, so he'd shore that up and then bring in some new drywall to cover the hole. But first he had to get something to open this window. He couldn't work in this heat anymore.

Mike walked through the hallway, wiping the sweat from his forehead and neck. He hadn't realised just how hot he'd gotten until he stepped out of the bedroom, which had to be one of the most stifling spots in the house, since he'd gotten all the other windows to open and shut.

He stepped out onto the front porch and the temperature dropped at least ten degrees.

"Whew," he said out loud. And then he realised that he wasn't alone.

A thin man with dark unruly hair leaned against the banister. He appeared to be sizing Mike up. But he didn't say a word.

"Um, can I help you?" Mike asked, wiping his wet hand on the thigh of his jeans.

The man nodded slowly. He looked to be in his thirties, and was slight of build – maybe five and a half feet tall. He had a narrow nose and dark, shadowed eyes, and when he looked down – which he seemed to do often – his hair covered his face.

"Sure," he said. "Can you show me the house?"

Mike was taken aback.

"I don't think so," Mike said. "It's not open for visitors."

The guy nodded his head. "Yeah, I know. But I'm not visiting."

"Who are you?" Mike asked.

"Sorry," the guy said, sticking out his palm. "They call me Argento. I'm in charge of decorating all the rooms in this place for the haunted house."

Mike grinned then and shook Argento's hand, which felt thin as a girl's. "That's different," he said. "I'm Mike, I've been fixing the place up for you."

The guy nodded, but said nothing.

"When are you planning to start working?" Mike asked.

"Tonight," Argento said.

"Oh," Mike said. "I didn't realise you guys were going to be coming in yet."

"So, can I see it?" Argento asked, ignoring Mike's comment.

"Yeah, sure," Mike said, and opened the door. "No air conditioning, so it's not exactly pleasant right now."

"No worries," Argento said. "I like to work at night. Should be just fine." He walked inside, and Mike followed with a frown. Something about this guy was off.

Argento stopped in the kitchen and pointed at the faucet. "Does that work?"

Mike shook his head. "No. I'm assuming it used to be connected to a well, but nothing comes out."

"Good, we can make a fountain of blood there."

"Yeah, sure," Mike said, and shook his head. *Of course*, they'd make a fountain of blood in the rusty sink. Why hadn't he thought of that? Ha.

They moved slowly through the house, Argento walking up to corners and touching doorways. Now and then he mumbled something to himself, but Mike didn't answer. The words weren't for him. And he honestly had no idea what they meant. It sounded like a barrage of random syllables.

"*Phenomena*," Argento murmured at one point, while touching a window. And then, "*Tenebrae, Suspiria…. Zombie. Duckling.*"

Zombie duckling? Mike thought. *What the hell?*

Every time Argento's finger touched a surface, it seemed to evoke a new disconnected word. "*Beyond. Demons. Fascination.*" At one point, he laughed when they were in the large master bedroom with a connected bath. He swung his hand out in a wide gesture and announced to a nonexistent audience, "*Bay of Blood.*" Then he shut up for a while, as he opened the closet and returned to the hallway to look in the other rooms.

After they'd walked the rest of the first floor in silence (aside from a couple more of Argento's nonsensical whispers), the thin man suddenly looked at Mike and said, "Stairways?"

Mike took him to the attic staircase, and they quickly ascended.

As soon as Argento reached the top, a smile broke out on his face. "Yes!" he said. "Oh, yes!"

Mike had no idea what he was agreeing to. The man continued to hold a conversation with himself.

"*Grudge. Suspiria.* Even *House on Sorority Row* maybe…" Argento said, peering into the side room that Mike had walled off.

"Are there any drains up here?" Argento asked after a moment.

"You mean, like bathroom faucets or toilets?"

The man nodded quickly.

"No," Mike said. "Only on the first floor."

"Pity," Argento said, and went back to touching the walls. He pulled out a phone and snapped some pictures, and Mike kept moving to stay out of the way. Then the decorator abruptly turned and walked back down the stairs without another word.

"Freak," Mike whispered to himself, before following.

When he got downstairs, he led Argento to the den and showed him the new flight of steps leading down to the basement. When he moved the bookcase, the man's eyes lit up. "*House by the Cemetery*," he whispered, and immediately disappeared through the opening.

Mike followed, and after watching the man skulk around in the basement for a few minutes, he walked to the exterior stairwell and called to the man. "You could have them either enter or exit the house here," he said, pointing at the stairwell that led back up to the outside.

"Yes, yes," Argento said, but didn't follow him out.

Mike shrugged and walked up the stairs. He waited for a few minutes on the porch, before noticing Argento's face peering out of the attic window. The guy was re-walking the whole place again, apparently.

"Whatever," Mike murmured, and pulled out his cell phone. He'd been meaning to call Perry all day to let him know that the watchman had apparently abandoned his vehicle and his job.

His friend answered on the second ring. "Hey Mike, what's going on? I've been meaning to call you this week."

"Well, it looks like we need a new night watchman," Mike said. "That Gonz guy hasn't been back in a couple days. But his truck is still parked here."

"Damn, when was the last night he worked? I'm not paying the service if he hasn't been showing up."

Mike frowned. "Tuesday, I think he was here? Not since."

He walked down the steps of the porch to move out of the sun and into the shade of the trees. He found himself in the graveyard, and sat down on the top of one of the taller stones.

"I'd call them, and have them send out someone else," Mike suggested.

"No need," Perry said. "I'll call them and tell them to have that truck towed if their guy isn't going to show up. And then I'll fire them. We won't need them anymore. The set people are going to start working nights on decorating the rooms you're done with. That's why I was going to call you today, to let you know."

Mike laughed. "Well, thanks for the warning but...you're too late. One of them is already here. Some nutjob called Argento."

Perry laughed. "Go easy," he warned. "He's a talented nutjob. You stay out of his way, and he'll stay out of yours."

Mike nodded. "I can see that. I'm not sure he's even aware that other people exist."

"How much more time do you need to finish your part?" Perry asked.

Mike outlined the few projects remaining, and said he should be done by the week after Labor Day.

"Good!" Perry said. "Though if Argento or the rest need any help building stuff, I'd like you to stay on though, and help them out. We need to open in a month. It's going to be a race."

"Sure," Mike said. After a few more words, they hung up, and he turned to look at the house.

"Who was that?" Katie asked.

Her voice made him jump; she was literally a foot from his shoulder. "Don't do that!" he complained.

She grinned and slipped a cool hand across his neck. "Do what?" she asked innocently as her fingers ruffled his hair and then trailed down the line of his spine. "This?"

"No." He grinned. "That you can do."

"So, who were you talking to?"

"That was Perry," he said. "The guy who's running this whole renovation. He was just telling me about the decorating crew that's going to start painting the place and I told him about our missing night watchman."

"What do you mean?" she asked.

"Guy who was keeping an eye on the place at night," he said. "Hasn't been here in a couple days, but you can see his truck still sitting right over there."

He pointed at the glint of silver through the trees.

"Huh," she said. "That's weird that he'd leave his truck. You're sure he's not around?"

Mike shook his head. "I looked. Plus, we've been sitting on the deck the past couple nights when he should have been here. Anyway, these other people are going to start being around, so it doesn't really matter, I guess. There will be someone in the house pretty much all the time from now on to get it ready."

Katie frowned. "Does that mean you're not going to have a beer with me at the end of the day?"

"I think we can still squeeze that in," he said with a grin. "Oh, right there. Don't stop," he begged, as her fingernails found the perfect place.

"Where, here?" she said. Suddenly she moved her hand from his lower back to cup the crotch of his jeans. Her fingers and palm moved up and down slightly as she put on enough pressure to feel his balls shift inside the heavy fabric.

"Um, yeah," he groaned with surprise. "That's really good."

"Okay," she said, removing her hand as fast as she'd surprised him with it. "Good to know."

She planted a kiss on his mouth, and then traced the outline of the chain and locket he still wore through his shirt before she backed away. "I've got something to do this afternoon, but I'll be back later and we can see if that is still really good."

Katie winked and turned around to walk through the gravestones towards the turnpike. She didn't follow the gravel path, but instead circled the lower half of the small pond before disappearing into the undergrowth.

Mike had to take several deep breaths before he finally got off the stone and walked back to the house. Going back to work was going to be a bitch after that tease.

He desperately hoped it wasn't an *idle* tease. She'd been leaving him blueballed for the past couple weeks, and he wasn't sure how much more he could take. On a couple nights, he'd literally been in pain as he'd driven home after the sudden cessation of her kisses, his testicles filled and anxious, with no release allowed.

As he stepped up on the porch, the front door opened and the wiry man stepped out.

"I'll be back," Argento announced.

"When do you think?" Mike asked.

"Maybe late tonight. Maybe tomorrow night. I need to get some supplies together, but I have to work until ten tonight."

"Do you need me to leave the front door unlocked?" Mike asked. "I'm not sure how that's going to fly, but I won't be here that late."

Argento shook his head and held up a bronze key.

"I'm good."

And with that, he marched down the steps to the gravel lane.

Mike shook his head and went to the truck to get the crowbar to force open the bedroom window.

After being outside for a while, once he was back in the bedroom, the air really felt stifling. Mike worked at shifting the window with his hands for a minute and had exactly the same success as he'd had this morning. None.

So, he finally sprayed some WD-40 on the dry-rotted window tracks, and then pressed the crowbar into the small gap.

The window ledge cracked as he pressed down.

But he moved the crowbar from side to side, pressing it down just a little, and then shifting it to the other end, trying to edge the window up centimetre by centimetre without having the frame skew further and get completely locked.

After a few moves from one side to the other, he had raised the window up enough to wedge his fingers in beneath the old wooden frame. He set the crowbar down and with both hands shoved beneath the window, gave a solid heave-ho...and the thing slid up another inch.

Air came rushing into the room in a welcome gust. It wasn't cool, but it was cooler. He kept working at it and could hear things shifting inside the wall as he jimmied the window another inch and then two more. Once he'd gotten it halfway up, he sprayed the track beneath it with WD-40 and pulled it down most of the way. He sprayed the top half again, and then pushed the window back up. It moved easier now. He repeated that twice more, until the window moved up and down without too much effort. The sides gleamed with oil, but he didn't care. The key was to be able to open the window without a crowbar. Hopefully, he'd worked out the seal that time had put in place.

Mike fingered the edges of the hole he'd made in the drywall, confirming it was solid. Then he lifted the biggest pieces of debris from the gap between the inner and outer wall and stacked them up with the pile he had accumulated in the room already. He'd bag and toss the whole mess once he finished mudding in a new piece of drywall.

As he reached in to pull one last piece from the area near the window, he saw a glimmer of something white on the ground. Something white but not drywall.

He reached over inside the wall and brushed off the dirt that partially obscured it. He could see a somewhat rounded knob; it didn't look like anything that belonged to the architecture.

Mike grabbed the end and pulled it towards him, and a long piece emerged from the dirt. He pulled it out of the hole in the wall and held it up, not quite believing his eyes.

It was a bone.

And not the skeletal remains of some mouse or rat or squirrel that had skulked in the passage and died.

This was a human bone.

Arm or leg, from the size of it.

As that registered, Mike opened his fingers and let the thing fall. It rolled across the floor to lie next to the pile of drywall.

He was reminded suddenly of Katie's story about people being hung and bled to death in secret, gruesome rituals in this house, and shook his head. He looked again inside the hole, and saw other bits of yellowed bone sticking up from the dirt and debris that littered the narrow passage.

Someone had walled in a body…or parts of one…behind this wall at some point long ago.

"Fuckin' A," Mike whispered to himself. He stepped away from the hole, shaking his head. "This is not a good house."

He took a deep breath and imagined he smelled the stench of dead bodies. He could guess at the horrible stench that must have once permeated this place, if Katie's stories were true. And with a human bone buried here in the wall, he thought that they very much could be.

"I need a drink," he whispered, and walked out of the room to head to the cooler in his truck.

The first PBR went down really fast.

He slowed down a bit with the second. He needed to. Because he wanted to close up that hole before the daylight waned. He pulled a fresh piece of drywall from the back of the truck bed and marched back into the house.

Some things should remain buried.

CHAPTER FOURTEEN

"Here's what I'm thinking," Argento said. Lucio, Lon, Jeanie and June all huddled around the kitchen table at June's house. Three pieces of paper lay in the centre, with boxes and notes sketched all over them.

"We've got three floors to play with," he continued. "But the place isn't huge. So, I think we set up the ticket taker outside on the deck."

He pulled one of the sheets of paper closer and pointed out a path with his pencil as he talked. "We have them enter through the foyer, walk through the front room and the dining room, then cross the hall into the kitchen. There's a back doorway to the kitchen, so we can have them go right through there and cross the hall into the back bedroom. If we have the carpenter cut through the back closet of that room, it would enter right into the den. And if we can cut through the back wall of the den, you'd be in the second bedroom. Exit through that main door, walk around a corner and you've got the stairs up to the attic."

"Do you really think he can just knock out the walls like that?" June asked.

Argento shrugged. "It looked like it to me. We'll have to ask him. If it doesn't work…then people are just going to have to go out through the same door they came in."

Lucio shook his head. "I don't like that. We want a straightforward funnel, no backtracking."

Argento nodded. "That's the goal."

At that moment, a loud yawn erupted from the hallway outside the kitchen. A moment later, Lenny walked in, stretching his arms towards the ceiling with his mouth wide open.

Lon turned and shook his head at June. "Does this guy ever go home?"

She shrugged. "When he needs to pick up his mail."

"Morning, haunters," Lenny said. "What are we all plotting today?"

"Well, for starters, it's afternoon," Lon said. "Didn't you go to work today?"

Lenny shook his head and walked to the fridge. "Didn't feel like it," he said, rummaging around inside. He came out with a can of Coke and popped the tab. "I called in sick. I'm *sure* I'll be fine by Monday." He grinned and took a deep slug of the pop.

"And that's what's wrong with America today," Lon declared. "No work ethic. You better not call in sick to the house."

"Don't worry," Lenny promised. "Showbiz is different. The show must go on and all that."

June sighed and rolled her eyes. Then she returned the conversation to the topic at hand. "Do you have ideas for the room themes yet?" she asked Argento.

"I have a few," he said. The way he smiled, it was clear he had more than just a few.

"I thought we could make the dining room a big *Texas Chainsaw Massacre* theme. And the den could be our giallo room. I'm thinking a combo of *Opera, Inferno, Suspiria, Phenomena*."

"I'd argue that those aren't really all giallos," Lon said, but Argento ignored him.

June leaned over to Jeanie and explained. "Those are all Dario Argento films," she said.

Jeanie nodded. "Got it."

"I thought the first bedroom could be the *Nightmare on Elm Street* room," Argento continued.

June and Lenny both lit up. "Now you're talking," Lenny said. He grabbed June's shoulders and squeezed.

"I thought we could borrow the stuff from your bedroom," Argento said, looking at Lenny. He shrugged. "Sure, why not?"

"We have to have a Fulci room," Lucio said. "It'd be cool to do something from a Jean Rollin film too – a *Living Dead Girl* or *Fascination* theme? I'm thinking we could stage the scene of the ghoul girl at the piano or maybe something like Brigitte Lahaie in that long cape threatening people with the big scythe. Or maybe have a vampire walking out of a grandfather clock? Or how about a Jess Franco thing…we could have the girl from *Countess Perverse* running around in a loincloth with a bow and arrow."

Argento laughed and shook his head.

"I don't think we're going to get away with having a nude girl sitting at a piano, or a bunch of women in see-through silk waltzing around," Lon said. "Or really anything from a Franco movie. This is a family show."

"But the girls could have long, fake-looking fangs," Lucio offered.

Lon shook his head. No.

Lenny laughed. "Yeah, gore is great, but no tits, God forbid."

"How about an homage to the films on the 1980s Video Nasties list?" Lucio suggested.

"I think 'banned in Britain' might be a little obscure for our audience," Lon said. "I don't think most people in the suburbs are too familiar with *Cannibal Holocaust* or *Antropophagus* or *Unhinged* or *Flesh for Frankenstein*."

"Maybe not," Lucio said. "But they know *The Evil Dead* and *I Spit on Your Grave*. And some will recognise *The Beyond*."

"I have white contacts, so we can have someone dressed up like that girl from *The Beyond*," June offered.

"That would be awesome!" Lucio said.

Argento nodded. "I think you get the second bedroom for Fulci stuff."

"So…it sounds like you have the first floor pretty mapped out," Jeanie said. "Where do they go next?"

Argento pointed at the thin hall that ran along the left side of the diagram. "They walk down this hall and reach the stairways. We want to have someone stationed there probably, to make sure people go upstairs first or else they'll miss the attic."

"Brigitte Lahaie lookalike with the scythe," Lucio suggested.

"Maybe," Argento said with a grin. "It would be better if the stairwells were in different parts of the house, but we're stuck with this setup. You go up or down right here."

"And what happens in the attic?" June asked.

"We've got rafters, so we've got to do a noose," Argento said. "I'm thinking we should play off the whole attic thing though, and have some old trunks up there that people can pop out of, maybe an old woman in a wheelchair, like Norma Bates, and then a row of old costumes that people have to walk past, like that room in *Curtains*. We could even have someone in the hag mask from there stalking the aisles."

"Nice," Lucio said. "I get to be the old crone with the sickle!"

Argento grinned. "Sold. But I thought you'd want to be a zombie?"

Lucio shrugged. "I can switch off."

Argento shook his head. Then he pointed at the large space at the far end of the attic. "Here we've got a nice back room which I was thinking we could turn into a creepy kid's playroom, like in *House on Sorority Row*. They'll have to criss-cross here to get back downstairs, because there's only one way up and down to the attic, so people will cross through the playroom and out the back door, which points them right back to the stairwell they came up on. We can divide the stairway, maybe?"

June pointed at the other piece of paper on the table and looked at Argento. "So what happens when they go in the basement?"

He grinned. "They enter…'The chamber of horrors'!" he declared.

Lon laughed. "So, you're decorating the basement to look like your bedroom?"

Argento snorted. "Downstairs, we've got two walled-in rooms, and a small area along the northern wall that's enclosed to hide the utilities. I thought we could set up an aisle of exhibits with iconic monsters there."

"An Aisle of Atrocities!" Lucio said.

"As people walked down the aisle they would see some of the most famous horror themes and film scenes. Countess Báthory, *The Exorcist, Hellraiser*, Romero's zombies…."

"How about Fulci's zombies?" Lucio asked. "They had better makeup. And maggots."

Argento shrugged. "Rotting zombies, clean zombies, whatever. We can have a dungeon, and I thought one room could be a Vlad the Impaler room – I've got a friend who works at Ellis Manufacturing. I've already talked to him and we could get a bunch of tall metal spikes from him and hang some latex bodies on them. Easy setup, great spot for gory makeup skills," he said, nodding at June and Jeanie.

"What about a *Re-Animator* set?" Lenny asked. "Or *Dead Alive*? That scene mowing down the zombies with a lawnmower is classic."

"Maybe," Argento said. He clearly had other thoughts and pointed at the corner of his diagram. "On one end of the aisle, there's another enclosed area that we could turn into a wax museum."

"And where the heck are you going to get wax figures?" Jeanie asked.

"They don't need to really be wax," Argento said. "I've got a couple manikins that look like wax…and I know Lon has a dead whore that we could use."

"What?!" Jeanie yelped. "What do you mean he has a dead whore?"

Lon laughed. "It's a conversation piece I got last year for my Halloween party. It's a latex body, but damned if it doesn't look completely real. You should see the detail in her toes. She's got bruises all over her and she's kind of scrunched up. When you walk into a room and see her lying in bed, she looks completely real. My parents walked in and saw her at the party last year and, I kid you not, they stood there waiting, watching for her to finally take a breath or jump up at them. They really thought I'd hired someone to lie there in the bed and spook people."

"That's fucked up," Lenny said.

"And having a bloody girl hanging from the ceiling over your bed isn't?" Lon asked. "Give me a break."

"That's a *Nightmare on Elm Street* homage," Lenny argued. "It's not the same as having a fake dead whore *in* your bed. And showing your parents!"

Lon grinned but said nothing.

"So where are you going to get all of these manikins and sets and everything?" Jeanie asked.

"Well, Lon and Lucio and June and I all have a bunch of stuff we can use," Argento said. "I've also got a lot of my own lighting equipment that I've bought for other houses I've worked on."

"And we do have a budget for buying stuff," Lon offered. "But it's not huge, so we really have to try to build or borrow as much as we can before we spend it."

June looked at Argento and Lucio. "Are you guys going to be able to build all of those sets? If we have an aisle of different exhibits downstairs, that sounds like a lot of false walls and stuff. We only have a few weeks."

Argento grinned. "That's why we have a carpenter on the payroll. We just need to tell him what to build."

"Within reason," Lon cautioned.

"So, when do we start decorating?" Jeanie asked.

"Tonight," Argento said. "I'm going there after work. Anyone who's free after eleven is welcome to join me."

CHAPTER FIFTEEN

"Did you miss me?"

Katie's voice echoed in the empty room. It sounded as if she was right behind him.

"Yeah, actually," he said. "Can you reach over my shoulder and hold this in place while I screw it in?"

He had just finished cutting the drywall to size and was holding it up to the wall joists.

"Sure," she said. Suddenly he felt the soft weight of her breast on his shoulder, as she draped her body over him and pressed her fingers next to his hands.

"I could hold it like this for you," she said.

"You *could*," he said. "The problem is, I need to move. The drill and screws are over there."

He pointed to one side, but made no attempt to leave the shelter of her chest. You took what you could get. And he was definitely taking this for all he could milk it for. So to speak.

"Emery can get it for you," she said.

As if on cue, a pair of hands held out his drill and box of drywall screws. When he took them from her, Emery leaned in front of them both and pressed her hands to the wallboard.

"Thanks," he said.

She didn't answer.

A moment later, the whir of the drill cut the air. Emery kept holding the board, but Katie let her hands drift back to Mike's neck and side. She ghosted his movements from behind, her arms draped over his, her chest pressed softly against his back; he found himself growing uncomfortably aroused as he punched screws through the drywall. He was pretty sure that he had never gotten a hard-on while working on drywall. Then again, nobody had ever touched him like that while he was working. He feared he was going to be incapable of work in a few more seconds. Which only made him work faster.

When he punched in the last screw, Mike leaned back into Katie's embrace.

"That's it." He looked at Emery and said, "You can let go now. We just have to mud it in and we're all set."

"Did I help?" Katie whispered in his ear.

"Couldn't have done it without you," he answered.

"Good," she said. "I wanted to help. Because I have something I need your help with later."

"What is it?" he asked, turning in her arms to look at her.

She kissed his lips and then sat back, releasing her hold on him. "Later," she said. "After you're done here."

"Just gotta slap on some mud, and it's Miller Time," he said.

"You don't drink Miller," she said.

"It's a figure of speech."

She smiled. "Should I go get a shovel from your truck?" she asked.

"Why?" He looked confused.

"For the mud," she said.

Mike laughed. "No, no," he said. "It's not that kind of mud. Come on, I'll show you."

He got up and led her out to the truck. Once he let down the bed, he picked up the can of drywall joint compound and a spreader. When they got back in the room, he popped open the lid and showed her the white paste within.

"If you like, you can spread it by hand," he said. "You just want to fill in all the cracks and cover and smooth it enough so that when you sand, you'll have a nice smooth surface. But you don't want to put so much on that you have to sand a lot, because then it's a pain."

He cupped his hand and dug out a big hunk of mud, and demonstrated working it into the cracks around the piece of drywall.

"Do you want to try?" he asked.

Katie shook her head. "I think I'll pass this time."

Mike grinned and slapped on a couple more handfuls before pulling out his joint knife and working the mud to an even covering across the edges of the piece. Katie sat and watched, keeping her hands to herself.

"I don't think I ever saw my dad do that," she offered at one point.

"Not something most people should have to do," he said. "Unless someone punches holes in their walls."

After another couple swipes of the metal blade, he finally sat back and nodded.

"I think that is about as even as we're going to get. Now they can paint it black or red or whatever the hell they want."

"Are you ready for a beer?" Katie asked.

Mike laughed. "I've been ready for hours."

He stood up and picked up the mud bucket, spreading knife and drill. "I just need a bag to put all of that crap in," he said, nodding at the pile of debris in the corner. "I don't like to leave a mess where I've been working."

He took all of the materials back to the truck and grabbed a black plastic bag to put the chunks of drywall and dirt and wood into. Katie followed him but Emery only sat in the corner of the bedroom, waiting for them to come back. When they did, she rose and took the garbage bag and he offered an end to Katie. He slipped the blade of a shovel under the pile and began moving the debris into the bag.

"I actually found a bone in that wall," he announced, when he recognised the long, ragged piece of wallboard that slid onto the top of his tool.

"Not surprising," Katie said. "They killed all sorts of people here. The walls are probably completely lined with bones. It keeps the wrong spirits out and leads the right ones in."

"And exactly which are the right ones?" he asked.

"That depends on who's laying the bones," she said.

"Touché," he said.

He picked up the bag, bucket and spreading knife and led the girls out to the truck to put them away. He set the joint compound bucket on the bed of the truck and used a paper towel and a splash from a water bottle to wipe off the spreading knife. Then he pushed the end of the bed up and slapped his hands together to knock off the dust and paste.

"That's it," he said. "Another day done."

"Well, not completely done," Katie said suggestively.

He grinned. "Nope, now it's time for a little relaxation."

He walked around to the cab of the truck and pulled the cooler from the passenger's side. "Who's up for a PBR?" he asked.

"I'd like one," Emery said. Her voice was low and strangely intense.

Mike was surprised to hear it, but glad at the same time. The girl's persistent silence creeped him out a little. "We can accommodate," he said.

They walked back to the deck and he opened the cooler, handing out cans to both girls before popping one himself.

"Oh yeah," he said, after downing the first three gulps of the can. "That hits the spot."

Katie grinned. "You looked like you could use a drink," she said, holding the can to her lips. "It was hot today."

"Hotter than hell," he said. "I thought I was going to melt."

"You don't know what hot is then," she answered, looking at him with eyes wide over the rim of her beer can. She didn't blink.

Mike suddenly felt aroused again.

"I think I'd like to know," he answered.

"I'd like to show you," Katie answered. Her eyes still didn't break contact with his.

"I don't think Emery wants to hear about that," he suggested.

Katie shook her head. "Em's cool. She knows me better than anyone."

At that moment, Emery held out another can of PBR to him. He emptied the last sip of his current can and cracked open the next.

"Whatever you say," he said, between gulps. The night suddenly felt both cooler and hotter than the sweltering humid soup of the day. And he was okay with that. On either extreme.

"So…what was the favour that you wanted to ask me for?" he said.

"It's kind of weird," she answered. "It's a family thing."

"Families are weird," he agreed.

"That's easy to say," she said. "Because it's really true. But…my family was *really* weird. Did you ever have an uncle who collected bugs?"

Mike shook his head.

"Well, I did. He used to say if you listened to them, you'd understand everything there was to know about the world. Personally, I thought he was crazy."

Mike laughed. "He sounds a little off."

She shook her head. "He was the least of them. My sister used to sleep with my cousin whenever our relatives came to visit. It started out that our parents put them in the same bed because they were little. But then when we were in our teens, they still did it. And they didn't sleep in pyjamas, once our parents were in bed. Do you know what I mean?"

"That...doesn't sound right," Mike acknowledged, taking another sip of his beer.

"What's your family like?" she asked.

He shrugged. "Not much to speak of. My dad died when I was a kid – heart attack. My mom is still around, but she's losing it at this point. Sometimes when I visit her she asks if I'll go tell my dad it's time for dinner. He's been gone thirty years. So...she's not all there."

"Do you have a brother or sister?"

"Brother," Mike said. "But he's out in Kansas City. I almost never get the chance to see him. And neither one of us is very good with the telephone."

"That's it?" she said. "No wife, kids, pets?"

"No pets, no kids...just one ex-wife," he said. "She left me last year for a guy who wears a tie and takes the train into work in Chicago every day. A guy who saws wood and hammers nails wasn't enough for her, I guess."

"Girls don't usually care what you do for a living," she said. "As long as what you do after the lights go out is good. Did you...."

"Please her?" he finished. "I did when we first got together. I'm not a pencil dick or something. But she wanted prestige and a fountain of cash. And after a while it was pretty clear that I was never going to give her either one of those."

Mike shook his head and pounded the rest of his PBR.

Emery popped the top on a new can and handed it to him. Mike didn't think twice; he upended it and sucked half of it down before slamming it to the wood. Thinking about Mia made him drink more. And faster.

"I was a good husband and I made a decent living for us," he said. His voice cracked a little and Mike looked out at the deep blue sky that shone just barely through the tops of the trees all around. Night had fallen fast.

Katie's arm slipped around his shoulder. Her lips tickled the edge of his ear. "I'm sure you were," she whispered. "Sometimes you just meet the wrong girl."

Mike nodded and took another pull from the can.

"And sometimes," Katie continued, "she rips your heart out like a fishing lure stuck inside the throat of a five-pound bass."

Mike snorted at that, and looked up from his contemplation of the deck wood. Katie's eyes were right there, and they didn't pull away when he met them.

"I wish I'd met you five years ago," he said.

"I wish I'd met you a long time ago too," she whispered. "But... you can't go backwards. Only forward. And you know me now. And I know you."

"Yes," he agreed. Mike realised he suddenly didn't know what else to say.

He took a sip and said nothing, and then suddenly heard another beer tab pop nearby. The can in his hand was pulled away, and a new cold one took its place.

"Thanks," he said, but even as he did, Katie's lips were on his, and her tongue tangled itself around his own. He set the beer down on the deck and slipped both arms around her. She not only accepted his advances tonight, but she made one of her own. Katie flipped one leg over his and smiled, her lips just inches from his own. She straddled him and pressed his head back to the post of the deck. Mike felt his head swimming amid the chiming hum of the crickets and locusts, and the call and response of the night birds throughout the forest, there on his deck beneath the light of the stars. He could feel her crotch shifting and grinding slowly against his as she nuzzled his lips and face with her mouth. Part of him knew that Emery sat quietly close by, and part of him didn't care.

"I want to stay with you tonight," she said at last, pulling back for a moment from kissing him. "I want to show you what it can be like to be with a woman who loves you."

Mike felt his heart thump hard. An explosion of pressure and need and blood. "You love me?" he whispered.

"Shhhh," she said, and buried him in her hair. When she pulled back from that kiss, she grinned slyly and whispered, "Don't tell Emery. She'll be mad."

She moved against him then, in a way that was more than just suggestive. It brought him to full erection in just seconds. He slipped his arms around her and ran his hands down to her ass, cupping the full, soft roundness of her, and pulling her even closer than she'd come on her own.

Her tongue slipped across his lips, tracing his smile, and she pressed him back until he lay down on the porch of the soon-to-be haunted house.

"Yes," he moaned.

"I need you tonight," she whispered, her lips just a breath away from his.

"You have me," he answered.

"There's just one thing we need to do first," she said.

"What's that?" he asked, moving his hands beneath her shirt to feel the soft curve of her waist.

"Not yet," she said, and slid her leg off him.

Mike blinked his way back into focus, and sat part of the way up. The sky was rich and dark blue above them, and the sounds of night filled his ears in a humming symphony. Thousands of locusts and insects and birds hummed and chirped in the distance. The sound was lulling; with Katie lying on top of him, he could have let himself go entirely. But she had moved.

"We need to do one thing first," she said. "Emery tried to do it on her own, but it's too much."

"What?" he asked again.

"I need you to help me move something," she said. "But we have to dig it out some more first."

"What is it?" he asked.

Emery held out a hand and pulled him to his feet as Katie rolled away.

"Do you have a shovel?" Katie asked. "We do need one for *this* kind of mud."

"Sure, in the truck," he said.

Together they walked to the bed of his truck and Mike pulled a spade out from the back.

"Do you have a light?" Katie asked. "It's dark over there."

Mike smiled. "I've got it all." He reached into the back of the cab, where he kept a large battery-powered lantern. You never knew when the power was going to go out on a new job.

"Follow me," Katie said, and led him down the gravel path a few steps, before veering into the woods. Mike followed, though the darkness and beer left everything around him in a haze.

At one point he stopped, and Emery slammed into him from behind.

When he turned around to apologise, she shook her head and put a hand on his back to push him forward.

They emerged from the short path through the brush at the middle of the small cemetery surrounding the pond. Katie turned around just as he realised where they were. She pointed at a small pile of dirt near her feet. A weathered grey headstone marked the top of a plot just a couple feet away. The inscription was lost in the shadows.

"Emery couldn't do this herself," Katie said. "I really need your help."

"Help to do what, exactly?" Mike asked.

Katie's eyes wouldn't meet his right away. She looked at the ground for a long moment, before they finally rose up, big and desperate looking.

"I need you to dig up my mother's grave," Katie said.

Mike's eyes grew wide.

"It sounds weird, I know," she said. "But it's really not. I told you my family was kind of messed up. Well, my mother took most of our family's money to the grave with her. She was buried with a family jewel, and I need it back."

"Oh no, no, no," Mike said. He dropped the shovel on the grass. "I've dealt with just about enough dead bodies this month. I am not about to dig one up on purpose. It's not right."

Katie shook her head. "I wouldn't ask you to help with this if it wasn't really important," she said.

"I'm sorry, Katie, but...I can't. I just can't."

Katie stepped closer, and leaned into him as she gave him a hug. She rested her head on his shoulder and whispered, "I promise you that if you do this for me, I'll do whatever you want tonight. Anything at all."

She raised her head up and met his eyes. "And I know what you've been wanting the past few nights. I'll do that for you, everything you've been thinking of. I'll be glad to do that with you. Just do this one thing for me before all those people start working on this house. You said this place is going to get crowded pretty soon, and it'll be impossible then."

The lights of a car passed by just a few dozen yards away on the turnpike.

"We're awfully close to the road to be digging up a grave," Mike said.

"That's why Emery couldn't do it alone," Katie said. "We need to do this fast and stay out of sight."

"I can't believe you'd want to dig up your own mother," Mike said. He still sounded unsure, though Katie's promises had nearly levelled any sane reservations he'd had. Beer and the promise of what he knew would be heaven had worn down nearly all of his will.

"She was buried with a family jewel that must be worth tens of thousands of dollars by now," Katie said. "And at the moment, I'm about to lose my house. If I can get the jewel back, I won't lose the house. You don't want me to lose the house I grew up in, do you?"

She looked at him with wide, dark eyes. For the first time since he'd met her, he saw the glint of panic, or at least, desperation, in her gaze. "I don't want to end up wandering the turnpike at night without a home like those lost ghosts you told me about."

Mike shook his head.

"Please," she begged, holding his shoulders. "Just get it out of the ground for me, and Emery and I can take care of the rest."

The night seemed to move like liquid around Mike's head, and he shook away the sense of disorientation as he reached down to retrieve the shovel he'd dropped. And then words came out of his mouth that he didn't think he'd say. But he heard his voice say them.

"Only for you," he said to Katie.

She smiled and leaned up to kiss him. "Thank you," she said. "I owe you. And I *will* pay you back."

Mike pushed the spade into the earth already loosened by Emery, and threw a load onto the small pile next to the grave. Emery herself held a shovel and did the same on the other side of the hole. Between the two of them, the piles on either side of the grave grew to be three feet high in almost no time.

A couple times they dropped their spades and ducked when cars passed on the turnpike, but it was later now, long after dark, and traffic was rare.

Mike dug until the sweat dripped off his forehead and onto his arm. At one point, the tip of his spade hit the iron of Emery's tool with a clang, and he looked up at the girl to apologise. Her face was flushed; her shirt covered in dirt and perspiration.

"Sorry," he said.

As usual, she said nothing. Emery only pulled her spade away and dug in to a new area of the grave.

Mike's spade hit the hollow sound of wood first, but Emery's was only a few seconds behind. And then her thrusts rang with the empty sound of hollow wood below. Together, they began to scoop instead of slice down, and in a few minutes, they had completely uncovered the surface of the casket.

"That's perfect," Katie said, standing watch nearby. "Can you lift it out?"

Mike looked at Emery, who had dropped her shovel and stood silent, arms at her sides.

"Want to give it a shot?" he asked.

The girl moved to the foot of the grave and reached down to find the handles they had exposed on the sides of the casket. She began to pull before he'd even bent over, and he hurried to get his hands placed on the other side of the wooden box from her.

The thing did not want to move.

Mike yanked and groaned and swore but it did no good. Finally, he pushed back from the edge and told Emery to stop. "We have to clear more from the sides."

He slid his legs back into the hole and stood on the top of the casket, and with the spade edged out the sides all the way around the wood farther than they had before, careful not to go too far so that the wall of earth above collapsed down. When they tried lifting it again, the casket moved. A little.

After shifting and moaning a few minutes more, the heavy box of wood finally jerked and shifted upwards. Mike and Emery dragged it to the side, away from the hole and onto the grass. As soon as they stopped, Mike fell back to the ground, panting. When he opened his eyes again, Katie and Emery stood there looking down at him. Their eyes were simply watching him. It was a little unnerving. Mike sat up.

"There you go," he said. "You can open it and get whatever you're looking for but...I'm not going in there. I dug it up, but that's where it ends."

"Can you at least help us move it to the basement of the house?" Katie asked.

"And just leave a big hole out here?" Mike asked. "No way! Someone would see that."

"Take it to the basement for me, so I can open it when nobody's around," she said. "I don't want to be doing it here, when someone could stop on the side of the road at any minute. The two of you can come back and fill in the hole quickly for tonight and nobody'll notice."

Emery stood on one end of the casket, grabbed the handles and lifted. Her end of the box rose a foot and she stood like that, casket partly raised, waiting. Mike shook his head, but didn't protest. It was all a little surreal and foggy right now, and he just wanted this inexcusable exercise over with. He took the handles on the other side and lifted. Seconds later, Emery was walking backwards as they moved through the cemetery and across the grassy clearing towards the house. She watched him, instead of where they were going, as they walked. He recognised that she was completely dependent on his navigation, and extra carefully guided them around the corner of the house towards the back.

"Down the cellar steps," Katie directed.

Mike shifted the box to the left and said, "Let me go first." Then he backed down the stairwell, grunting with each step. When Emery and he were both on level ground, he asked, "Okay, where should we set her?"

"Let's go to the old cellar," Katie said. "That way if any of the decorating people come down here...."

He nodded and hefted the casket higher. "You got it," he said, and began walking backwards once more. At last they stepped down a few inches to the original earth floor and walked through a door to go behind the barricade wall he'd set up. It was effectively a secret, hidden room in the cellar.

"Here?" he asked.

"Perfect," Katie said.

Mike dropped his end and sat down on top of the coffin. His underarms were soaked, his forehead dripped sweat into his eyes.

"I'm not opening it," he reiterated.

"No need," Katie said. "Emery will help me. But...I really do need your help with one more thing."

Mike let out a faint moan and Katie grinned. She stepped up to him and bit the bottom of his earlobe before whispering, "I promise I'll make it worth your while."

Her lips felt like an electric shock, and he straightened. He was stung but it felt like the prod of heaven.

"What else?" he asked.

"Fill in the hole?"

He sighed and nodded, and then walked back through the 'public' basement and up the steps.

The night felt good. The air had cooled since the hot August afternoon, and once alone, Mike was lulled by the steady oscillating hum of the locusts in the trees. Their call was warm and placating, as he scooped the loose dirt shovel by shovel back into the hole. He only ducked down twice when lights from the road announced themselves through the forest trees.

After he patted the earth down and tried to loosely rearrange the hunks of sod on top, Mike took the shovel and dropped it back in the bed of his truck. He grabbed his cooler then, and walked towards the house. Half of him expected to find the girls gone; how many times over the past month had Katie ditched him?

But the memory of her electric touch kept him walking quickly to the house. And as he stepped up on the porch, he found Katie waiting there, in the shadow of the doorway.

"All done?" she asked.

He nodded.

"Then I think you've earned a reward."

Mike felt a stirring below the belt and couldn't help but smile. "Do you want to go back to my place for a while?"

She shook her head. "Actually, I had someplace else in mind."

A pair of headlights broke through the tree line, and Mike heard the crunch of gravel as a car pulled down the entry road from the turnpike. The first of the decorator crew was probably here.

Katie opened the door to the house and disappeared inside. Mike followed, and a moment later they were walking up the stairs to the attic.

"They're going to be working up here tonight," Mike said as he followed her across the floor.

"Not where we're going," she said. Katie led him behind the barricade he'd constructed to hide the laundry chute secreted in the flooring.

"Well, it's tucked away," he said. "But I think they'll still see us back here."

She shook her head and pointed to the floor. "We're going down there."

Just as she said it, the trapdoor opened, and Emery's head emerged. She climbed up the ladder stairs and stood beside the entryway, holding the door open.

Katie stepped into the hole and began to descend. When her head disappeared, she called up from below.

"I don't have all night."

Mike put his foot on the ladder and stepped down into the darkness.

"Or maybe I do," Katie's voice whispered, as his right foot suddenly left the ladder to touch hard floor at the bottom.

"This isn't really a laundry chute," he observed. He had been so focused working on other areas of the house over the past few weeks that after Katie had given him the glimpse of the trapdoor in the floor of the attic, he'd never bothered to pull it open again to look more closely inside. It simply wasn't part of his plan.

She didn't answer, but her hands slipped over his shoulders, and her lips brushed against his neck. He closed his eyes, and let the feeling wash down his skin. And then he jumped as the trapdoor above them slammed shut.

He heard Emery's feet creaking on the ladder near them in the dark, but couldn't see her. With the upper door closed, the room was absolutely pitch black, a silent tomb of a space. No exits, no windows. He should have felt a touch of fear, or at least claustrophobia. But all he could focus on was the tantalising whisper of Katie's fingers on his skin. He felt as if he were floating in an endless dark, as tiny orgasms of touch moved across his body.

A light flickered on then in the corner of the room; just a single candle flame. Emery stepped away from it and suddenly Mike could make out the basics of the hidden space. It was very small with a low ceiling; he almost needed to duck. The walls were dark wood varnished planks, which seemed to mimic the floor, if they weren't made from the exact same material. The result was that even with light, it was a very dark room. Stifling. You could touch the ceiling just inches above your head and probably lie down on the floor and be able to reach the far wall. There was a small dresser in the corner, which was where the candle was perched. A scattering of matchbooks and pools of wax surrounded it. Given the small size of the room, one thing took up almost the entire space.

The bed.

Or, maybe more correctly stated, the torture device.

There was no mattress on this bed, though there was a headboard, and the wrinkled rumple of a blanket bunched up at the end. But it was the uncovered portion of the bed that made Mike blanch.

The sleeping area of the bed was not a solid surface, but instead, it was made up of row upon row of thin metal spikes. They were close together, but there was no question about what the owner of the bed slept on.

It was a bed of nails.

"This is Emery's bed," Katie said. "She says all of the points remind her to feel. We can use it tonight, though I don't think you'll need the reminder."

Mike considered the potential feeling of a hundred sharp-spiked nails all digging into his back as he lay down and shook his head.

"I don't think so."

Katie laughed. "Are you afraid of a little poke and bite?" she said. "I'll give you more than that. You'll forget all about the nails."

She pointed at the blanket and another bundle of fabric lying on the far side of the bed on the floor. "Emery, why don't you make your bed for us so it's not so scary?"

Katie moved in front of him and raised herself on tiptoes to press her lips to his. "It looks like it would be painful, but it's really not," she said. "It's just firm. Very firm." She pressed her hand to his belt and ran her fingers down. "Like you."

Mike took a deep breath and the whole room seemed to spin. He didn't think he'd had that much beer, and all the digging should have sobered him up regardless, but....

"You should lie down," Katie suggested. "Trust me, you'll be okay."

Mike put the cooler down next to the bed, and sat on the old blanket that Emery had pulled over the top of the nails. She was right, he didn't feel the nails digging in at all. The nails were close enough together that with a little fabric over them, they absorbed the weight with an evenness that avoided the presumably unavoidable spiky pain.

He heard the cooler click open and then a cold can was pressed into his hand. He saw Emery's dark eyes for just a moment before she stepped back and out of sight. Almost without thought, he popped the tab and took a drink.

"Relax now," Katie said. She sat down on the bed next to him. "Thank you so much for helping me tonight. I couldn't do it myself."

Mike shrugged. "You know I'll help you however I can."

She slipped an arm around his shoulders and kissed his cheek.

"I know you've been really patient waiting for me," she said. "And I really appreciate it."

She slipped a hand under his shirt, and he felt the tee riding up. Hands pulled at the ends and he lifted his arms without thinking, holding his beer can in the air. Then the can suddenly disappeared from his fingers and his shirt soon followed before the cold aluminium of the can returned.

"You don't have to be patient anymore though," Katie said. "Lie down."

He took a gulp of his PBR and set the can on the ground before lying back on the *very* firm surface of the bed. Hands worked at his belt, and then his jeans were falling to the floor. It was hot in the enclosed room, and finally being out of his clothes was a welcome relief. He closed his eyes and took a breath as his briefs slid down his thighs and away. His penis felt thick and instantly alert as it tasted the open air, and felt the faint brush of a woman's hand.

"I've wanted to bring you here since the first day I met you," Katie whispered.

The floorboards creaked above them, and Mike began to sit up.

Katie pressed him back, rolling over on top of him. She bent down and kissed him and then made the faintest "shhhh".

"What if they hear us?" he whispered.

"Don't scream and we'll be fine," she said. "You're not going to scream, are you?"

He shook his head, and she smiled before melting her lips over his.

Mike slipped his hands beneath her shirt and pulled her tight. Katie shifted against him, her lips now urgently hard on his. As he breathed, he breathed her. His thighs ached at the silk of her skin. His hands moved across her back; he wanted to feel every pore of her.

"Oh my God," he whispered, when she broke their kiss. "I've wanted this for so long."

Katie smiled, and with one hand fondled the evidence of his need between them. "I know," she said.

He moaned at the attention, and then lifted his hands to push her shirt up. He couldn't wait anymore. He wanted to have all of her, naked, pressed against him. He couldn't get close enough to her body.

Katie pulled out of his embrace and lifted her arms to let him strip her.

"There's just one thing," she said, as the shirt came off. The first thing he saw in the dim candlelight was that she wasn't wearing a bra underneath.

The second was that her chest and belly were crisscrossed in ragged scars. They still showed twists of black thread from the stitches that had obviously pulled her back together from whatever hideous accident had ripped her open.

"What happened?" he whispered. His fingers traced a line from her sternum to her groin, and he felt the hard points of the stitches shift like stubble beneath his hand.

"I will tell you all about that day," she said. "But…not tonight, okay?"

She pushed his hand down to the silver buckle of her belt, and Mike didn't argue. He was not going to screw this up, after waiting so long, by asking questions. There would be time enough for answers later. He unzipped her shorts and began to slip them down her thighs. She moved down to the bed so he could pull them past her knees and off. When he dropped them off the bed on the floor, he saw the shadow of Emery still standing at the back of the room. His stomach constricted for a moment; he'd been so lost in Katie, he'd forgotten there was anyone else in the room. But the other woman didn't move or say anything and again, his crotch told him not to fuck this up. If Katie didn't care, why should he? He slid his fingers up Katie's inner thighs, and slipped his thumbs beneath the elastic band of her panties when he reached them. She arched her back and he slid the silk down, gasping with desire as he exposed her.

"Hurry," Katie whispered. She spread her legs apart and held her arms open for his embrace. He accommodated, pressing himself between her thighs and diving into her kiss. She took his breath away; her every touch sent jolts of fire down his back, up his thighs, into his crotch.

It had been months since Mike had had sex, and foreplay with Katie had gone on for weeks. He wasn't slow or tentative about pressing inside her. He literally couldn't wait. She accepted his entry with a quiet moan, and then Mike felt the threads of her scars – or wounds – scratching against his belly as he moved with her. The sensation was strange, but weirdly exciting. He had all of her, even if it was a ragged her, against him. He poured himself inside Katie, rolling her back and forth on the bed in the dark. Her hands pressed against his thighs and ass, massaging him and stroking his body as he moved the most sensitive part of himself inside her. At one point, he felt lips and breath on his neck even though

Katie was beneath him. But he didn't question it; his climax was too close to think.

Katie groaned and gasped in small tight sounds, and he struggled to hold his own sounds in, still aware that the decorators were working just a few feet above their head. When he finally let go inside her, a warm weight pressed down on his back. The soft flesh of breasts and the hot lips of a mouth that was not Katie's kissed his back and neck, as he moaned into Katie's shoulder.

Emery was lying on top of him, naked and hot. He was pinned between them, and his eyes rolled back. This was the strangest heaven. And then Emery's hands were urging him to roll over, off Katie to lie on his back. He did, and before his thighs had fully touched the bed she was on top of him, her wetness pressing down on his erection, still bone-hard from the excitement of plumbing the depths of Katie.

"Oh my God," he whispered, as the heat of her engulfed him. Compared to Katie, she was like a furnace, dripping with desire and panting with need. She pressed his wrists to the bed and rode him hard, with each motion bleating a tiny catch of a sound from her throat.

Mike couldn't believe he was still hard enough for her to use; he couldn't possibly come again, but Katie leaned over his face and kissed him as Emery used her hips and worked him inside her. He could feel the nails in his back now, as she pumped herself to orgasm, slamming his ass again and again towards the thousand nails beneath the sheet.

And then it was over. Emery let out something that sounded like a wounded animal caught in a trap. She froze above him, her breasts hanging down to just barely brush his chest. Then she lifted her hips and pushed off the bed, leaving him alone again with Katie.

"Thank you," Katie said. "She deserved that. It's been a long time for her."

"Nice of you to share," he said, laughing just a little. Nervously.

"If you take me, you get Emery," she said. "We're like a set."

"Whatever you want," he said.

Katie's eyes squinted with humour. "I didn't think you'd mind," she said. "You're a man, after all."

"What are you saying?"

"I think you know," she said. "None of you can say no to the kitty."

He snorted and slipped his hand between her legs. She was still wet with the evidence of their orgasms. "You weren't exactly resisting, yourself," he said.

She ran her hand up his arm to touch his chin. "No," she admitted. "But women can choose to resist. Men are slaves to their penises."

Mike ran his fingers over the rough stitches that marred her middle. The flesh felt angry, puckered and hard. The black stitches scraped his fingers like wires.

"What happened to you?" he asked. "How did you get all cut up?"

"Are you sure you really want to know?" she said.

He nodded.

"They did an autopsy on me," she said.

Mike made a face and shook his head. "They can't do an autopsy on you while you're alive," he said.

Katie nodded.

"I know," she said. "They did it after I died."

PART TWO
THE HAUNTING

CHAPTER SIXTEEN

"They're lined up all the way to the turnpike!" Jeanie exclaimed. She pushed the black drapes back over the window and walked across the room to her impromptu makeup station. This was the *Nightmare on Elm Street* room, so it was decorated like a girl's bedroom. Which meant she had a full vanity where she could work on makeup. Once the house opened for business each day, she could easily stow her stuff in a drawer as the house haunters made their way to their stations in all of the themed rooms. At the moment, everyone was gathered there for a last makeup check and a pep talk from Perry Clark, the guy who had masterminded this whole thing. Lon, the house production manager, stood at his side. Lenny and June stood in the front row waiting for Perry to talk. Both of them were visibly beaming with excitement. This was the night they'd been working towards for the past two months.

"Quiet down for a second," Lon called. "It's almost show time."

Jeanie slipped past Lenny to stand next to Bong. She'd played off his ethnicity and turned him into a pale Asian ghost with a long wig and black contacts. Against the pancake white of his face, his eyes were like dark pools of hell.

"Thank you all," Perry said. "You have done an amazing job here. Lon just gave me the tour, and I have to say, this place gave me the creeps – and you all weren't even in your places to jump out at me. Thank God!"

Perry grinned and nodded at the grizzled carpenter in the corner. The thin, quiet girl who was always with him, Katie, stood at his side.

"The first time I saw this place, I didn't think it would be safe for people to walk through without tearing it down," Perry said. "But Mike, here, managed to bring this place back from the dead."

He pointed at Argento and Lucio. "And you two...well, you made it *look* like the dead! I don't even want to know how you got the blood splatter to look so real. It's disturbing, I have to tell you."

Perry waved his hand around the room at the collection of ghouls and zombies and gutted 'haunters' and grinned. "And all of you look... disgusting. Huge thanks to June and Jeanie for turning you into...well... whatever you are. You're all amazing. And that's really all I have to say. I just wanted to let you know that I'm so proud of what you've all done. This is the first time in decades that Bachelor's Grove has had something positive happening within its gates. So, I just want you to go out there tonight, and the rest of the month and...have fun scaring the hell out of people."

Lon grinned and held up his hands. "Thanks to Perry for making this all happen. Haunting Bachelor's Grove was a stroke of genius. Once they walk through, I know people are going to be talking about this house for the rest of the year. Just remember, we're here to have fun. If you see someone having a real problem – like they get so freaked out they're crying or won't leave a room or something, fade back and text me. I'll be just outside or downstairs in Ops every night to deal with anything that comes up. I want the rest of you to stay in character for our guests."

He looked at his watch and nodded. "Front door opens in fifteen minutes. So...places, everyone. Let's haunt this house!"

The cast began to file out of the room, and Jeanie walked over to her makeup station to hide the rest of her things for the night. As she passed Perry, the businessman shook his head.

"That's disgusting," he said.

"What, this?" she asked, turning her belly to face him. She had worked with latex to create a grisly twine of guts. It was held fast to her back with flesh-coloured straps, allowing the fake intestines to literally hang and sway out of her belly. They glistened with something that looked like blood mixed with a yellow slime.

"Go ahead and feel it," she offered.

Perry grimaced, but put a finger out to touch one curled rope of guts. He instantly pulled his hand back.

"It's good, isn't it?" she asked.

"Maybe too good," he said, and shook his head, grimacing. Then Lon came up and grabbed him away to talk about some issue with ticket processing out front.

She saw that Katie and Mike still remained in the back of the room, talking quietly. Katie's face was pale, and she wore a crop top halter and Daisy Dukes to show off her midriff to maximum effect. Her midsection was crisscrossed with scars and stitches. The effect was striking, yet also subdued. Jeanie wondered if everyone moving through the house would catch the grotesquerie of it, especially with the low lighting and moving quickly through the rooms. Jeanie stepped over to the two, interrupting their conversation with a smile.

"Do you want me to add some blood to that?" she asked, pointing at Katie's belly.

The other woman shook her head. "Nobody does my makeup but me," she said curtly, and went back to saying something to the carpenter. Mike had gotten her the job as a 'floater' at the last minute. She was not assigned to a particular room, but would simply be wandering the house looking spooky. But she had refused all of Jeanie and June's offers to help with her makeup. Jeanie didn't like her; she seemed just a bit too full of herself.

"Suit yourself," she said, and went back to her vanity to put the last tubes of blood and spirit gum to attach all of the latex appliances to the haunters back in the drawers.

"Ten minutes," Lon called from somewhere out in the hall.

Jeanie felt a lump in her throat and shut the last drawer. Bong stood next to her, and she leaned up on tiptoes to give him a small peck on the lips. She barely brushed them but apologised. "Don't want to ruin your lipstick," she said.

"I can't believe you made me wear lipstick," he complained.

"I can't believe it's opening night," she said. "Are you excited?"

He shrugged. "I can think of better ways to spend a Thursday night."

Jeanie frowned. "But think of all the nights we'll be together this month," she said. "We'll see each other more than ever."

"I like seeing you better without your guts showing," he said.

"I don't know," she said. "I might like you better with lipstick." Jeanie grinned and took his hand. "Come on, it's almost time to begin."

Mike bent down to kiss Katie, now that they were the last people remaining, and she shooed him from the room. He would be hiding out with Lon in Ops each night, helping with any problems. His official job had really ended three weeks ago, but Lon and Perry kept finding new reasons to keep him on the payroll. He didn't mind, since it gave him a good excuse to hang around Katie. "See you later," he told her, and exited the room.

*   *   *

Emery emerged from the closet then, wearing a black cowl and holding a long, curved butcher knife.

From somewhere in the house, someone yelled, "It's showtime. Let's get bloody!"

Katie nodded, and whispered, "Oh, we will."

CHAPTER SEVENTEEN

There were far more people tonight in Bachelor's Grove than had ever been there before for a funeral. And the people in line were buzzing with excitement. Many of them had heard of the haunted cemetery, but never actually been there before.

"...I can't believe they actually are doing this here..."

"...what if it really is haunted, like they always said..."

"...best gimmick for a haunted house ever. As soon as I heard about it, I was in..."

"...I'm going to scream, I just know it..."

Jillie Melton heard it all, and shook her head. She stood near the front of the line with Ted. She hadn't been able to enter the house or get it shut down since the carpenter had sent her away, so she'd bought a ticket to get in on opening night. They couldn't keep her out with a valid ticket. The county forest preserve commissioner had listened patiently before dismissing her as a kook with the explanation, "This is the best way to put all of that haunting nonsense to rest. Instead of having people sneak past the police and possibly get hurt in there at night in October, we're turning it into an attraction. For the first time in years, Bachelor's Grove will actually be a safe place to go at Halloween. The only ghosts that will be there will be the ones we *put* there."

Jillie didn't believe that for a heartbeat, but she knew when to give up on a full-frontal assault. She was going in tonight to feel just how dangerous this attraction was likely going to be.

"I'm really worried about this," she said.

Ted shook his head. "I think you're working yourself up over nothing," he said. "All this construction, all these people? I think they've probably driven away a lot of the energy here."

"You know better than that," Jillie said. "Spirits don't just get up and move. Most of them can't leave the place they're tied to without intervention. That's why you see the repetition over and over. The ghostly hitchhiker getting in cars on the turnpike happens again and again and again. The mother and her baby. The apparition of the house, with blood painted all over its front door. That energy is tied to the graves and the house, and all this activity is going to feed it, not send it away. And the spirits here have never been happy ones."

"Most of the negativity that's been here was because of the devil worshippers that desecrated this place in the Sixties and Seventies," Ted said. "The dark stuff that happened here was all caused by living, breathing humans, not ghosts."

She shook her head. "There were sacrifices here," she said. "That blood remains in the ground. The darkness may have been started by the living, but the spirits they tied here remain. There's been death here, violent death. And I just have this horrible feeling that there's going to be more."

The line suddenly shifted, as the first ticket holders were ushered past the gate on the front of the porch. As they stepped up on the first wooden stair, Jillie felt a chill down her back. An invisible pressure, like two cold hands, pushed against the front of her shoulders, trying to repel her backwards. Trying to send her away.

"I can feel them now," she whispered. "Stage Three and we're not even inside the house."

Ted looked at her with concern.

"I don't know what we're going to find once we actually get inside. But I don't think these kids have any idea what they're going to be dealing with."

She nodded at the group of high schoolers ahead of them. There were a half-dozen of them, and two were wearing black and gold Oak Forest High School jackets.

A man wearing a hideous mask that looked like the skin of someone else's face held up a chainsaw as he stood guard at the door. He only let in one group at a time to the house. He opened the battered screen door and motioned with the chainsaw for the high schoolers to move forward.

"Step inside," he said. "Don't slip on the blood."

CHAPTER EIGHTEEN

Larry led a group up the steps to the house at Bachelor's Grove. They had all met for drinks at The Edge and planned to head to Naperville for a Halloween movie night with friends afterwards.

"We're going to get as much horror in as possible tonight," Diane had told the bartender just a half hour earlier, before her husband Troy had pulled her back to their table with Larry, Lisa, Amy and Pam.

"Everybody in the world doesn't need to know," Troy said.

"But everybody in the world should be going to haunted houses and watching scary movies this week," she'd insisted.

Now that they were finally about to enter the haunted house, Diane could barely contain herself.

"Who's ready to scream?" she asked.

Amy smiled and shook her head. But Lisa grinned. "Let's see what they got!"

They crossed the porch after getting their tickets. The door was opened by a man dressed as Leatherface.

"Good thing I wore my red shoes," Larry said, as the *Texas Chainsaw Massacre* doorman ushered them inside. "You won't be able to see the blood on them."

Lisa laughed and bit his ear. "After what you drank, you won't be able to see anything soon," she whispered.

"I can see just fine," Larry said. "Like right there. Isn't that a human thigh on the dinner platter? I'm gonna pass on that, but the liver and onions might be good if it's not overcooked."

The dining room table was made of weathered wooden planks and set with three table settings. A series of serving plates covered the middle. It looked like the preparation for a feast…if you were a cannibal. A pale, grey, disembodied head perched at the top of the table, and a silver platter was piled high with amputated hands and feet. The bloodied fingers and toes were piled next to a long hunk of human thigh. Behind the table, a blond girl in a thin blue shirt was tied to a chair that appeared to be made of human arms. Her hands shook and pulled hard at the bindings, trying to get away from the dead fingers that made up the ends of the chair arms beneath her.

"Help," she pleaded at them. "Get me out of here."

At that moment, a chainsaw growled to life in the background, and a hulking man wearing a pig's head stepped out of the shadows behind her.

"Holy shit," Amy said from right behind them as the smell of gasoline and blue smoke filled the room. She shoved at Larry to keep walking, and he and Lisa laughed and stepped through the doorway back out into the hall, and then into the kitchen. Diane and Troy followed with Pam lagging just behind.

"That was pretty awesome," Troy said.

"Gross," Pam complained. She had not wanted to come, but Lisa had insisted. "You are not pussying out on this one," Lisa had said. "A Bachelor's Grove Haunted House? And Lon managing the props and shit? It's gonna be epic."

The kitchen was lit with one bare bulb, which hung from the ceiling on a wire that swayed back and forth, throwing weird shadows on the room. The place looked as if it had recently been used as a slaughterhouse. Blood was splattered on the peeling old country wallpaper, and an axe was embedded in the far wall. A woman's body lay on the floor, blood pooled all around her head. A butcher knife handle stuck out of the back of her head; the silver tip of the blade protruded from her forehead. The tip of it gouged the floor.

"Damn, that looks real," Troy said.

Lisa laughed. "You know it's all just for show. I don't know how anyone could be scared of this shit."

She looked pointedly at Pam, who looked away. She stepped closer to the sink. One side had what looked like a human heart sitting in the middle of the basin. Around it, a thousand squirming maggots jittered and shifted.

In the basin next to it, a human head sat with its neck over the drain. Its hair was matted with blood, and gore streaked its cheeks.

"Oh my God," Pam said and stepped away.

"You are such a baby," Lisa said, and bent closer to the sink. "They sure did good work here though."

The eyes of the face were bloodshot and glossy; she could have sworn she saw the damn thing blink.

"Hi there," the bloody lips suddenly said.

Lisa shrieked and jumped back two feet.

"Gotcha," the human head laughed.

Behind her, Troy and Diane were bending over the woman with the knife in her head. Just as Lisa jumped, the dead woman began to rise up from the floor.

"That's it," Diane said, and bolted for the next room.

The rest of them followed, and a moment later, they found themselves in a bedroom with floral wallpaper. The sheets of the bed were rumpled, and a pool of red marred the centre. The reason hung from the ceiling above. A girl in a white nightgown drenched in crimson hung from the ceiling. She looked as if she were crouching there; both of her legs were stretched out like a sprinter at the starting gate while one hand clutched the ceiling, surrounded by bloody handprints. Her other arm reached out towards the bedroom door, as if she were begging for help.

"She better not move," Diane said.

"No way they could hang someone up there every night," Troy said. "I don't think we have to worry."

The closet door creaked open at that moment, and they suddenly heard the singsong chant of a group of children. "One, two, Freddy's coming for you...."

A hand emerged from the closet, wearing a glove tipped with long knife blades. The blades trailed down the wall with a faint scraping sound, before Freddy Krueger emerged in his familiar red and green sweater from the closet, his face a burned mass of scars. "Welcome to my nightmare," he said and started towards them.

"Time to go," Pam said, and bolted back out of the room. Lisa laughed and followed her down the hall to a room that offered two exits. The walls shimmered with red and blue light, and hidden speakers played a taut, synthesiser-dominated soundtrack that gave Pam the creeps almost as much as the setpieces of the house. A sign seemingly written in blood said 'Don't Go In The Basement'. A human skeleton seated in what looked like an electric chair pointed with one bony finger towards the stairs that led upwards.

The darkened stairs that led down had another placard nailed to the wall next to them. 'No Exit', the sign said. Screams erupted from the dark below, and they didn't sound like a recording.

"I guess 'up' it is," Pam said.

She started up the steps. The walls were covered in a strange array of taxidermy. There were animal pelts stretched out with pins, and the full heads of a raccoon, a squirrel, a goat and other creatures emerged from the wall at odd intervals.

There were also the stretched-out skins of three human faces.

As she passed one, it let out a scream, and Pam jumped. "Jesus," she complained. Her heart was pounding a mile a minute now. "I really just want to get out of this place," she murmured.

"Gotta love a skinhead," Larry laughed behind her.

The attic was creepy. The music here was louder, and the first thing they saw was a girl's head lolling through the broken glass of a window. The shards had clearly punctured her throat, and her mouth hung open in a silent scream.

"Ouch, I bet that had to hurt," Larry said.

To their left an old woman sat in a wheelchair. A rope was fastened around her neck and stretched up to a hook in the ceiling. To their right were racks and racks of what looked like costumes. It could have been the props department for a horror movie. There were lots of velvet vests and gowns on hangers, but there were also rubber masks of all sorts of monsters, from the overt Frankenstein's monster to more freakish things with three eyes and hag hair.

The floor had an arrow painted on it in red pointing the way into the aisle in the centre of the costume collection. Words were painted on the floor next to the arrow.

'Shed Your Skin and Choose Another,' they said.

"I'm not going first," Pam announced.

"Chicken," Lisa taunted. "Let me show you how it's done."

She held out her hands and began to walk through the aisle of outfits, making them all shift and move as she passed through.

Larry grinned and patted Pam on the head as he passed her, pulling Lisa by the hand behind him. Amy followed closely behind them.

"Come on, Pam," Diane urged, as she and Troy walked into the aisle. "The sooner you get through it, the sooner you'll get through it."

Troy laughed at that, and the two passed into the aisle of clothes. Pam was about to follow, when she heard Lisa scream ahead.

"Oh shit," she whispered. Her knees were shaking and she couldn't seem to walk forward.

Just then, someone in the mask of an ancient woman with frizzy hair and a horrible wrinkled face poked out of the aisle. She held a sickle in her hand and made a pass of it through the air in front of Pam.

The girl shrieked and leapt backwards, shocked out of her paralysis. The figure disappeared back into the aisle and a moment later, Diane screamed.

Pam staggered backwards, past the old woman in the wheelchair. That monster, at least, she knew wasn't real.

She rounded a corner and bent over, trying to catch her breath. "I just want to go home," she whispered. "I just want to go home."

From the far end of the attic, she heard Larry laughing, and then another shriek. It sounded like Lisa. Then Diane was demanding, "Go, go, go."

The upstairs grew silent, except for the eerie music overhead. Pam took a deep breath, steeling herself to follow them alone through the costume maze.

Something creaked in the floor in front of her, and Pam looked up to see two hands reaching out of a door in the floor towards her. Before she could move, the hands grabbed her ankles and yanked. Pam fell backwards, as her legs slid forward.

She hit the ground hard, her head bouncing on the wooden floor. Pam opened her mouth to scream, but hardly any sound came out.

And then the hands pulled her down into darkness, and the door above her head slammed shut.

She hadn't had the chance to voice even the faintest scream.

CHAPTER NINETEEN

"Perfect," Jillie said. They had just entered the *Nightmare on Elm Street* room. "There's a bed in here," she whispered. "Unless someone's already under it, that's where I'm staying."

The sound of children singing the Freddy Krueger song suddenly began, and Jillie pushed Ted in front of her. "Don't let anyone see me," she said, dropping to the floor.

The closet door opened and a moment later Ted was face-to-face with the infamous boiler room killer.

"Welcome to my nightmare," Freddy said, clicking his finger blades together.

"I was just leaving," Ted said. He turned and hurried back out of the room.

Jillie lay perfectly still beneath the bed. There was nobody else there, and she held her breath until she heard the closet door close again. She intended to stay here until the place closed for the night. And then, once she was alone, she'd be able to walk around and really take the pulse of the house. She would text Ted to come back then, and let him in so they could set up their EMF meter and take some readings. Not that she couldn't feel some of the energy here herself. But she wanted recordings and scientific readings. Maybe with some evidence, she could get the county to reconsider what it was doing. Show them the danger they were exposing all sorts of people to, especially all the kids who would be walking through here in the next three or four weeks.

Jillie edged her way to the centre of the space beneath the bed, put her hands on her chest and closed her eyes. For a few hours, she needed to be very quiet.

Outside in the room, the closet door opened again and Freddy said, "Welcome to my nightmare."

He was greeted with the shriek of a teenage girl.

CHAPTER TWENTY

"That's a wrap," Lon called. "All of the living have left."

Argento stepped out of the closet on the first floor. He pulled the black hood from his head and began to peel off his black leather gloves as he joined the others in the gathering room.

"How was your body count tonight?" Lon asked with a grin.

"I think I made a woman pee," Argento said.

"Nice!"

Lucio came walking down the stairs first, still wearing the old hag mask and carrying the sickle. Bong was just behind him, and June followed. Her throat appeared cut from ear to ear and one of her eyes appeared gluey white.

"Oh my God, that was so much fun," Jeanie said, emerging from the basement stairs. She was followed by three zombies. They made for a strange sight, as all of them were laughing.

Chelsea, the girl with the knife through her head, came staggering out of the kitchen. "Lying on the floor all night is going to get old really fast," she complained.

"Did you freak anyone out, though?" Jeanie asked.

"I made one guy scream like a little girl." She grinned. "He really thought I was just a dummy, and was about two inches from my face when I jumped up."

Lenny came out of the back bedroom still wearing his Freddy mask. He clicked and clacked his blade fingers together while the family room filled with the cast of the house.

"All right," Lon said. "Great job, everyone. That was an excellent night's work and we sent a lot of people home happy. With wet underwear, maybe, but happy. But now it's late and we do it all again tomorrow. So, get out of your costumes, leave them on hangers upstairs, and let's get the heck out of here. Thanks for making it creepy!"

"Did you have fun?" Jeanie asked Bong. She gave him a much longer kiss than she had at the start of the night.

He shrugged. "People don't seem to like Asian ghosts who crawl down the hallway at them. So I really didn't meet any new friends, although I talked to June a bit. Plus, now my arms are tired."

"I'll rub you down when we get home," she promised.

"I'm counting on it," he said.

"Somebody help Allen out of the sink in the kitchen," Lon called.

Jeanie grinned and patted Bong's shoulder. "I'll be right back," she said.

She walked to the kitchen and found June already there, with the front cabinet open. "I'll lift while you push," Jeanie offered. The counter creaked upwards on hinges, and Allen rose up slowly, rubbing his neck.

"Damn, that's a long night," he said. "How long are we doing this?"

"All month," June said. "We'll get you some Bengay."

Allen snorted and staggered off towards the bathroom.

"How are you doing?" Jeanie asked.

"What do you mean?" June answered.

"Well, it's none of my business, I guess, but…I thought you and Lenny…."

June snorted. "Lenny spends too much time at my place, that's all."

"But," Jeanie began. "With the *Nightmare on Elm Street* room and all, I thought…."

June grinned, but she didn't look happy. "Yeah, a lot of people think. But, if you're interested, he's available."

Jeanie's eyelids shot open. She put her hand up. "No, I didn't mean…."

June shook her head. "Look, I don't care," she said. "He crashes at my place a lot, that's all."

"I have Bong," Jeanie said. "I'm not after Lenny."

June shrugged. "Suit yourself," she said, and began to walk away. But then she looked over her shoulder and said something that made Jeanie's stomach go cold.

"Lenny's a good lay if you're feeling dry. Just sayin'."

Jeanie took her time putting the kitchen countertop back in place and closing the cabinet doors before she returned to the bedroom where Bong waited. She didn't know why June had said that, but she couldn't stop hearing it in her head.

She shook her head until it went away, and then she raised her chin and kissed Bong on the lips.

"Hey," she said. "Wanna take me home?"

*   *   *

The voices had been silent for a while now. Jillie slid out from her hiding place beneath the bed and stretched. Her back was stiff. She walked over to the window and peered out the black curtains. The forest outside looked completely dark. No headlights in sight. She pulled out her phone and texted Ted.

> *Jillie: Where are you now?*
> *Ted: Went home. Are you ready for action?*
> *Jillie: Think so. All is quiet.*
> *Ted: Be there in ten.*
> *Jillie: Cool.*

She walked to the hallway and peered up and down it for several seconds, listening for any sound in the house. Hearing none, she finally stepped into the hall, and walked down to the dining room and kitchen. There were no lights on. She hit the flashlight app on her iPhone and shone it around the rooms. Nothing there but props. Grotesque, red-splashed walls and chains and furniture.

Jillie walked to the other end of the house and found the room with the stairs to the attic and basement. She shone the light on the darkness going down, and carefully stepped on the first stair. She hadn't gotten this far on her tour earlier.

One by one she crept down, pausing to listen at each step. When she reached the bottom, she flashed her phone in a 360-degree arc, absorbing the layout. The place looked like a junk shop, with mirrors and bureaus and boxes all stacked in rows. She peered at herself in one mirror and almost jumped. A ghostly white face appeared just behind her own. Then she realised the 'ghost' was fastened to the beam just above her head – so anyone who looked in the mirror (which was tilted upwards) would get a shock.

She moved down the row of junk, strategically placed to allow 'zombies' or other 'monsters' to hide and jump out, no doubt, while corralling the patrons down a specific path. And that path now resembled a museum of horror. Every twenty feet or so, there appeared to be a small set constructed to represent some kind of horror theme. To her left, she saw the half-nude manikin in a tub of red, meant to depict the Countess Báthory. But that gory tableau wasn't what made her pause.

There was something wrong here.

Jillie had followed her career as a ghost hunter because she had always been sensitive to things. She knew most people thought she was a nut, but that didn't change the fact that she *sensed* things. Her spine seemed like an antenna for ghosts; it chilled and sparked whenever she was in areas reputed to be haunted…and often in places that were not. She could always seem to find cold spots in old buildings where there was no breeze. There had been many times walking through a cemetery that she had felt fingers brush across her face when she bent over a gravestone to read the inscription. As if the dead were reaching up from the earth to greet her softly. She had felt things that other people didn't ever since she was a kid. It had all started when her family moved to an old house in Virginia for a couple years when she was four. Every time she'd gone into the basement, her mother had found her standing in the corner, talking to someone. She barely remembered those early years, but her mom had told her later how unnerving it was to see her conversing with the wall. But kids often had imaginary friends, so her parents had chalked it up to that.

When they moved across country to the Chicago area, she no longer talked to walls…but there was one place in the house that bothered her. It felt wrong. Every time she'd walked into the room she'd felt cold, sometimes to the point of shivering. It was her dad's den, and over time she began to avoid going there, which her father never questioned, because he didn't want to be disturbed when he was working there anyway. Every time her mother sent her there to call her father or take him something, she'd complained that it was too cold in there.

"It's the same temperature as the rest of the house, baby," her mom insisted. And Jillie had argued over and over again that it was not.

"It's like walking into a freezer," she remembered saying.

Later, as an adult, she'd researched the house and found the probable cause. In the Forties, there had been a horrible crime committed in that room. Domestic violence that had turned into a murder-suicide.

That had always given Jillie proof and validation that her 'feelings' were not imaginary. She had lived with ghosts and felt their frozen rage. The dead were not gone, she knew. The dead were everywhere. So now, when she reached the end of the basement and felt something twist in her stomach, and a chill begin to creep up her back, she trusted her instinct. There was something here.

She walked through a tableau inspired by *The Exorcist*, pushed an old dresser out of the way and stepped behind the construct to the other side of the aisle, towards the back wall of the basement. It was a newly constructed wall. A quickly thrown together barricade of plywood and 2x4s.

What was it here to hide?

She moved the light along its length until she found a hinge. Three hinges actually. She moved the phone around until she discovered the foot-long piece of board that served as the knob and lock. It was positioned horizontally to hold the door in place, but when she twisted it vertically, the plywood swung inward. There was another small room here in the basement, hidden away from the 'attraction' area.

Jillie stepped down a few inches from the wooden floor to an earthen one. The air here was immediately more dank and chill than in the rest of the hastily 'finished' portion of the basement.

There was a coffin against the wall to her right, but she barely noticed it because in the middle of the small room, lying with her face to the ground, was a teenage girl. She looked like one of the kids in the group that had entered the haunted house before her earlier tonight – the girl wore a thin Oak Forest High School jacket, and a swirl of long brown hair covered her eyes and cheek before cascading to the dirt.

"Hey, are you okay?" Jillie called softly. When the girl didn't answer, she repeated the question, a little louder. And then she stepped closer.

There was blood on the girl's neck. Jillie bent down and brushed some of the hair from the girl's face; her skin felt cool and Jillie could now see the long gash that cut across her neck. The ground beneath her chin glistened with the girl's blood. She hesitantly reached out her hand to touch the darkened earth, and her finger came back wet with blood.

"Oh no," Jillie whispered, just before her spine suddenly turned cold as ice water.

A woman's voice spoke from behind her. It sounded deathly serious.

"Get out!" it said.

Jillie looked behind her but saw nothing. However, her legs suddenly felt like wet spaghetti. The ice spread from her spine to her chest, and Jillie held a hand to her breastbone as she found herself struggling to breathe.

"Get out now!" the voice demanded again. She couldn't see where it was coming from, though it sounded like it was right next to her. She backed away from the girl.

Jillie staggered to the door and dove through the furniture to return to the haunted house path. It felt as if two fists were beating her back, and she stumbled and half-ran back along the aisle until she came to a door. It was locked, but she fumbled with the doorknob until the metal latch turned. Then she ran up the steps, not closing the door behind her.

When she reached the grass, she fell to her knees. When she got back up, she realised the pressure inside her was gone, and the hands no longer pushed her. But she wasn't going back. Jillie moved quickly towards the front of the house. Behind her, she heard a door slam shut.

"There you are," Ted's voice said from across the clearing. "I was looking for you. Are you ready for us to set up?"

Jillie shook her head vigorously. "No," she gasped, bending over and putting her hands on her knees as she caught her breath. "Call the police. There's a dead girl in the basement."

Ted shook his head. "They did a really good job decorating the place," he said. "But I can't believe they freaked you out."

"I'm not joking and the body wasn't a prop," Jillie said. "I touched her face. There was blood all over the ground. Somebody was murdered in there tonight. And that's not the worst of it."

"What could be worse?" Ted asked.

"I *felt* her," Jillie said. "*Physically*. She wanted me out of there so I wouldn't interfere. She actually pushed me. But I know it was her, and I think I know what she wants."

"She who?" Ted said.

"The witch of Bremen Coven," Jillie said.

"She died fifty years ago," Ted said.

"Exactly," Jillie said. "And she's been trying to come back ever since. I think that girl in the basement was a sacrifice, and if I'm right, she won't be the last one."

She looked at him with wide eyes. "Now call the police!"

CHAPTER TWENTY-ONE

Two cop cars arrived a few minutes later, with red and blue lights flashing, but no sirens. They pulled past the gravel onto the grassy clearing just in front of the porch, where Jillie and Ted waited.

Four officers emerged. A tall, thin one with a day's growth of stubble and tired eyes walked quickly towards them. He introduced himself as Officer Mulkin and pointed at Ted. "Did you call in a homicide?"

Ted tilted his head at Jillie. "I did, but she's the one who saw the body. It's in the basement."

The cop nodded and looked directly at her. "You're sure you saw a body and not a prop?" he asked. "This is a haunted house, after all. I'm sure they have some very realistic-looking stuff in there."

Jillie shook her head vehemently. "It was real," she said. "It was a girl from Oak Forest High. Her throat was cut."

The cop looked sceptical. "What were you doing in the building after hours?" he asked. "Are you working in the house?"

"No," Jillie said. She looked at Ted and made a face before continuing. "I'm a paranormal investigator, and I was here trying to see what kind of impact turning this place into a circus has had on the ghosts inside."

"Uh-huh," Mulkin said. "So you were trespassing."

"I think the fact that there's a dead girl in there is more important right now," she said. "I bought a ticket to go inside tonight, and then I waited until the house was closed to look around." Briefly she explained how she had hidden beneath the bed and then used her cell phone to explore the house in the dark.

Mulkin pursed his lips and nodded. "Show me."

Jillie stepped down the deck and began to walk around the perimeter of the house. Ted and the four officers followed right behind her, but then they stopped as two headlights cut through the forest and moved straight up the gravel path towards the house.

A silver Mitsubishi stopped right next to the police cars, and a stocky man in Dockers and a blue polo shirt got out.

"What's this all about?" the man called, as he walked towards the group.

"Are you in charge of this place?" Mulkin asked, as the man reached them.

"Yeah," he said. "I'm Perry Clark. Someone from the police station called and told me there was a problem out here."

"This woman has reported a dead body inside," Mulkin said.

"There are all sorts of 'dead bodies' in there," Perry said angrily. "It's a haunted house, for Christ's sake. And it's closed. Nobody should be here at all right now. I don't want anyone messing with our sets for tomorrow."

"This is county property, so we were going to take a look," Mulkin said. "You can join us and make sure we don't damage anything if you like."

Perry glared at Jillie. "I should have known," he said.

"Do you know this woman?" Mulkin asked.

Perry snorted bitterly. "Yeah, she's the ghost hunter nut who tried to get the house shut down last month before we opened," he said. "I'm guessing this is another one of her stunts."

"You're welcome to press trespassing charges if you like," Mulkin said. "But first let's see exactly what she saw."

He pointed at Jillie. "Let's go," he said.

Jillie walked around to the side of the house and led the way down the steps to the door. She paused at the bottom and took a breath. She did not want to go back in there. When she put her hand on the knob and turned, it didn't budge.

"It's locked," she said. "But I didn't lock it. In fact, I left the door open when I left."

Mulkin showed no expression. "Do you have a key?" he said to Perry.

The businessman nodded. "Yeah, but it's to the front door, not this. C'mon."

They walked back up the steps and around the house to the front. Perry let them in and flipped the switch for the lights. Then he led them down the hall to the basement stairs. When they reached the bottom, Jillie pointed to the far end. "It's over there," she said.

When they threaded through *The Exorcist* exhibit and reached the false back of the basement, she lifted the wooden latch and pushed the door.

Mulkin stepped inside, followed by the other three officers. Jillie did not go in. Instead, she looked around the area, now that the lights were on. She didn't feel the sensations she had down here just fifteen minutes before.

"Ma'am," Mulkin called. "Can you come in here please?"

She stepped down onto the dirt and walked over to where the officers huddled over a figure on the floor.

"Is this what you saw?" he asked, looking up from the body to meet Jillie's eyes. She could see the legs and pale bare feet, but the rest of the girl was blocked.

"Yes," she said. But then she saw the face through the gap as Mulkin straightened up and her forehead creased in confusion. "I mean, no! That's not the girl who was here before."

The body on the floor was clearly a manikin. It wore jeans and an Oak Forest High School jacket. But the face was clearly plastic. A wig lay slightly askew, covering part of the face, and a line of red – maybe lipstick – cut across the neck.

"Somebody took her. This isn't what I saw."

"The basement lights were not on when you were here, were they?" Mulkin asked.

She shook her head. "No, I used my iPhone as a flashlight."

One of the cops was grinning and Jillie closed her eyes for a moment to still her frustration. "You have to believe me," she said finally. "This is not the body that was here earlier. I touched the skin, I had blood on my finger. Somebody moved this here after I left – probably the same person who shut and locked the cellar door. There must have been someone else in the house with me."

"If it's okay with you, we'll take a quick look around," Mulkin said to Perry. "Make sure nobody else is in the house."

Perry nodded.

"You can go outside, but don't leave the premises," Mulkin told Jillie. "We'll want to talk further with you."

He motioned to one of the officers who started walking the perimeter of the basement, as the other three headed upstairs.

"Let's wait outside," Jillie said to Ted.

Perry glared at the two of them, but held his hand out to point the way to the stairs. "After you," he said with mocking politeness.

Ten minutes later, the officers all returned to the porch.

"Well?" Perry said.

Mulkin shook his head. "There's nobody else in there. You have some very sick artists, however."

Perry grinned. "They're the best."

Mulkin turned his attention to Jillie. "Breaking and entering is a crime. Filing a false police report is a crime. It could be a felony."

"I didn't file a false report," Jillie said. "And I didn't break and enter...I just didn't leave on time."

Mulkin ignored her and looked at Perry. "Would you like to press charges?"

The other man frowned and opened his mouth to say something, then thought better of it. After thinking another moment, Perry shook his head.

"No," he said. "I don't want to waste any more time on this and I don't want to encourage any other stunts through media coverage of this."

He turned his gaze on Jillie. "However, I don't ever want to see you near this house again."

She opened her mouth to protest and he put a hand up. "Seriously. You had your say to the county and they ruled against you. I do not appreciate getting calls from the police at one in the morning. If you cause any more trouble here this month, I will make sure they throw you in jail."

Perry turned and thanked the officers and then walked back to his car.

"I think you'd be best served by listening to him," Mulkin said.

"Do we have to go to the station with you?" Ted asked.

Mulkin shook his head. "Not this time. However, I would advise you to not come back here again."

Ted nodded and took Jillie's arm in his hand. "C'mon," he said, and guided her across the grass to his car.

"There was a body there," Jillie said. "I'm not lying."

"I believe you," Ted said, though he didn't sound one hundred percent convinced.

Neither of them saw the curtains in the attic of the house move as they pulled out onto the path around the cemetery.

But Jillie felt a tremor in her heart. The witch who had led Bremen Coven had been associated with other murders at the house in the past. Jillie knew all the stories, and more than one said the witch had been working with an incarnation spell that needed blood. Lots of blood.

"Something bad happened in there tonight," she whispered. "And I think it is going to be just the beginning."

CHAPTER TWENTY-TWO

Mike lay beside Katie on the bed of nails. With one hand, he traced the puckered lines of her ravaged body. She shifted next to him, and then tilted her head to gaze into his eyes.

"I don't think I've ever been this happy," Mike whispered.

In answer her hand reached down to his thigh and with one fingernail drew a line from his knee to his balls. Then she cupped his manhood in her hand and squeezed just a little.

"I'm glad," she said. "It's hard to find a good guy when you're dead."

"I still don't buy the dead thing," Mike said. "You seem perfectly alive to me. And you're not some brain-eating zombie or anything."

Katie slipped her fingers around the knuckles of his right hand, and drew it up to her breasts. She held it between them, and whispered, "What do you feel?"

"A beautiful woman," he answered.

"No," she said. "What do you feel? Do you feel warmth? Is there a heartbeat?"

Mike paused. He let his fingers spread out, for once not with erotic intent, but simply to feel more of her. And then he finally had to admit the answer to both questions.

"No."

"There you go," she said.

Both of them were silent for a minute. Mike ran his hand over her breast, lingering for a second on the hard nub of a nipple before slipping his fingers across her bellybutton and down into the soft hair of her pubes. He was so confused. She felt so good; she wasn't some rotting corpse. How could he be making love to a dead woman? How could a dead woman talk to him? For a moment, he thought about all of the beer he'd been drinking. Could he be hallucinating? For two months? That thought was more disturbing than lying with a dead woman who talked to him.

"Okay, then how did you die?" he asked finally. Maybe knowing more about how she had gotten this way would help?

"Does it matter?" she asked. "The end result is the same no matter what."

He shrugged. "I'd like to know."

"My husband stabbed me with a butcher knife because he thought my baby wasn't his."

Mike's eyebrows rose. "Why did he think that?"

Katie's lips gave a faint smile. "Because it probably wasn't."

Mike's eyes bugged a little. "Oh."

"I loved a lot of men," she said. "I didn't want to only give myself to one and he said he could handle it. But in the end, he got jealous and crazy."

"Did it happen...here?" Mike asked.

She nodded. "Downstairs, in the master bedroom. I'd just come home from being with some friends and he had been drinking. He was passed out on the couch when I came in, so I just went to the bedroom. I had just taken off my clothes to put on my nightgown when he came in. His eyes looked all wild. 'Slutting around again?' he asked me, and I just ignored him. But that just made it worse. 'Who was it this time?' he asked. 'Randall? Ted? That black guy? Tell me you haven't been sleeping with him at least. I will not be the laughingstock of this town walking around with you holding a little mulatto. Because that bump in your belly isn't even mine, is it? Tell me the truth.'

"I told him, 'It could be from any of you, but it won't *belong* to any of you. The baby will be its own person, just like me.'"

She shook her head. "Things got ugly then. He slapped me around and I kicked him. Then he raised his fist to punch me and stopped. He got a look in his eyes that was just pure crazy, and he walked out of the room. I should have run then, but I didn't. And he came back a minute later holding the butcher knife. 'I should never have married you,' he said. I can remember every word. 'You're the devil herself,' he said. 'You probably conceived that kid on the altar during one of your pagan rituals that you never want me to be part of. But I have eyes and ears. I've seen things when you didn't know. But I'm not going to be the cuckold for someone else's brat. I won't do it. We'll just cut that thing out of you right now and be done with it.'

"I screamed and threw stuff at him but he was bigger than I was, and eventually he caught me and pinned me to the bed. He smelled like a whiskey bottle and I pleaded with him to see reason, but he was seeing something else entirely. He had the knife at my throat and then all of a sudden, he raised it and jabbed it just below my chest. 'We'll see if you've got that dirty black guy's kid right now,' he said. 'Or maybe that Mexican you were hanging around last fall.'

"The pain was horrible, and I screamed and screamed, but he just laughed and twisted the knife around until he could reach his bare hands inside me. I could feel something horrible moving and pulling inside and then his hands were in my face all covered in blood and he was saying something about the baby but...I didn't hear anything else. That's when I died."

"Jesus," Mike breathed, and took her into his arms. "I am so sorry."

After a few minutes, he loosened his embrace and asked the most obvious next question. "But, how did you come back?"

Katie smiled. "Emery did it," she said. "She's my anchor. If it wasn't for her, I'd be in that cemetery out there right now."

"Emery?" Mike asked. His voice sounded more than a little incredulous because, well, from what he'd seen, the other girl didn't seem to have a lot going on. "How did she manage it?"

"She was one of my secret sisters," Katie said. "There were five of us. We weren't related by blood but we were closer than family; you'd say we were a coven. That's part of the reason I moved out here to the forest. So we could practise our rituals without being seen. We came from different mothers and backgrounds, but together we formed a circle of unified power."

"You were witches?" Mike asked. This just kept getting weirder.

"That's the way most people label it," she said. "We were connected to something bigger, that's all I know. And Emery used her connections to stop me from leaving this world behind, even though Patrick had gutted me and killed my baby. She used her power to keep me from disappearing into the void, and I used mine to keep her alive all these years, just as she was then."

She rolled over on the bed to lie across his chest and stared down. Her face looked worried. "Are you okay?" she asked. "Do you still want to be with me?"

Mike wrapped his arms around her slight bare shoulders and crushed her against him. "Yes," he said. "I don't care what happened in the past. All that matters is that you're here now. And you might be the only woman I've ever really loved."

Katie smiled and planted a soft kiss on his lips.

"You don't know how glad I am to hear that," she said.

CHAPTER TWENTY-THREE

Bong got down on his hands and knees in the attic room and steeled himself for another long night. June walked up the stairs and into the room a moment later and took her place on the chair. People would focus on her and assume she was the 'jump scare' of the room, when actually, it was Bong's job to jump out and scare people. She was the distraction.

"Looks like you nicked yourself shaving again," he joked as she lolled her head back, exposing the red gash.

She held up the large straight razor from the table next to her. "Yeah, seems like it happens every day. This job is a killer."

"I'm not sure my knees are going to take this abuse for an entire month," Bong said. "I may end up becoming the scary Asian ghost in a wheelchair!"

"I'm not sure that's going to have quite the same impact," she said with a laugh.

Her voice made him grin. She was one of those people who always made people feel up.

"Are you wearing kneepads?" she asked.

He shook his head. "Nah, hadn't really thought of that. I don't think it's part of the costume."

"I think we can find some pads that nobody will notice," she said. "I think that's a much better plan than the wheelchair."

He shrugged. "Probably a lot cheaper too."

"I work at Oak Forest Hospital," she said. "I think I can find something that won't cost you a dime."

"That suits my budget perfectly," he said.

Just then, Lon's voice interrupted from the base of the stairway.

"The living are coming!" he said. "Let's make some screams tonight!"

That was the cue to shut up because the doors were opening. Bong flashed June a row of blackened teeth and moved back into the closet out of sight.

Someone downstairs shrieked, and Bong grinned. It wasn't really the kind of job he was interested in doing, but there was very clear affirmation if you were doing the job right. And so far, based at least on the number of screams, jumps, squeezed hands and quick exits, they all seemed to be haunting the house well.

Bong wondered how Jeanie was doing. She was one of the floaters on the first floor, and sometimes played the ravenous zombie, while other times she simply held out her guts, trying to get people to touch them. She said the guys sometimes would, but usually the girls yelped and said 'no way'.

This was supposed to be a job that brought them closer together, but honestly, Bong felt like it was going to have the opposite effect. He'd been so tired the past few nights that he'd passed out as soon as he took her home. The only time they'd had to talk was on the car rides to and from the house.

Three boys walked into the room. They looked college age and one of them was prodding the other one forward.

"Touch it," he said. "You know that's a dummy."

They stepped closer, and the provocateur pushed his friend to bend over.

"Ten bucks if you give her a kiss."

The other one stepped forward then, so all three of them were hovering over June, who managed to stay amazingly still. "Hell, I'll do it for ten bucks," he said.

Bong couldn't watch anymore. He pressed the button to start the strobe and began to crawl quickly towards them just as the guy bent down over June's face.

"Oh shit," the ringleader said when he saw Bong coming out of the dark, eyes and teeth blackened, his movements made more jerky and strange by the lights.

They were all so focused on June, that Bong's entry really freaked them out. The 'brave' one probably leapt the most. Bong kept relentlessly moving towards them, and while one of them started laughing at their surprise, the threesome quickly exited the room. Bong crept back to the closet.

"What did you do that for?" June asked before the next group arrived. "You didn't wait for my cue. I think I could've made one of them piss his pants!"

"Sorry," he said. "I knew I was early, but they were just making me nervous with all the kissing talk. They were getting a little too close, I thought."

"Thanks," June said. "That's sweet, and I appreciate it, but I can handle the frat boys, don't worry."

Bong nodded and ducked back out of sight as the next group entered the room. *Stupid, stupid, stupid*, he told himself, and steeled himself to make sure to wait this time for June to move. Then he laughed inside at his own private joke. Seemed he was always waiting for a girl to make a move.

June jumped, and Bong started out of the closet towards a handful of high school girls.

When they saw him, they screamed. "It's like *The Ring*," one of them said.

He had to grin at that. Sometimes the wait was worth it.

CHAPTER TWENTY-FOUR

Mike walked the attic, making sure all of the props were where they should be. He rehung a costume that had fallen to the floor and pushed a trunk back in place with his foot. Then he shut out the lights and went down the stairs to do the same on the first floor. He and Lon were taking turns handling lock-up each night, so one person didn't always have to be at the house insanely late.

It was hard to even recognise this as the same smelly, rotten and forgotten house he'd walked into less than three months before. Between his renovations, coats of paint, props and gelled spotlights, it was like a whole new, ancient museum of movie sets.

He walked down the stairs and shook his head at the dining room, decked out in the most suggestive cannibal décor possible. The leg bone – red with fake meat – still gave him the creeps and Argento and Lucio had finished what they called the 'Tobe Hooper Room' over a month earlier. It was their first project, because they wanted people who walked into the house to be immediately reminded of Hooper's most famous, most harrowing film.

Mike flipped off the hidden red spotlights and then walked down the fingernail-etched hallway towards the den. That remained one of his favourite spots in the house. He still couldn't believe that someone had built a hidden bookcase/stairway there, or that it still actually functioned, decades later. But he'd oiled and cleaned it, and now the room served as a great scare for the house. When a group entered the room, they found a suspiciously cosy spot with a glowing fireplace (electric) and a smoking pipe in an ashtray next to an easy chair. But then they noticed the pool of blood on the floor beneath the chair, and then maybe they noticed the giant framed portraits hung all around the room depicting serial killers, each grinning and holding his or her weapon of choice.

That's when the door slammed shut, and something groaned behind them. Some patrons screamed, some turned and ran for the door. But either way, they were forced back into the centre of the room, faced with a man in a terribly deformed rubber mask who was holding a large axe. When they became sufficiently freaked out, the bookcase would click and swing open with an extended creak. The flickering red and orange lights that escaped from the dark stairwell behind it did not provide any confidence for the haunted house visitors, but the room's axe-wielding mutant didn't give them much of a choice. They headed towards the stairwell down to the basement every time. For those who did get past the axeman (or when they needed to jam groups through the house faster), there was a back door that led back out to the hallway where both the stairwells up and down were. But Lon wanted them to use the bookcase basement entry as much as possible. It was a great gimmick and they hadn't even had to build it.

At the moment, however, nobody was in the house but Mike. He walked over towards the coffin that leaned sideways against the far wall and reached behind it to shut off the glow of the fireplace and a couple other quietly shifting LED lights tucked around the room. The cords were hidden behind the coffin, so patrons couldn't see the source of the 'atmosphere', which Argento said ruined the effect.

As Mike reached behind the coffin for the switch, someone screamed in the basement.

His heart froze.

Nobody was supposed to be left in the house.

"What the fuck?" he asked. Luckily, nobody answered.

Mike walked towards the bookcase and fingered the hidden latch that remained where it had been set up dozens of years before. The wall of books and skulls and other arcane decorations swung inward at his touch.

The scream did not repeat, but now Mike's ears were tuned. He listened to the air move as he stood at the top of the steps, waiting for some sign that someone was alive and moving downstairs.

None came.

Mike took a deep breath and forced his foot down on the first rung of the staircase he'd rebuilt. He had heard something down here, he was sure of that. And he couldn't leave the house without checking it out.

Carefully he eased his foot down another step, and then the next. He didn't want to make the steps creak. He still had visions of some coven of devil worshippers stabbing wild animals in the heart and then hanging them to bleed out over the original earth floor of the basement, as he'd discovered in his first couple weeks on the job. Whoever had been responsible had never been caught, and he didn't fully believe that they were gone. It occurred to him suddenly that Emery may have actually been the culprit, which was something he would have to ask Katie about. But if she hadn't been…well…the haunted house activity may have chased them away for now, but….

When he reached the bottom, Mike blinked as a red spotlight moved across his face. The room had been set up to have slowly shifting colours and hues, and noise or not, he would have needed to come down here regardless to shut everything down. He stepped to the side wall and lifted a fake wood shingle to expose the lighting switches. He flicked the coloured bank off, and then flipped a switch to light the downstairs in a series of cool white lights. The non-haunting bank.

The bulbs lit the long expanse of the basement without revealing any people. Just long empty aisles in between setpieces of horror.

Mike stood and simply listened for a moment, waiting to hear if any sound repeated the anguish he'd heard before. He could hear his heart beating louder than any sound in the room. But the sound, whatever it had been, didn't reoccur.

He turned to flip the downstairs lights out completely, when something thumped at the end of the aisle. It seemed to come from somewhere behind the Báthory and *Exorcist* tableaux.

Mike frowned.

There was nothing down there, except the long false room where the water heater and furnace were. The small room where he'd put Katie's coffin was also down that way. Nobody should even know that room existed, let alone be in there. Even the haunted house cast didn't know about Katie's room. They knew about the other section though, because Lon ran Ops out of the utilities room. Mike started walking down the aisle.

As he drew closer, he heard another noise. Something like a gasp.

Mike's chest constricted. Nobody should be down here. Especially not in the hidden basement room. He'd seen all of the regulars leave the house.

"Why me?" he asked silently, and then reached for the inset latch of the door. It opened quietly, and for a moment he was able to see what was going on within without alerting the people inside.

The glimpse made his heart ice over.

Inside the small hidden room, Emery held a long knife to the bare side of a man who'd been stripped naked. The man appeared to lean heavily against his captor. Mike couldn't see his face, but Katie was walking around the two of them in a circle, whispering things. Emery spoke along with her in unison. As Mike watched, trying to figure out exactly what Katie and Emery were up to, he saw Emery lift the silver blade higher in the air. Before he could react, she brought it down and drew it across the man's side. Then she reached across his middle and ran her hands over the wound, cupping and gathering the blood that welled.

Katie walked around and around the two of them, but Emery never looked at her. Instead, she moved to where the coffin that they had dug up sat. Only, the cover had been removed since Mike was here last. Emery held her hands out over the open coffin and let the blood drip off her fingers. She shook her hands then, sprinkling it on the bones that Mike dug up from the cemetery.

The victim himself didn't move, he just stood there in a trance, bleeding and blinking until Emery turned back and rubbed her hand over the crimson wound again.

Mike couldn't hold back then, and stepped down onto the dirt floor.

"What the hell are you two doing?" he asked. His voice was quiet, but his tone told how freaked out he was. Katie moved away from the still, naked man who, strangely, remained standing, and put her hands on Mike's shoulders. "It's okay," she said. "We just need to siphon a little life from him for me to hang around." She kissed him, wrapping her arms around his neck to pull his eyes away from the naked, bleeding man.

"What are you talking about?" he asked, moving to push her back. But she didn't let him get away. When the touch of her lips had calmed him somewhat, she pointed to the wooden box at the far side of the room. "That coffin that you dug up for me?" she said.

He nodded.

"Those bones are mine," she said.

"What are you talking about?" Mike asked. "You're right here. You're not a ghost."

"Aren't I?" she answered. "Take the chain off from around your neck."

"The one I found in the house?"

She nodded. "Give it to Emery."

He frowned, but raised the necklace past his chin and over his head. Emery took the chain and locket from him and slipped it into her jeans pocket.

The naked man now stood abandoned in the middle of the room; he remained still as a statue, though he could have easily walked out of the room.

"So now what?" Mike said, when Emery had hidden his locket.

"Now try to touch me," Katie said.

Mike shrugged. He had held Katie before they'd gone to the stupid expensive Red Robin for half-assed burgers a few hours ago, and he'd held her again later tonight when she'd dressed up in her witch-ly 'haunt' costume and prepped to walk the halls and scare people. Not to mention touching her as she kissed him seconds ago. He didn't see why taking off a necklace would change anything there.

He held out his arms to pull her close but instead she sidestepped them, and whispered in his ear. "I need you to finally understand," she said.

"Understand what?" he asked.

"Understand that I'm dead," Katie whispered.

When he shook his head and turned to look at her, she kissed his lips and pulled away. He felt the faint spark of electricity that he did every time her mouth met his.

"You're not going to like hearing this, but it's true," she said. "I died a long time ago, and while I've told you that, what I haven't told you is the body you've been holding isn't real. But I want it to be. I want to come back. And if you help me…you can be with me forever. I've kept Emery with me all these years… I can do the same for you."

Mike shook his head. "You're real," he said. "I can feel you. I've kissed you."

Katie smiled, but it was a sad smile. "You think you have. Now give me a hug," Katie urged.

Mike put his arms around her and started to pull her close.

Only.

His hands went right through her.

"What the hell?" he whispered.

"I'm dead," Katie said. "I've been telling you."

"That's insane," Mike said. "I've been with you for weeks. We've made love; we've eaten and drunk beer together. You've been working in the haunted house – other people have seen and touched you."

"You *thought* you felt me in bed," she said. "And you've dumped out a lot of nearly-full cans of beer after our nights together, haven't you?"

He shrugged at that. He had simply figured that Katie was really a lightweight.

"I can make people see me pretty easily," she said. "But without the locket, nobody can feel me. I've been careful not to get too near to anyone in the haunted house, so nobody has touched me."

Mike kept shaking his head, as if in pantomiming *no* he could make the past few minutes disappear.

"I have been dead for a long, long time," Katie said. "But I don't want to be any longer."

"So…" he said.

"So, I need the blood," she said. "Living blood to touch my bones. Every night. And with every drop, I'll come closer to being real again, instead of a ghost."

"But I've touched you," he said. "You're not a ghost. I've felt you."

"You *think* you have," she said. "That locket is the key. It lets you feel me when I'm not really here."

"What about Emery?" he asked. "I've touched her. She's shovelled dirt and lifted boards with me."

"Emery's not the one who's dead," Katie answered. "I've kept her just as she was on the night she saved me. She sleeps on that bed of nails to constantly remind herself that she's still alive. She grows distant, but she's not dead like me."

She waved a hand at the still silent man standing alone by the coffin. "If we can dress my bones with the blood of thirty victims – one every night in October – on Halloween night, my body will be reborn and my spirit will finally be able to walk again in the flesh. You'll be able to hold me again."

Mike shook his head as the enormity of what she suggested dawned on him. Katie was talking about stabbing people down here every night for the rest of the month. "No, no, no," he said. "You can't do that. If people start disappearing every night from here, they'll shut this place down. And they'll find you."

Katie laughed. "They won't find *me*," she said. "They might find my bones. But I don't think they'll know what to do with those. They're not taking a skeleton to prison."

Mike couldn't help but smile at that idea.

"But it doesn't matter," she said. "People aren't disappearing. We're not killing anyone. In fact, right now you can help Emery bandage this one up and take him back to his natural habitat."

Mike frowned at her. "This guy is going to go straight to the police and tell them about the two women who cut him. And now he'll probably mention me too."

"He won't remember anything," she said. "He'll wake up and wonder how he got hurt and who bandaged him… but that's as far as it'll go. He'll count the money in his wallet, count his blessings that he's alive, and do his best to forget about it all. Does he look ready to tell tales?"

Mike looked at the man, who remained staring straight ahead, slack jawed. Blood dripped down his waist from the slice in his side.

"Fix him up," Katie said to Emery. "It's getting late and we don't want him to be missed."

Mike watched as Emery retrieved paper towels, tape and gauze from behind the coffin. She wiped off the blood, then held a piece of gauze over the wound. She looked up at him then, as if waiting for him to do something. When he didn't move, she spoke softly. "Hold this," she said.

Mike held the gauze in place and she covered it with medical tape. Moments later, she was guiding the man's legs back into a pair of jeans, and Mike helped her pull a t-shirt over the man's head. They might as well have been dressing a warm dummy; the man hadn't moved on his own or said a word.

"When will he wake up?" Mike asked, as Emery worked on getting his shoes back on.

Katie shrugged. "Once he gets away from this house, the spell will wear off. Emery will take him to his car and drive him down the turnpike a ways. When he comes to in his car, he'll wonder how he got hurt, but won't remember anything. He might not even remember coming here. But a little piece of me will be reborn from the wash of his blood."

"This is crazy," Mike said, shaking his head in disbelief.

Katie leaned towards him and planted a kiss on his lips. He felt the spark, but as his arms instinctively went around her, they passed right through her shoulder blades.

"If you want to feel me again, you need to help Emery," Katie said. "This is a matter of life and death. Mine."

Mike took a breath and nodded. "C'mon," he said to Emery and took the man's elbow. Together they started walking the zombie-like man towards the door. When Mike looked over his shoulder to catch Katie's eye, the room was empty.

All he saw behind him was the coffin.

CHAPTER TWENTY-FIVE

"I knew it," Jillie said. She pointed at a small article in the Oak Forest *Daily Southtown* and then reached over the table and grabbed a handful of Ted's fries. "There was a Missing Persons Report filed a couple days ago with the police. A girl from Oak Forest High School didn't come home, and her friends said they didn't know where she disappeared to. They said they lost her inside the haunted house."

Ted's eyes rose. He took another bite of his greasy cheeseburger.

"They said we were nuts. Well, I'm sure this is the same girl that I saw in the basement of that house. I'm going to the police station to show them this missing person notice. Maybe now they'll want to talk more about what I saw."

She reached across the table and Ted slapped her fingers away from his plastic container.

"I'm going to file a Missing Persons Report on my fries if you keep that up."

"They're not good for you anyway," she said, and avoided his hand to snatch one.

"And they're good for you?"

She shrugged. "I have more nervous energy than you. I'll work it off."

She crumpled up her sandwich wrapper from inside her red plastic container and stood up suddenly. "C'mon, let's go over to the station."

Ted shook his head. "I don't think that's a very good idea. They already let you go once. You want to tempt fate?"

"No, I want to prove that they should have listened to me," she said. "And then I want to get that house closed down before the witch gets anyone else."

She snatched up Ted's basket of fries as he shoved the last bite of his burger into his mouth.

"C'mon," she said, and walked the basket to the trash. She took a handful of fresh cut fries and stuffed them in her mouth before emptying the rest in the trash.

"Damn, those are good," she said, as Ted launched himself from the table to try to stop her.

His hands passed through air as she emptied the basket and set it on the top of the garbage can.

"Drive me to the police station?" she said. It was framed as a question, but there was no query about it. Ted sighed and looked longingly at the garbage can for a moment, before walking to the exit.

*　　*　　*

Jillie was three steps ahead of him as they walked into the station. She marched up to the intake window, where a woman in a blue uniform shirt sat behind a (presumably) bulletproof pane of glass. Her voice came through a round silver vent in the glass.

"How can I help you?" the woman asked. She sounded bored.

Jillie waved the paper in the air and then set it down and pointed at the Missing Persons Report. "I need to talk to an inspector," she said. "I saw this girl murdered at the Bachelor's Grove Haunted House two nights ago."

The woman behind the desk looked sceptical. Then she fingered a button on the phone next to her. "Hey Bill, can you come up here a moment?" Then she pointed at an uncomfortable-looking plastic couch with orange vinyl cushions on the side of the room. "If you would wait over there…"

Jillie walked triumphantly over to the couch and flopped down on the edge. She could not wait to let the cops know they'd screwed up when they refused to listen to her. She felt bad about the high school girl, but she felt good about the chance to shut down the house before more people were killed.

Ted sat next to her, but he slouched into the chair. He did not look anxious to face the police for the second time this week.

A minute later a white steel door opened to the right of the reception booth and a big man in full officer uniform stepped into the lobby.

"Can I help you?" he asked the two of them. A silver rectangle pinned to his blue shirt said 'Richton'. Above it, a thin badge boasted, 'Detective'.

Jillie leapt back to her feet, and crossed the room in a heartbeat, holding out the newspaper.

"This missing girl from Oak Forest," she said. "I saw her dead the other night at the Bachelor's Grove Haunted House. She was downstairs in the basement after the house closed."

Detective Richton nodded slowly and took the newspaper from her.

"You're the one they found trespassing there, aren't you?" he said.

"Yes," she said. "That doesn't matter though. The point is, I saw the girl. She was lying in a pool of blood and the cops that night didn't believe me because someone came back and put a manikin in her place before they got there. Now you need to listen to me, because she's missing. I was right. And someone or something at that house did her in. You need to shut the place down and actually investigate it."

The officer looked at the newspaper article and shook his head. "I don't think so," he said.

"Why not?" she said. "I'm telling you, the house is connected with this girl's disappearance. And you're not going to find her alive. She may be at the bottom of that pond by the cemetery."

Detective Richton shook his head again.

"No, she's not," he said. "And we are not looking for her either."

"What do you mean?"

"That article was out of date before the newspaper was even printed," he said. "That girl is safe and sound back home with her family. She bumped her head, got lost and scratched up wandering around in Bremen Woods, but found her way out the next day. She's fine."

Jillie frowned. "You're sure?"

He nodded. "She'd been in the haunted house the night before and got separated from her friends. But she's fine."

"Maybe the girl I saw was someone else then," Jillie said. "Are you investigating any other missing persons?"

Detective Richton handed her back the newspaper. "No," he said. "We are not."

He turned to return to the interior of the station, but then paused.

"Remember what they told you," he said. "Stay away from that house. Stop making trouble where there isn't any."

Jillie's eyes caught fire and she started to spit back a retort, but Ted grabbed her arm.

Detective Richton disappeared through the door without another word.

"C'mon," Ted said. "Let this one die."

"I swear that girl already did," Jillie said.

CHAPTER TWENTY-SIX

The night was alive with screams. Recorded, and real.

Mike stood behind the barricade on the left side of the attic in the dark, and watched groups of patrons thread their way through the costume aisle at the right. Periodically one of the haunters would jump out at them from a hidden location and someone would always let out a yell. Then they'd disappear into the room at the end of the path and be sent down the back stairway before the next group came into the attic.

One thing that Lon and the rest of the group had been good about was separating the groups. Some haunted houses just jammed people through in an endless line, so the rooms were never vacant enough for the scare factor to really work. Sure, there were jump scares, but it was all too fast and crowded. Lon had insisted on limiting the flow of people into the house, so they could really 'work' each room.

That was playing well for Mike now, as he waited in the dark.

A hand gripped his shoulder from behind. Mike jumped a little. The pale face of Emery emerged from the shadows. She said nothing, but pointed at the stairwell coming up from downstairs. Mike nodded. Then he walked out into the main room and stood next to the stairs on the other side.

When a single girl stepped up and into the room, Mike said nothing. As she saw him, he stretched out his right arm and pointed towards the small entry to the alcove that led to Emery's secret bedroom.

The girl had neon-blue hair and wore a black t-shirt with a pattern that glowed in the black light beaming across the stairwell to illuminate a pile of bones in the corner. She was chewing gum and grinned as she saw him. Without questioning him, she moved into the small side room where Emery waited. She assumed he was a haunted house guide. Mike followed her.

When she walked two steps in and reached the centre of the small space, she stopped and looked confused. Her face turned one way, and then the next, searching for where to go next, and then she turned to walk back towards Mike. There was only one way out, and that was the way she had walked in.

He said nothing, but shook his head. No exit.

Then he pointed at the floor.

The girl gave him a look. "Okay," she said. Then she bent down and looked at the floor where Emery's door was concealed. Mike noted that she wore a black skirt and ripped fishnets above black boots. A goth chick. Probably here on a dare that she wasn't afraid to do the house on her own. Nothing could scare her.

We'll see about that, Mike thought.

The door in the floor suddenly opened and Emery's face emerged from the darkness. The goth girl jumped backwards, but Mike caught her in his arms easily. Then he lifted her in the air and dangled her feet into the opening in the floor. Emery grabbed the girl by the waist as Mike took over holding the door.

"What the fuck?" the girl yelled.

But before she could get out another word, she'd disappeared down the stairs pounding at Emery's shoulders. Mike lowered the door gently back to the floor, and the sound of her struggles disappeared. In moments, the girl would be silent, captured in whatever spell Emery and Katie wove.

He looked out at the empty attic, making sure none of the haunters had seen the girl's abduction. At that moment, a gang of rowdy teens ascended the stairs and a few seconds later the room was echoing with laughter and screams again.

Mike watched them disappear down the hall and nodded to himself. Then he opened the door in the floor and slipped down into the secret heart of the house.

*   *   *

Jeanie walked down the hallway with slow, exaggerated steps. She was roaming tonight, moving from one area of the house to the next, making sure there were no stragglers. With one hand, she cradled her fake guts to her middle, as if preventing her intestines from completely falling out of her body. With the other, she touched the wall. It was a convincing gimmick that usually sent patrons moving quickly to get out of her way.

A middle-aged guy in glasses and a blue polo shirt walked out of Argento's favourite room, with two teenage boys behind him. The group stopped when they saw Jeanie, and she reached out a hand to them and let out a horrible moan. The older guy smiled and nodded, clearly impressed with her makeup. But the younger-looking teen led the trio quickly ahead, sidestepping past her in the hall.

They ducked into the next room, and instantly she heard a scream from one of them. One of the haunters, Darren, was in there, with a huge machete. Jeanie grinned and slipped into Argento's room for a moment to check it out.

The room was awash in red and blue spotlights, and a tapestry shivered on the wall to the left. A woman's head was impaled on the blades of glass remaining in a broken window on the far end of the room. Overhead, the ceiling was a moving mass of maggots. When someone stepped on the spot in the centre of the room, a handful of the tiny rubber things fell from the ceiling. That typically elicited some solid shrieks from any women who walked through and suddenly saw white maggots stuck in their hair.

Jeanie didn't walk to the centre of the room, but before she'd gone inside two steps, a black-gloved hand grabbed her from behind, and held her mouth shut. The cool touch of a metal blade touched her neck. "Take another step and I'll cut your guts out for real," a voice growled in her ear.

Jeanie laughed. "And I'll shove fake bugs in your mouth."

She turned around and grinned at Argento. The set designer loved playing the part of a giallo killer.

He dropped the knife (which had a completely filed down rounded edge) to his side, and smiled through the black latex hood that covered his head.

"Getting hot in there?" she asked. "Need me to give you a break?"

He shook his head. One of Jeanie's roles as a floater was to give the other haunters a chance to go to the bathroom, or take a breather from sweaty costumes for a few minutes each night.

"I've got to rack up more kills tonight," he said. "Can't afford to stop."

He and 'Lucio' had a bet going. Every time one of them used their favourite director's 'weapon of choice' on a guest, and that guest screamed, it counted as a kill. Whoever elicited the most total kills in a week bought the other's bar tab on their night off.

So far, Lucio was winning this week. They turned in their totals to Lon each night at close, and he was keeping the running totals on the notes app in his phone.

"What's the score so far?" she asked.

"It's 113 to 97," he said. "People hate zombies."

Lucio's makeup this week was that of one of Fulci's zombie creations, and featured an eyeball hanging down his face. He'd flipped from wearing the murderous crone mask when one of the other haunters had developed a rash from the zombie makeup. The hanging eyeball was a particularly gruesome bit of makeup that Jeanie wished she had done. But June had designed it.

Outside the door, they heard steps moving quickly in the hall. "You better walk," he said.

She nodded, and exited the room, just as a new group rounded the corner of the hall. She held her arms out to them, and a girl with blond hair laughed and shook her head upon seeing Jeanie's guts. "That's so gross," she said. But her friends dragged her into the room Jeanie had just left, and within a few seconds she heard a scream.

Jeanie smiled.

"Ninety-eight," she murmured, and walked towards the stairs to the attic. She wanted to check out how Bong and June were doing.

The eerie keyboard-driven music of a band – that Argento had once impatiently explained to her was called Goblin – jittered and added to the creepy atmosphere as she walked up the stairs. She abandoned her shambling gait to reach the top floor before a new group caught up to her from behind.

She slowed for a moment though, as she saw a lone girl with blue hair walking up the stairs ahead of her. Jeanie stopped on the stair and waited. Someone upstairs yelled, "What the fuck," and Jeanie grinned. Probably the blue-haired girl meeting up with the old crone mask…and the sickle. A guy named Ben was playing that part tonight, and he loved to wave his weapon.

Jeanie counted to thirty, and then walked up the rest of the stairs. The blue-haired girl should be through the costume aisle and past the old hag slasher and in Bong and June's room by now. Another few seconds and she'd be on her way back down the stairs to head towards the basement.

When she stepped onto the floor of the attic, the room appeared empty; she headed towards the costume racks. She waved off Ben and walked down the clothes aisle and into the room that Bong was haunting. But when she stepped inside, neither of them were to be seen.

"Bong?" she called.

There was a creak on the other side of the room.

A second later, the black hair and white face of Bong emerged from the space behind a large old projection television set. Someone had donated it from their basement since it didn't work well anyway, and it was a great prop for an 'Asian ghost' to hide behind, since it brought back thoughts of *The Ring*. They ran a loop of TV static on it to help set the mood.

"Hey," Bong said. He pursed his lips like she'd taught him to spread his black lipstick better. "I was just talking to June. It's been a while since anyone came through…is someone behind you?"

Jeanie frowned. "Didn't a girl with blue hair just go through here?"

Bong shook his head. "I don't think that was the last one."

June walked out from behind the TV then, and pulled down the hem of her white, bloodstained dress. Her milky eye was creepy even to Jeanie, who knew it was just a contact.

"Do either of you need a break?" Jeanie asked.

June shook her head and looked at Bong. "I think we're both okay right now."

He nodded quickly. "Yeah. You'd better head down before the next group gets here."

"No worries," Jeanie said. "I won't blow your scare!" She stepped up to Bong and pecked his lips lightly. He instantly rubbed his finger over his lips to smooth out the black. Jeanie frowned before walking to the back stairwell beyond them. "I'll be back in an hour."

"Cool," Bong said. "We'll be here."

As Jeanie walked down the back stairwell, she had a cold feeling in her stomach that had nothing to do with scares and haunting. She couldn't help but feel as if she'd just been pushed out of the attic room.

CHAPTER TWENTY-SEVEN

Emery stood next to the blue-haired girl in the basement. She held the docile girl's arm out over the coffin on the back wall, and massaged the biceps until ribbons of red dripped out of the cut she'd made and onto the bones below.

The house had been closed for a half an hour now, and Mike had turned off all of the upstairs lights before descending into the basement. When he arrived, he found Katie and Emery whispering strange words together as Katie walked round and round the punk girl, who stared off into some space that nobody else could see.

It was eerie to see, but also something he was used to by now. He'd helped Emery for the past two weeks to pick off lone victims towards the end of each haunted house night. The women somehow quieted and calmed their 'bleeders' and kept them hidden away in the secret room until the house was closed. Then they bled them in the basement over the casket, before bandaging them up and sending them back out in a confused and disoriented state to the world. Mike had helped drive a couple of them down the road to the parking lot of a strip mall, when the victims lacked any car keys. If the lot was empty when they took the bleeder out of the house, they knew that they'd picked on someone who'd been dropped off or had come with others, even if he or she had been walking the house solo.

He stood back and waited until whatever magic the two were spinning was spun; he'd learned quickly to stay out of their way when they bled their victims.

Emery slid her knife across the girl's arm in another spot, an inch or so away from the first cut, and fresh blood surfaced on the white skin of her lower biceps instantly. They cut every victim in a slightly different place. Katie smiled and nodded, and the two began a chant once again.

Mike pulled his cell phone out of his pocket, and skimmed his email. It was hard to believe, but after watching this strange ritual night after night, he no longer was fascinated or repelled by it. This was just what Katie and Emery did...and he would be there at the end, ready to help take their 'bleeders' outside to safety, so that they weren't missed. His biggest fear was that sooner or later one of them would remember how and where he or she was cut...and the whole thing would be blown before Katie's resurrection was complete. But Katie assured him that none of the victims remembered a thing. He had to believe her, since so far not a single one had come back to the house with the police in tow the next day.

He looked up from his email, which was empty other than spam from banks that he didn't hold accounts at, and coupons from White Castle and TGI Fridays.

What if this was all just bullshit? he wondered. What if, after a month of cutting people, Katie remained a ghost, a phantasm who slipped through his fingers when he went to hug her?

The thought made his stomach churn. Since the night that he'd discovered Katie and Emery's ritual, Katie had remained noncorporeal to him. Emery had kept the locket from him, and Katie used it as a bit of sexual blackmail. "I need you to help Emery make me whole," she'd said, when he asked for the necklace back. "I want you to remember that I can't really touch you until we're done with all of this. So, for now, Emery is going to keep the necklace."

He'd not been happy. Every night, he asked the same question: "Can we be together tonight, please?"

Katie only looked at him with wide, sad brown eyes and whispered, "Soon."

Having sex with her again was bait – so he would keep bringing her people to bleed. Mike thought about it a lot at home, in his bed at night. But every time he questioned himself, he came to the same conclusion. She was worth it.

But now, as Emery moved the girl away from the coffin, and beckoned him over to help her bandage the wound, Mike found himself doubting again.

"Is all of this really doing anything?" he said, as he held the gauze in place and Emery taped it down.

Katie's eyebrows creased, and her ethereal fingers stroked his forehead. He couldn't really feel her, but there was still some connection, some spark that his skin felt as she brushed her spirit over him.

"You still don't believe me?" Katie whispered. Her voice sounded girlish. And hurt.

Mike licked his lips and clenched his fists before he answered. He didn't want to say the wrong thing. He didn't want the necklace to be withheld forever. "I believe you," he said. "But I just worry if something doesn't go right...."

Katie smiled. "Everything is going fine," she said. "Come here and see for yourself."

She motioned him closer to the coffin, as Emery led the punk girl away.

"Look at me," Katie said.

"I am," he said.

She shook her head and pointed into the open coffin. "No, look at *me*," she insisted. He leaned over to peer inside the wooden box.

"Do those look like the bones you brought here?" she asked.

As Mike peered into the cavity, he gasped.

He'd expected to see white bones stained in blood, because they'd been drenching the coffin in it every night.

He hadn't expected to see bones with sheaths of...meat covering them. In fact, there was so much pink in the coffin now, he could barely see the shards of white where Katie's skeleton had once lain dry and white. The bones of her feet and hands still were clearly naked in the box, but even those had a spiderweb haze of *something* starting to grow on them.

"It's actually working," he whispered.

"You doubted me?" Katie asked.

Mike shrugged. "I didn't know what to think. It all seems so unlikely."

Katie smiled, sort of, but her lips stretched thin. "You have to learn to trust me," she said. "Relationships are built on trust, right?"

He nodded, and the words hit him. He had a *relationship*. Sure, it was with a ghost but...he hadn't had a relationship with a woman since his wife had left him. And arguably, he hadn't really had one with her for months, or maybe years, before that life-decimating event.

Mike found himself smiling for the next fifteen minutes as he walked the blue-haired girl to the lone remaining car in the parking lot, fished out her keys from her purse, and then drove her a few blocks down the turnpike before putting the car in park, and moving her over to the driver's seat. He knew from past experience that by the time he locked up the last rooms of the house and drove past here himself, the girl would have woken up, and the car would be gone.

When he walked back into the haunted house, it was silent. Emery and Katie had disappeared. But it was late and Mike knew that he'd see them again tomorrow. And that was one day closer to the day when he could hold Katie in his arms again and actually feel her. He felt better about that day coming than he had before. Because…they had a relationship, right?

CHAPTER TWENTY-EIGHT

Jeanie wondered if she really had a relationship. Over the past couple weeks, Bong had grown increasingly quiet. Admittedly he was always quiet; it was just his nature. But the past couple nights, he hadn't even come inside with her when he'd dropped her off after the house had closed.

"I'm really tired and tomorrow is going to be a long day," he'd said last night. He'd planted a kiss on her cheek and sat back, waiting for her to get out of the car. As she did, she'd seen his phone light up with a notification. "Who's texting you?" she wanted to ask. But she didn't dare. It probably wasn't even a text, just a Facebook notice or something.

The problem was, she'd wanted to ask.

She had never felt like that before with Bong. And that sucked. She wasn't really sure what had changed. She knew he'd never wanted to do the haunted house, and had agreed to do it for her. So, he had been a little grumpy for the past month or more. But she figured that would pass and he'd have fun with it, the same as she did.

But instead, he'd just grown quieter.

And then last night, when she'd seen him talking animatedly to June, when he'd not said more than a few sentences to her all day, well…that's when her heart suddenly screamed a warning klaxon. Was he just unhappy with her, or was he getting happy with June?

Fuck.

June was her 'boss', and she seemed really cool. She knew more about monster makeup than Jeanie had ever dreamed of knowing. Jeanie had already learned a tonne from her.

So she didn't want to think that June was making time with Bong. She wouldn't do that, right?

Jeanie walked back into her kitchen and pulled a Milky Way bar from the cabinet. She always craved chocolate when she got upset. She ripped the paper wrapper off and bit down hard.

When Bong rang the doorbell a few minutes later, the candy bar was gone and Jeanie sat on the couch in a worse funk than before.

"Ready to go?" he asked through the screen door.

She didn't answer, just stood and grabbed her purse.

"How was your day?" she asked once they were on the road.

Bong shrugged. "Same as ever. Wish it was Friday night."

"Me too," she said. "Maybe you can stay over this weekend."

"Maybe," he said, staring straight ahead.

Her belly felt a pang of ice, and she said nothing else for the rest of the ride.

★   ★   ★

"Okay, it may be hump day, but I don't want to see any humping going on in these halls tonight," Lon said. He was giving their nightly pep talk in the *Nightmare on Elm Street* room. "I want to see people too creeped out to kiss," he said. "So, let's get our game on and keep the blood flowing fast. Less than two more weeks to Halloween, you know that?"

Lon pulled his phone out of his front jeans pocket and thumbed it on. He hit the touch screen a couple times and then held the phone in the air for everyone to see. Not that anyone really could.

"Last week, you know that Lucio took home the scream prize. So far Lucio is poking out Argento's eye this week. He's already ahead 77 to 49 on the scream-o-meter. Maybe people just aren't a-scared of black-gloved, leather-masked killers these days. But they still do love their zombies. At least, that's what these two are reporting. Maybe neither one of them is getting the scream on, I don't know."

"Hey, hey, hey!" a voice called out of the crowd. It was Lucio, wearing his trademark *Zombi 2* shirt, with maggots crawling out of a decaying face's eyeball.

"I have earned every one of those screams. And you can audit me if you want. Maybe you'll scream too while you're at it."

"Somehow, I doubt that," Lon said with a grin. "All right, the point is, let's give 'em our best tonight and make 'em wanna come back and do it again. And good luck catching up tonight, Argento. Creeps dismissed!"

"See you later," Bong said, and reached down to fondle her fake intestines. "Maybe suck it in?"

"Ha ha," she said, and grinned in spite of herself. That was more like Bong.

But then she watched him walk through the crowd to catch up with June. And she saw June's face light up with a smile before the two of them exited the makeup room to head upstairs to their spots.

All of a sudden, her stomach felt like her guts were all twisted up again. The weird thing about it was…if she looked down at her waist, they were.

Jeanie realised suddenly that this wasn't fun anymore.

And that sucked.

★   ★   ★

"How are your knees?" June asked.

Bong shrugged. "Dreaming of the day after Halloween," he said.

She snorted. "Not enjoying your nights as a Korean ghost?"

"I think I'm supposed to be Japanese," he said. "But what difference does it make? I mean, jet black hair, slanty eyes, we're all the same, right?"

"You don't think Jeanie knows the difference?" June asked. "C'mon, I don't think she's that clueless. She really likes you."

"All she thinks about is this place," Bong said. "That's what she cares about."

June shook her head. It was a little disconcerting to see the bloody gash in her neck twist in the flickering red light. "She's living a dream right now," June said. "But in a couple weeks, she'll be all yours again."

Lon's voice echoed up the stairs. "Get your spook on!"

June gripped Bong's arm and leaned in close to him. Close enough that he could smell the faint flower scent of her deodorant. "Of course, in a couple weeks, you may be in a wheelchair," she laughed.

"You're evil," he said with a grin. "Now go…slit yourself."

★   ★   ★

Argento adjusted the black leather hood over his head. Damn thing was hotter than hell, and the sweat dripped around his ears and down his cheeks. But no matter how uncomfortable the getup was, he was bound and determined to get ahead on the count tonight. Truth be told, he wasn't aggressive enough on the floor. He knew it. He loved decorating the rooms and setting the lights and coming up with the 'look'. Because every 'look' was really a homage to his favourite movies and director. But when it came to playing a part…he was, by nature, too shy. And shy monsters didn't scare people.

Lucio wasn't that much more outgoing than he was, but he had more disgusting makeup. That trumped a 'quiet killer' every time.

"Not tonight," Argento whispered. He walked to the back of the room and reached behind the set tapestry to turn up the Goblin soundtrack to *Suspiria* two more notches. Music helped set the mood.

So he'd let the masters talk for him. He just needed to act the part more.

He just needed to be more menacing with the (fake) knife.

The first footsteps sounded in the hallway outside, and he held out the knife and assumed the position.

Tonight, he was going to freak people out.

Or he'd sever his own neck on a broken window.

★ ★ ★

Tonight's bleeder, according to Emery, was a forty-something guy with a long ponytail and a Dio t-shirt with ripped sleeves.

Mike wasn't real happy when he saw the guy stomping up the stairs. Emery had done her usual quiet appearance behind him and pointed at the stairs. Meaning, corral the next person who came up here. But railroading a big dude was way different than scaring a thin girl into the hole in the floor where Emery waited. Hell, how did Emery even think she was going to carry this guy down her secret ladder?

"Fuck," Mike whispered under his breath. But he'd learned not to question Katie. And if Emery said it, it was Katie who spoke. He'd realised that much a while ago. There was only one girl calling the shots here.

Mike pointed towards the alcove behind the bureau, and the guy looked at him hard for a second, and then started walking towards the entry point without a question.

Thank God for small favours.

Mike followed him into the half-hidden area and pointed dramatically down at the floor. They guy looked confused for a moment, and then as if on cue, the floor door opened and Emery came out.

She stood next to the open door and pointed, just as dramatically as Mike had, for the man to walk down the ladder.

The guy hesitated for just a moment, and then turned and began to descend the stairs.

Emery looked at Mike and for the first time in the entire time he'd known her, he swore the girl smiled.

When the big guy had stepped down four or five stairs and the door was closing behind him, Emery took it in her own hands, and waited for him to disappear below her before she followed.

When the door closed, Mike heaved a sigh of relief. Whatever shit happened down there, it was on her, not him.

After the next group passed by on the stairs and began screaming down the aisle as haunters with hag masks and knives jumped out at them, Mike quickly slipped down the stairs before the next group could ascend.

He was going to check in with Lon and see what else was up for tonight. Because his job for Katie was done. At least for the next 24 hours.

CHAPTER TWENTY-NINE

Thirty-seven out-loud screams tonight. Argento was happy. He hadn't heard Lucio's score yet, but his own was better than he'd charted on any other night for the past two weeks.

Sometimes pressure was what drove you to succeed.

And sometimes you were just lucky.

He didn't know which of those scenarios he owed his numbers to, but he was proud of the rank he'd racked up. It ought to put him back in contention with his friend.

Lon had just called the 'spooks out' call, which meant that all guests were out of the house, and they were closed for the night. He walked out of his room with a faint grin and headed to the makeup room to get rid of his gear. There was a line at June's mirror, but he didn't need to worry about that shit. He pulled the gloves and mask over his head and went upstairs to hang it on the rack with the others.

"So, what did you hit?" he asked Lucio when he got back down.

"Twenty-nine," Lucio said.

Argento grinned. "Creeping up on you, man. Thirty-seven."

"Bastard," Lucio said. "I even made a girl piss her pants, I swear I did."

"Sometimes the knife is better than the maggot," Argento said.

"Yeah, sometimes." Lucio grinned. "But rarely. You want to grab a drink? A few people are going."

Argento shook his head. "Wiped. Maybe tomorrow. I just want to head home."

Lucio shrugged. "I hear ya. See you tomorrow."

Argento smiled as his friend headed out the front door. There was one thing he wanted to do before he left. Lon had mentioned earlier that a couple of the lights in the basement were out. So he grabbed replacements from a pack he kept in the *Nightmare on Elm Street* bureau and headed to the hall. Lon was talking to Lenny at the end of the hallway, but looked up as Argento came out.

"You're gonna be the last one out," Lon said.

Argento shrugged. "Nah, you guys are still here. I just wanted to fix those lights before I go."

Lon nodded. "Fair enough. Mike's closing up tonight, so we were just leaving. You want to meet us up at The Edge in a few? We're going to have a beer."

He shook his head. "Lucio already asked me. I gotta get some sleep."

Lon grinned. "Save up your energy for another big scream night tomorrow? Got it. See you then."

Lenny waved and the two of them walked toward the front foyer.

Argento had second thoughts for a moment about following, and then shook his head. He needed some sleep; his throat had been scratchy earlier, and he couldn't afford to be sick for Halloween.

He descended the 'Don't Go In The Basement' stairs and saw the problems. There was a floor spot out on the far right, which was easily fixed. But there was also a top spot out near the middle of the maze, and he needed a different bulb for that. He replaced the first one, and smiled as a red glow instantly lit the wall. It was a small change, but every light made a difference.

Argento went back upstairs, but left the lights on. He thought he had a replacement for the other spot in his trunk; he hadn't used many of those and they were LEDs so they should have lasted the whole show. He replaced the other extra bulb and went outside.

The night air was cool, but a little humid. It smelled of the forest, and he took a deep breath. There was nothing better than the night. He preferred to sleep all day and work at night, when he had a job that allowed it. For a long time, he'd been a stock boy at a Jewel supermarket, and it was perfect. He had a night shift, but could drive home long before the sun came up.

He stood still for a few minutes, just breathing the air and listening to the chime of the night bugs. They buzzed and droned and chirped like an orchestra, a steady, constant background of natural music.

Argento smiled and finally walked to the car to retrieve the bulb. He opened the trunk and found he did, indeed, have a pack of them tucked in the back. He grabbed the box and decided he might as well keep some extras in the house with the other bulbs.

When he went back inside, he paused for a moment, listening for any sound to tell him where Mike was. He hadn't seen the carpenter in hours, though Lon said he was here. He should let him know that he was still here so he didn't lock Argento inside.

"Mike?" he called. "You around?"

When there was no answer, he shrugged and dropped the spare bulbs in the *Nightmare* room and grabbed a screwdriver before heading down the stairs. The mount for these spots was a little more difficult to get to – he had to take off a plastic guard – but he should be out of here in a minute anyway. Maybe the guy was taking a dump somewhere.

Argento walked over to the dead lamp and reached up to unscrew the housing. The whole mount moved, instead of the screw, and he frowned. With one hand, he held it fast to the beam and tried unscrewing it with the other hand. The screwdriver promptly jumped out of the hole and gouged a hole in the joist.

"Damnit," he whispered, and tried it again. He tapped the back of the screwdriver to jiggle the screw mount, and then twisted...this time it unlocked. He grinned and got the rest of the housing off and then swapped out the bulb. A blue halo appeared, bringing out a splatter pattern on the wall nearby that he was particularly proud of. It was all a part of a whole. No light, no swatch of paint was unnecessary.

Some artists worked on canvas, but Argento liked to think that he worked in three dimensions. Five, really, because he also used music and sometimes scent to fill out the atmosphere of a room.

Something thumped at the end of the basement.

Argento froze. The aisle he was in appeared completely empty, just shadows of red and blue and green light melting and merging across the empty plank floor.

Another noise then. A scraping. As if something was being dragged across a floor. For a second he thought maybe it was Mike putting something back in place, but the noise sounded closer than that. And he saw nobody else in the basement. Could an animal of some kind have gotten in? Raccoon?

"Shit," Argento whispered. Slowly, he began to walk towards the back of the basement, where the source of the sound seemed to be. It was dark back there, by design. Every few seconds a strobe went off and illuminated a gutted man that June had created. It looked pretty good, but Argento didn't think it was quite good enough to have a solid light trained on it.

The impression the strobe made was better than letting people stare at it too closely.

He stared at the area behind the gutted man for a moment, watching as the strobe illuminated the dark space near the back wall three or four times. Nothing.

He walked over to the wall at the right. It was the back of the house, the side that faced the cemetery. But there was nothing there. He stepped around the false prop wall to look behind the room that the public saw, and the space was dark.

Then he heard a voice through the wall. Someone was talking in low tones close by. It sounded like a man. Mike?

Argento frowned and stepped closer to the back wall. He cocked his head to see if the sound was coming from upstairs, but no. His ear said it was directly in front of him. Behind a wooden wall which he thought butted up to the cement foundation. But maybe not.

He ran his hands over the wood, pressing on it to see if it gave somewhere. That's when he found the cavity in the wood. And when his hand slipped into it, he found the door knob. There was a room down here? How had he decorated this space and not known this?

Argento turned the knob and the door swung inward. The hinges were on the inside – so that's why you couldn't see the door from inside the basement.

He stepped inside and saw Mike standing on the right side of the room. Katie, his girlfriend, was next to him, and another girl, a stocky woman with a head of knotted brown hair, stood next to them. Only, she was propping up a body that appeared to be slumped against her. If the guy really was relying on her for support, he couldn't figure out how she managed it. The guy looked like a construction worker; his shoulders were broad and he must have stood well over six feet.

Argento opened his mouth to call out to Mike, who still hadn't noticed him enter the room. But then he shut it. The slumping guy was naked from the waist up, and the chunky girl was holding his arm over what looked like a casket at the end of the room.

He frowned. What the hell was going on here? Then he saw the girl lift a silver blade, and swipe it across the guy's arm. A spout of blood erupted from the man's bare arm to spray across the casket, and a light went off in Argento's head. That's not makeup, he realised.

"What the hell are you doing?" he yelled and bolted forward.

Mike turned and moved to intercept him but before he could, Argento had grabbed for the knife arm of the girl. She didn't flinch. Instead, she released her hold on the big man and lunged.

Something cold touched Argento's neck. He opened his mouth to cough, and then the whole world lit on fire. He grabbed for his neck but it was too late. Emery pulled back the blade and the knife left his throat, which instantly filled with blood. Argento choked and blinked and struggled to scream. This couldn't be happening.

He heard Mike yell something but he couldn't understand the words. Everything seemed like it was closing in and he felt hands grabbing at him, but Argento found that he could only see the thick lips of the big girl as she bent over him and stared at him with dull brown eyes.

Argento kicked and twisted on the floor as he clutched his neck and tried to stem the tide of hot blood flowing out. And then all of a sudden he was lifted into the air by the girl.

"We need to get an ambulance," Mike said.

CHAPTER THIRTY

Mike's stomach sank as he turned and saw Argento standing in the hidden basement room. They'd managed to keep the room secret this whole month, but now, as they approached the final days, the set guy had stumbled not only on the room, but on the bloodletting.

"Shit," he said under his breath and turned to head the guy off. Emery was busy washing Katie's bones with blood, but maybe he could steer Argento off before he really got what was going on.

"What the hell are you doing?" Argento yelled and bolted towards Emery. Mike moved to intercept him, but missed. And the next thirty seconds played out like a slow-motion film in his eyes as Emery's knife swung around and stabbed, catching Argento right in the side of the neck, piercing, sliding in like it was a sheath and then pulling back. And then the wiry little set and lighting guy was clutching at his neck, as red blood splashed through his fingers and he fell to the floor.

Emery scooped the man up and Mike grabbed for her arm. "We need to get an ambulance," he yelled. "Put pressure on his neck."

"It's too late for that," Katie said behind him. "He's going to be gone in seconds. Just look at his eyes."

Emery struggled to hold Argento over the coffin so the blood dripped inside.

"Help her," Katie urged. "Don't waste his life. He's going to be dead in seconds no matter what."

Mike's head swam with conflicting emotions but he had followed Katie this far, and somehow that made him go once more with what she said. He grabbed Argento's black-booted feet and hefted the man up and over the coffin, trying to hold him steady as the man's feet kicked and his middle tremored. Emery gripped him by his shoulders and tilted his upper half so that the blood dripped in a steady river across the raw sheaths of muscle and meat that had taken shape in the coffin. After a couple minutes, the body grew still, and one arm hung limply across the meat of the growing body below.

"Lift his feet higher," Katie urged, and Mike did, closing his eyes when he saw the blood flow increase.

This wasn't happening. None of it. Mike held his eyes closed and wished himself back to that meeting with Perry. He imagined himself turning down the job, and muddling by these past few weeks with normal jobs. Maybe he would have fallen into a full steady gig without Perry's help. Or maybe he would have lost his house. But either way, he wouldn't have been standing here holding a man's legs in the air so that he could bleed the body's last blood onto a ghost's reborn corpse.

"That's enough," Katie finally said softly.

Mike opened his eyes as the body began to move – because Emery was pulling it. He followed her lead to lay Argento on the ground. The man's eyes were wide open, staring at the wooden ceiling as if in shock at what he saw. Mike swallowed hard and reached over to finger the man's eyelids closed.

He couldn't look at him that way.

"What the hell are we going to do now?" he whispered. "You promised that we weren't going to kill anyone. They'd all go home and wake up with a bandage and a weird scratch on them that they couldn't recall getting and that was it."

"Curiosity killed the cat," Katie said. "He shouldn't have come here."

"That doesn't help," Mike said. "The police are going to come. They'll arrest me and Emery and this whole thing will have been in vain."

Katie shook her head. "No, they won't," she said, and then pointed at the big guy who lay unmoving on the floor next to Argento. "First, you're going to take our friend here for a walk so that he can get home and not wake up here. Then you're going to come back and help Emery bury this other one."

Mike felt a tear running down his cheek. "I can't," he whispered.

"You have to," Katie said. "You want to hold me in your bed every night, don't you?"

He nodded.

"In just a few more days, I'll be yours to hold forever. Right now, we have to finish the plan. This is a setback, but we need to work with it. You need to make it right."

"We can't make it right," Mike said. "Argento's dead."

"And his death will help in bringing me back to life. It's a trade. Don't waste his life by stopping on me now."

Emery was starting to bandage the arm of the big man who remained alive, and after a minute, Mike bent to help her. When the gauze was taped in place she began to pull a t-shirt over the guy's mostly bald head.

Then the two of them put the man's arms over their shoulders and lifted him to his feet. His body seemed to unconsciously respond, and together they walked him like a zombie out of the basement.

There was a pickup parked just down the gravel path, and Mike patted the man down and found the keys in his right pocket. Emery helped load the man into the passenger's side and then Mike drove the truck down the road towards Cicero Avenue. He pulled off on the side of the road and pushed and pulled until he'd shifted the guy into the driver's seat, all the while looking over his shoulder to make sure no cars were coming. An unlikely, but occasional, risk at one a.m.

Once the man was in the seat, Mike rolled down the window and closed the driver's side door.

"You should go home," he said in the man's ear. He repeated himself twice more, and then stepped backwards, away from the truck. He was only a few yards down the road when he heard the crunch of gravel. He turned and saw the pickup moving slowly down the shoulder of the road. After a moment, it eased hesitantly onto the asphalt. The brake lights went on and off a couple times, but then the truck suddenly accelerated.

One problem out of the way.

*　　*　　*

"What are we supposed to do with him?" Mike asked when he got back to the basement. Emery had closed the casket and put away the bandages. But Argento still lay, very dead, in the middle of the floor.

"Put him in my grave," Katie said. "The earth should still be loose there."

"And his car?"

"Find his keys and drive it away from here. I'm sure you can lose it somewhere."

Mike wanted to protest, but what was the point? If he ditched the body somewhere so that someone could find it, the police would be all over the haunted house. And if he tried to come clean about what had happened… he'd be in jail. To be honest, he was more worried about getting rid of the car than the body.

With the latter, the only option was to bury Argento and hope that the body was never found. And who was going to look in an existing old grave for a new body? So that was a good solution.

After he searched Argento's pockets and found a set of keys, he looked at Emery.

"Let's go," he said, and the two of them picked up the body by its arms and legs and walked it across the basement and up the stairs outside. They laid it on the ground near the grave, and then Mike retrieved two shovels. In a half hour, the two of them were dripping with sweat, but the pile of earth on the side of the grave was high. When they'd gone down about as far as they'd dug originally, Mike stopped and put up his hand. "That's enough."

They lifted Argento's body once again, and held it over the centre of the hole. "One, two, three," Mike counted aloud. They both let go, and the body dropped with a thud to the clay base below. Part of him wanted to straighten the arms and legs, which twisted at odd angles. But instead, Mike just took a deep breath, and started shovelling earth back into the hole. He moved fast, anxious to stop seeing the empty face of the haunted house decorator.

When they were finished, Mike patted the earth down firm, and got down on his hands and knees to push the piles of brown and red leaves around, hiding the evidence that the ground here had been disturbed.

They walked back to the house in silence, and Emery didn't slow when they stepped inside. She walked down the hallway and a moment later he heard her feet on the stairs going up to the attic. Apparently, she was going to bed.

Mike went downstairs and walked down to the hidden room behind the sets. It was empty. Katie was gone. Part of him had thought maybe she'd be waiting here for him. He was disappointed, but also relieved. Part of him didn't want to see her now. All he wanted was beer. Many beers.

There were splatters of dark on the floor, but other than that, you couldn't tell that a man had been murdered here just an hour before. Mike shook his head and backed out of the room, closing the door behind him.

He quickly made the rounds of the rest of the house, turning out lights. He fumbled with the keys to lock the front door, and swore. When he finally got the lock to click shut, he looked over through the forest to the faint silhouettes of the tombstones nearby.

Then he pulled the keys from his pocket and got into Argento's car. There was a road a quarter mile down the turnpike that led back into the heart of the forest preserve. He could drive the car back there and off the road into the trees. It should stay undiscovered for a while if he went back far enough.

Mike started it up and eased the car across the gravel road and onto the asphalt. A few minutes later he was manoeuvreing through brush and trees until he was well off the small access road that led into the forest preserve. At this time of year, nobody came back here.

When he was satisfied that it was well secreted behind a thick wall of scrub and branches, he turned it off, but left the keys in the ignition. It would be a favour if someone found it and stole it. Mike looked at the car for a minute under the light of the stars and shrugged. Then he began the long walk back to the turnpike and the haunted house.

When he finally got back to Bachelor's Grove, he was sweating. And exhausted. He looked at the dark, silent house across the clearing and considered going back inside to look for Katie. Then he shook his head in denial and walked quickly to his truck. He needed to be away from here. When the truck started and he pulled on to Midlothian Turnpike, Mike reached up to scratch his cheek. His fingers came back wet, and angrily he wiped the back of his hand across his face.

When he walked in to The Edge, he went straight to the restroom and washed his face and hands clear of tears and dirt. And any blood that he might have touched. Then he took a seat at the bar and ordered a PBR.

"Last call in a few minutes," the bartender said.

Mike nodded and shotgunned the beer. The bartender looked at him with concern.

"Been a long day," Mike said. "Hit me again."

CHAPTER THIRTY-ONE

"You good?" Jeanie asked.

Lenny shrugged. "This hood is sweaty, but I'm all right. I don't know how Argento's been wearing this every damn night though. He better show up tomorrow, because I'm not doing this all weekend."

Jeanie grinned. "I thought being the masked killer was a step up from being just another zombie."

Lenny shook his head. "Black guys don't wear masks and gloves. We don't need to hide – we put it out there."

"So, you're breaking typecast now," she said. "You're always saying black guys get all the shit roles...now you've got a lead shot."

Lenny shook his head. "The masked killer always gets killed in the end. He's not the hero."

"Maybe," Jeanie said. "But I think some people think Jason is the hero. And he never seems to die."

"Oh, he died," Lenny said. "He just keeps coming back from the dead."

She grinned. "Whatever. I'll be back later. People on the floor."

She quickly exited the room before the footsteps of the next group reached them. She turned to face them before they entered Lenny's room and let out a horrible moan as she massaged her bloody guts. One of the girls in the group turned her head away and complained, "Oh my God, that's so gross."

Then they disappeared inside, and Jeanie headed upstairs to check on Bong and June.

* * *

"This is driving me insane," June said.

"What's the matter?" Bong asked. He crept out of his hiding spot. A group had just exited the room and they should have a minute or two before the next.

"I got like five mosquito bites on my back last night. There must have been a swarm of them in my bedroom."

June twisted and turned, pushing on her elbow with her hand to try to guide her arm to an untouchable spot on her back.

"Fuck," she complained. "I can't reach it." She backed against the wall and started to rub her back against it.

Bong laughed and stood up.

"Here, let me," he said.

He reached around her back and began to scratch. "Tell me where," he said, watching her eyes. He knew that he'd be able to see it when he found the spot.

"A little to the left," she said. "And up."

He moved his fingernails up and over, and then he smiled as her face suddenly took on the look of an orgasm.

"Holy shit," she moaned and arched her back against his hand, expanding the radius of his scratching.

"God yes," she said. "That's it, right there. Dig in. Rip my fucking back open, I can't stand it anymore."

"I don't want real blood on my hands," Bong said. He kept scratching for a few more seconds, and then began to slow. "We probably need to stop. I think I heard someone on the stairs."

June nodded, but her eyes looked up at him in pure adulation. "Thank you so much. I can't tell you how good that felt. It's been driving me crazy for hours."

She tilted her face up and went to kiss him on the cheek. But Bong moved. He couldn't have told if he did it on purpose, or instinct, but his lips connected with hers and instead of jumping back, he only pressed forward.

He loved Jeanie, but there was something about June that drew him so much. Talking with her every night for the past month…he felt close to her. Closer to her than Jeanie lately. He welcomed the intimate touch of her lips on his.

"We shouldn't," June whispered, but didn't pull her lips away.

"No," he agreed, and kissed her harder, wrapping his arm around her back and digging his nails in where the mosquito bites were.

"We should get in position," he said, his lips still touching hers. He could taste her breath in his mouth.

"Yeah," she said, not moving. "We should."

Bong's eyes met hers, and saw the desire and anxiousness there. This was wrong, and they both knew it. Might never act on it again. But it had happened.

He pressed his mouth to hers one last quick time and then pulled away.

"Showtime," he reminded her, and moved away from her to hide again.

*   *   *

Jeanie walked down the long attic floor to the back room that June and Bong 'haunted'. As she reached the threshold and opened her mouth to ask how they were doing, she suddenly bit her tongue.

Bong's hands were all over June, and then their mouths were touching. They kissed again and again, and Jeanie felt an icy stab in her heart.

She wanted to run into the room and punch them. She wanted to kick Bong in the nuts and pound June in the face with her fist.

But instead, she stood there rooted to the floor as her boyfriend kissed her monster makeup mentor.

The dream of this haunted house was now a nightmare.

Jeanie wanted to scream, but instead she backed quietly away. She couldn't face them now. Maybe not ever.

On the far side of the room, a group of people were just stepping into the attic from the stairs, and Jeanie ran towards them. The group split, one of the women screaming at her aggressive approach, as one of the other couples moved quickly to one side.

Jeanie didn't slow until she was down the stairs. Then she ran out the front door, surprising the group in line outside. She ran around the house and into the trees, stopping only when she came to Bachelor's Grove Cemetery. There, she sank down on the toppled stone of a grave and finally let out one long, plaintive howl.

The tears came hard and ruined her makeup.

And for the first time, Jeanie didn't care.

PART THREE
CLOSING NIGHT

CHAPTER THIRTY-TWO

"Looks like you were celebrating a little early," Lon said.

Mike moaned, and then held a hand to his forehead. It hurt to moan. "Yeah, I might have crushed one too many cans last night."

"You know *tonight's* closing night, right? Post-party at The Edge?"

Mike nodded, and moaned again at the ache. He had to stop doing that. "Oh yeah, right."

Lon tilted his head slightly and stared at him. "You gonna even make it through tonight?"

"Yeah, I'll be fine in a couple hours," Mike said.

"Good, because I think things are going to get a little crazy later."

"What do you mean?"

"It's Halloween, man," Lon said. "The big night. People are going to be lined up down the turnpike to get in here. And the gang is psyched. I know they're going to be working overtime on the scream factor tonight. Wait until you see Lucio. I think he's been working on his makeup since three o'clock."

"How gory can a zombie get?"

"You'll see."

"I guess I will," Mike agreed. "I'm going to go set up downstairs."

"Don't go to sleep down there," Lon warned. "We open in a half hour."

"The basement is the last place I want to fall asleep," Mike said. Lon could have no idea why the basement was any different for Mike than the main floor or the attic, but in his head, he had visions of the bloody meat-covered bones that lay pulsating in the coffin behind the door of the hidden room. Lon just looked at him and shrugged.

"I dunno. It's cool and dark down there. If I was you, that's where I'd head for a nap. But…don't do it!"

"All right, all right!" Mike said shaking his head. And then he put his hand to his forehead and mumbled, "Ow," as he walked away.

Lon grinned and turned his attention back to the room of bloody, creepy, excited people and held up a hand to get their attention.

* * *

In the back of the room, Lenny pulled on the black leather giallo killer hood.

"I did not want to still be doing this," Lenny said. "Where the hell did Argento disappear to this week? I can't believe he's missing closing night."

The man with the hanging eyeball and gory cheeks next to him shook his head. "I wish I knew. I'm pretty worried."

Lenny nodded. "Yeah, I know man. I'm sorry. I'm sure he's okay, just got called away on a family emergency or something."

"Argento doesn't have any family," Lucio said.

Lenny didn't have an answer for that.

"Hey," Lucio said. "I know you hate the outfit but…make 'em feel like you're really gonna kill them tonight, okay? For him?"

Lenny suddenly felt his throat closing up. He opened his mouth to speak but instead, just nodded.

* * *

"All right!" Lon yelled from the front of the room. "This is it. I can't believe I'm saying this, but…it's fucking Halloween!"

The room erupted in cheers.

"I can't believe it's all come down to this. Hell night. Hallowmas. All Hallow's Eve. Night of the demons. We have been scaring people almost every night for a month, and tonight's the final night. This is our last hurrah. Last time to make one of those girls from Tinley Park High pee her panties. Last time to make one of those jocks from South Suburban College run like a baby out of your room. So, let's make it happen. Let's scare the hell out of them!"

As the motley, blood-soaked crew exploded in whistles and claps, Lucio walked up to stand next to Lon. The house manager nodded and took a step back, ceding the floor.

Lucio didn't talk much, and so the room quieted when he stepped up to speak. His voice was quiet and a little shaky as he began.

"You all know that this place looks like it does because of Argento. He designed most of these sets and this lighting. I don't want to bring anyone down, but I know that he'd be here tonight if he could. This should have been his crowning night, and I know he would have been challenging me for the scream title big time tonight. I don't know what's happened to him this week. I know...." His voice broke and Lucio hung his zombie head for a moment before continuing. "I know he'd want us all to scare the shit out of people tonight, so...." Lucio raised one blood-streaked hand. "Do it for him."

Lenny raised a black-gloved fist in the air and yelled, "Hell yeah!"

Jeanie raised a hand next to his and grabbed on to his hand as she yelled out, "For Argento."

Everyone around the room joined suit, and raised their fists as they yelled in unison, "For Argento."

*   *   *

Lon retook the floor and closed the 'rally' down after a couple chants. "I know that there's one thing for sure that Argento would say if he was here: Quit jerking around and get the fuck out there and scare people."

People laughed and clapped and Lon pointed towards the door. "Go out there and get it done. Let's have a good time tonight!"

*   *   *

Lucio walked out of the makeup room and down the hall to his station. Part of him wished that the night was over now. And part of him wished it would never end. He was here because of Argento. And his friend hadn't answered a call, email or text in a week. From what he could tell, he hadn't been home either. His car was missing, so the police suggested that maybe he'd left town.

Lucio didn't believe that.

He believed something horrible had happened, though he hoped it wasn't the case. Still, his friend had always been a strange one. Anything was possible. In his heart though, he knew better. If Argento was alive, he would not have missed the chance to wear the leather mask and gloves on the final night of the haunted house.

And while part of him wanted to just walk away, the part of him that had been friends with Argento heard the same words in his head that Lon had suggested just a couple minutes before. "Go out there and get it done."

CHAPTER THIRTY-THREE

"You don't look so good," Katie said.

Mike looked up from the spotlight he was adjusting and smiled. Thinly. "I don't feel so good," he admitted.

"Why don't you come upstairs?" she said. "I might be able to help."

"I don't see how," Mike said. "I can't even feel you anymore."

Katie nodded. "I know," she said. "But that's all going to change soon."

"You keep saying that," Mike said. "But we're kind of out of time. After tonight, this place is closed."

"Tonight is the last night I need," Katie said. "And I want you to be ready when it's all over."

"I'll be fine," he said. "I've had a hangover before."

Katie raised her eyebrows. "Yeah, I'm sure. Come upstairs, okay?"

He nodded, and once again cursed himself. Then he finished resetting the light and turned to follow her.

"Shouldn't you be staying here to haunt the basement?" he asked.

Katie nodded. "Yeah, I'll be back. But let's get you set first. They haven't opened the front door yet."

She led him up the back stairs, and a moment later they were in the attic. After ensuring that nobody was in the vicinity to see, Mike opened the door in the floor and let Katie step through. He followed and pulled the door down behind him.

In the hidden room, Emery stood in the corner.

But Mike was used to that by now. He ignored her and only looked at Katie.

"Why are we down here?" he said. "I can't even touch you anymore. Coming here is pointless."

Katie shook her head and held a finger to his lips. He couldn't feel it.

She looked at Emery and motioned with her other hand. The surly girl moved from her spot across the room. Katie leaned towards her and whispered something in her ear. Then she leaned back, and Emery reached into the pocket of her jeans.

When her hand came out, she held the locket that Mike had once found lying on the floor of the old house, before ever meeting Katie.

The locket that had allowed him to touch Katie.

He snatched it out of her hand, and pulled it over his head. When the cold kiss of metal met his chest, he turned from Emery and looked at Katie.

"I hope you mean this," he said.

Katie grinned. "Of course I do," she said. "You've been so good to me the past couple weeks, I wanted to give you something special so that you'd know I was serious."

"Serious about driving me crazy," he asked.

She took his hand, and a spark shot up his arm as he realised he could feel her grip. With her hand, she pressed his fingers to her chest. Mike's heart jumped as he felt the swell of her breast beneath his fingers. "Only in a good way," she said.

Katie stepped backwards, towards the bed, and Mike couldn't help but follow.

"Come here with me," Katie whispered, drawing him down to the bed of nails with her. Mike melted into her arms. The touch of her on his skin felt like heaven. For days, he had only been able to *see* her. Every brush of her skin, every kiss, had been like touching the wind. He'd felt a spark now and then, but no substance.

Now she hugged him and he actually felt her body there. Mike didn't resist; he wrapped his arms around her slight shoulders and pulled her close.

"God I've missed you," he whispered.

"I don't know why," Katie said. "I've been right here all the time."

"I've missed feeling you," he said.

"Oh, that," she said. Katie laughed, and he couldn't help but smile at the wide grin that she gave. Her teeth were long and white and she looked mischievous and happy. "I wanted you to remember what it was you were fighting for," she said.

Mike had no answer for that, so he bent down and kissed her. Her tongue answered his with electric energy. In seconds, she had wrapped her legs around him as well, and rolled him over and back on the hard, pointed bed. Somehow their clothes disappeared, one piece at a time, and Mike realised that most of his headache was gone as he moved between the silken skin of her naked thighs and pressed himself into her.

"Oh, I have missed that," she gasped, as he rolled her beneath him, tilting her head back against the bare nails.

Mike groaned and pulled her tighter. "Then you should have left me with the necklace," he whispered, as her lips brushed his.

"Shhhh," she said, and pressed her mouth hard on his lips. When she pulled back, she said, "Soon you won't need it."

"Jesus, I hope so," he gasped and thrust his hips hard against hers.

"Jesus has nothing to do with it," she answered, and pressed his hips back to the bed.

Then they were quiet, at least with words, and focused on moving together across the bed of nails.

When their motions finally slowed, Katie pushed Mike over and onto his back. "How's your head now?" she asked, licking a pink tongue across his lips.

Mike smiled. "Better," he said. "But even sex can't cure a hangover."

Katie nodded. "I figured," she said. "But Emery's got something that does."

She motioned behind her, and Mike's heart skipped a beat as he saw the chunky girl move out of the shadows towards the bed. Once again, he'd forgotten she was there. He shouldn't care if Katie didn't, but there was something creepy in having sex in front of a big wallflower girl who just stood…still…against the wall. (*Kind of the definition of a wallflower, moron*, he said to himself).

Emery dropped three white tablets on the small table next to the bed, and set a bottle of water next to them.

Mike didn't question it. He knocked back the tablets and slugged down the bottle of water. When he'd swallowed them, Katie wrapped her arms around him and straddled him. She kissed him again and again until he felt almost smothered; the room began to fill with amber shadows.

"I am so exhausted," he said, stifling a yawn.

Katie smiled. "Then you should sleep for a while. I have work to do downstairs anyway. I'll be back."

She got up from the bed, and then, as Mike felt the waves of dark and sleep wash over him, Emery took her place, and reached down to take the necklace back from around his neck. He wanted to protest, but realised that he really couldn't move. His limbs felt like lead.

"Wait," he whispered, suddenly feeling helpless and wondering what had become of his arms.

"Shhhh," Katie said, returning for a moment to push a finger across his lips. Without the necklace, he only felt the hint of a spark.

"You won't need that again," she said. "I told you, tonight's the night. Now…get some sleep so you can really enjoy it."

He wanted to argue, but dimly he saw Katie walk away, and then Emery, too, disappeared from the range of his vision. He wanted to sit up and see where they were going, but instead, his eyelids slipped closed, and Mike let the heavy cloak of sleep spill over him. He didn't fight it.

* * *

Lucio went to his room but he couldn't settle in. Jeanie had helped him put on what was probably the best, most elaborate makeup he'd had all month, but he just didn't feel like scaring people tonight. It was a weird feeling, but all he wanted was to know what had happened to Argento. The guy had been his best friend for three years now, ever since they'd met at a Terror in the Aisles film night in Chicago where they were showing *Suspiria* and *The Beyond*. They'd talked, at first haltingly, about their favourite directors, and quickly realised that they not only loved the same era and style in films, but that they lived close to each other, too.

It was a match made in heaven. Or hell, as Argento would have insisted. They quickly began getting together on the weekends and staging film fests. It was Argento who had introduced Lucio to Lon, who didn't fixate like they did on Eurosleaze, but still had an amazing library and palate for obscure horror. Lon had actually convinced the two of them to watch some comic horror movies from Australia, which they were sceptical of, but ultimately loved. Lucio would never forget the time they all got together for beer at some log cabin bar near Lon's place, and the guy had suggested they watch a horror movie about a tyre.

"C'mon," Lon had said. "It's a killer tyre. The audience breaks the barrier of the fourth wall. It's called *Rubber* and I know you're going to love it. Plus, I've got bourbon."

Argento had shaken his head in feigned sadness, but Lucio had grinned. "I'll watch any movie if bourbon is involved."

"Be careful what you promise," Lon said. "I've got an Australian movie about killer sheep too."

"Oh my good lord," Argento had moaned.

And in the end, they'd all loved *Rubber*. And had watched dozens of crazy horror films together ever since.

Only…maybe they wouldn't be doing that anymore now.

Lucio pressed his eyes closed. He needed to take a walk before the house opened. He stepped into the hallway and then remembered that Argento had always checked the lights in the basement before the house opened. He had a bunch of sets going down there, and some of the incandescents seemed to burn out quick. As far as he knew, nobody had really looked at them since Argento had disappeared early this week.

Lucio shrugged and took a walk down the hallway towards the stairs. It was something to do. Something that Argento would have wanted done.

Even with his costume on, Lucio felt the chill as he stepped down the stairs into the basement. The house had been hot most of the time when they'd first come here to decorate and set it up, but now, at the end of October…it was draughty and cold. There was no furnace, so some nights over the past couple weeks, he'd been able to see his breath as he closed up at the end of the night. It wasn't that bad so far tonight, but the temperature had definitely dropped since the sun went down.

Lucio stepped onto the floor of the basement and stood still, taking stock of the room. His glance went from one spotlight to the next, and the spaces in between, where perhaps there was supposed to be a light, but wasn't. The front end of the basement looked good. He walked down what Argento had dubbed the 'Aisle of Atrocities', where they had constructed several sets that played off famous horror tales and grinned at the setpiece that took its premise from the story of Countess Báthory. A half-nude woman hung from the ceiling, tied with her wrists and feet behind her back to a hook in the ceiling so that only her belly hung down. Her gut was…gutted. Intestines hung out like a rope, and a steady stream of red dripped into the white porcelain tub below, where another woman luxuriated in the deep red bath.

Argento had outdone himself there – he'd rigged a hidden fish pond pump that took the red water out of the tub back up in the air and into the 'corpse' so that it could be a continuous blood fountain.

Something rustled in the blue shadows down the aisle and Lucio walked towards it. The 'haunters' of the basement ought to be down here any minute, but he hadn't seen anyone yet.

Someone flipped on the music soundtrack then and the room was filled with the eerie synthesiser tones of Goblin. Argento had nicked the soundtrack from *Suspiria* for this area. It worked great in a heavily shadowed basement. Lucio turned towards the back of the room, but didn't see who had turned on the music.

"Andy?" he called out. "Karen? Is that you?"

Nobody answered. Lucio shrugged and continued his survey of the lights. Something moved amid the hanging chains of the *Hellraiser* display. He walked across the aisle and saw the shadow of someone standing still there, in front of the tortured body strung up with hooks and chains. They were in front of the lights, so he couldn't make out the face. But whoever it was wore a dark cape and cowl, and held a long blade in front of their chest. It looked like a classic devil worshipper pose.

"Very funny," Lucio said. "But you're in the wrong Atrocity for that outfit."

The figure didn't answer, but instead raised the knife with both hands in the air. As it did, the cowl fell back and Lucio saw that it was a woman. She was a big woman, with ratty brown hair. He didn't recognise her at all.

"Hey, who are you and what are you doing down here?" he demanded.

She didn't answer, but instead suddenly lunged forward and brought the knife down.

Lucio was caught by surprise and started to jump backwards to avoid the attack, but he was too late. The knife plunged right through the false eyeball stem that hung from the rubbery mask he wore.

Lucio felt a white-hot explosion in his eye, and grabbed for his face. But the woman pulled the knife right back out of his skull, and brought it back down in his other eye.

The world became a sea of hideous, bloody black pain.

But only for a moment.

Then Lucio didn't feel anything anymore.

CHAPTER THIRTY-FOUR

Bachelor's Grove had never had so many people trying to get in. Word of the haunted house had spread throughout the south suburbs of Chicago over the past few weeks and everyone wanted a look before it closed for the season. The line of people stretched from the ticket taker on the porch all the way down the gravel road past the cemetery and pond, and out onto Midlothian Turnpike. Both of the forest preserve parking lots that served the attraction just down the road were full, and police were directing and stopping traffic on the turnpike to allow people to cross the busy street safely in the dark.

"This is crazy!" Jeanie said to Lon. She had ducked into the hidden main level Ops room – the converted master bathroom. The cast needed to pee over the course of the night, so they'd cordoned this room off from the rest of the rooms as a refuge. And when this was in use, Lon used the hidden room downstairs for Ops. "We're never going to get all of these people through the house in one night!"

"Yeah, I know," Lon said. "Can you let everyone know that they have to speed up their throughput tonight? I don't want to ruin the impact, but we have to move this line faster."

"I would, but Lucio has been missing for the past hour, so I've been working his room. That's why I'm here. Have you seen him?"

Lon shook his head and frowned. "Fine time to get lost. Parker is a zombie – he's downstairs in the basement near the Romero Atrocity. Can you grab him and send him up to the room? We have plenty of people down there tonight and I need you roving to help people out. I need to go back outside and help with crowd management."

"Sure," Jeanie said. "But I wish I knew where Lucio was. I spent a tonne of time on his makeup tonight. I wanted him to be seen."

"Yeah," Lon agreed. "I'm just glad we got some extra haunters for this week. Because we sure need the help tonight."

He got up and closed the laptop screen where it sat on the sink. "Just four more hours until the witching hour!" he announced.

Jeanie held her guts out for several groups as she tried to move down the hallway to the basement. She had to stay in character, which meant that every few steps she had to stop and mug for a group of visitors. The house was alive with screams and laughter – though mostly screams. Eerie music streamed from every room and groups of people were going room to room just yards apart from each other. They'd never allowed people to stack up this thick before. The ticket takers were already moving people through the house at twice the speed and volume as they had earlier in the week.

She reached the basement finally, and quickly moved to the left side of the room before another group confronted her. She saw Parker lurking to the right of a prop zombie. He stood still as a statue, but she knew the makeup. She stopped and waited, as there was a crowd of people moving towards the exhibit ahead of her.

Parker's gimmick was to let the group be lulled by the 'fake' bodies in the display space and then, just before they moved on to the next display, he came to life. His grey hands touched the shoulders of one of the women, and she shrieked as if she'd been stabbed. Her boyfriend or husband laughed, and she slapped him. "Ass!" she said, but he pulled her down the aisle away from Parker, who was now lurching towards another girl in the group. The girl had her own zombie makeup on and Jeanie grinned as she saw it. Peeling flesh, glistening red blood around her mouth…the girl had done a good job.

Parker held out both hands towards her, as if to hug her. "Friendddd," he growled.

The girl laughed and swatted his arm away. "Freshhhh!" she said, and quickly ran to rejoin her friends.

Jeanie hurried forward then, before another group turned up behind her.

"Nice one," she said. "I thought you had a new recruit there for a minute."

"She just doesn't appreciate my sensitive side," Parker moaned.

"You mean the side that has watched *Return of the Living Dead* thirty times?"

"It's a deeply moving examination of the youth culture in our society and their need for connection."

"That and Linnea Quigley lies naked on a gravestone."

"You just don't appreciate the deep and life-changing symbolism of that moment," he said.

"Uh-huh," Jeanie said. "Hey, Lon asked me to come down and get you. Lucio disappeared somewhere and we need a zombie in his room. He wanted to move you up there."

Parker shrugged. "I can stagger and beg for brains wherever he wants me."

"Cool," she said. Then she nodded towards the exhibit, which had both the standing zombie at the side and another one half crouched in the back. In between was a row of gravestones. Next to one of them, a hand emerged from the fake earth. And nearby, a body lay bloody and dishevelled. One hand was draped over a gravestone, as if it were trying to crawl away when the end came.

"Did Lucio add that this week?" she asked, pointing at the bloody body. "I don't remember that prop there before."

Parker nodded. "Yeah – he must have brought it down this afternoon, because it wasn't there yesterday. Pretty freakin' awesome though, isn't it? You almost feel like the blood is fresh and wet."

Footsteps tramped down the stairs behind them, and Jeanie grinned. "You better take care of this group and then head up," she said. "I'll go check on Maggie while I'm down here."

"She's by the Wax Museum," he said.

"Thanks," Jeanie said and began walking as quickly as she could without attracting attention towards the middle of the basement. Behind her, she heard the chatter of a group, and then the sudden growl and scream as Parker leapt out at them. Jeanie smiled. Damn, she was going to miss this. She was already thinking ahead to next year.

CHAPTER THIRTY-FIVE

"He's asleep now?" Katie said.

Emery put her hand on his forehead and drew her fingers lightly across his forehead.

Mike didn't stir.

She nodded.

Katie pointed at the small dresser. "Take the knife and the glass, and get some of my blood in it."

"But I can't cut you, you're not…" Emery said slowly.

"From my real body," Katie said. "Go downstairs. I need my blood to be inside him tonight."

Emery nodded, picked up the implements and climbed up the steps to leave the room.

Katie stood over Mike's body and smiled. "Soon," she promised. "You and I will truly be bound together as one, just as you've wished for. I hope you'll still feel the same when it happens."

*   *   *

When Emery's feet returned a few minutes later, and stepped slowly down the ladder, she set a glass down on the tiny nightstand next to the bed. It was about a quarter full of a dark liquid. She set down the blade next to it. The blade was stained.

"Now what?" she asked.

"He needs to drink this from me," Katie said. "Once he does, I can join with him for a short time, while my blood is mingled with his and running through his veins. Lift his head and feed him my communion."

Emery put one hand behind Mike's snoring head and propped him forward. He was heavy, and she didn't get his head far up from the pillow. But it was enough. With her free hand, she held the glass to his lips. His head remained angled backwards, his mouth parallel to the ceiling. Emery pressed the glass down on his lower lip until she could see the dark space between his teeth.

And then she poured.

Mike's throat gulped automatically and he choked. Flecks of blood escaped the sides of his lips, but the majority of the blood from Katie's 'unborn' body remained in his throat.

"Perfect," Katie said, and Emery let his head rest back on the bed. A trickle of blood slid from the corner of his lips to disappear down his neck. The ghost of the witch climbed onto the bed and lay down on top of the carpenter's body.

She kissed his sleeping mouth briefly, and then said something. Her voice was silent, but her lips moved and she stared into Mike's sleeping face.

A moment later, her body began to sink, as if he were quicksand and she was trapped in his pull.

Just seconds later, she had fully disappeared into his form.

Mike's head shook, as if fighting off a bad dream. His arms moved too, grabbing at the steel points that served as the mattress of the bed.

Then he opened his eyes, and sat up to slide his legs over the side of the bed. He raised one arm and looked at it. Then he flexed the other hand in front of his face.

Mike's lips split into a wide smile.

He stood up, walked past Emery, and climbed up the stairs.

CHAPTER THIRTY-SIX

"You've got the switchblade, right?" J.T. asked.

Nikki nodded. "How many times are you going to ask that?"

"I'm just anxious," J.T. said. "Did you put the blood packs in or do we need to find a bathroom?"

Nikki shook her head. "If I slap you in the head a few times, do you think it would break some of your brain free?"

J.T. grinned. "This is going to be so awesome. We'll just see about who is scaring who here tonight."

J.T. and Nikki had gone through the house the weekend before, and when they'd reached the Argento room, a man in a black mask and gloves had leapt out at Nikki so fast and threatened her with the knife so close that she'd literally peed her pants. J.T. had jumped, himself, but when they left the room, he was not amused. When Nikki whispered to him that she needed to change her pants, he shook his head in anger.

"That's too much," he'd said. "They're going too far. I'm going to get our money back when we get out of here."

But the ticket taker had refused a refund, suggesting that if they got the piss scared out of them, the house had done exactly what it promised.

That had not set well with J.T., and he'd stewed on it for a couple days before coming up with his solution.

Scare the crap right back out of the people in the haunted house. How? By surprising them with something they wouldn't expect.

"We'll start with that bastard in the black mask," J.T. said.

"If we ever get inside," Nikki said.

"Almost there," he said. Then he pointed. "Look, they're taking that whole group in at once."

A dozen people in front of them all marched up the steps and disappeared inside, and then one of the wranglers walked down the line asking for the number of people in each party. A group of three and another group of five were ahead of them. J.T. held up his first two fingers and the wrangler nodded and checked on two more parties before returning to the front of the line. They only waited a couple more minutes and then they were being ushered up the steps and into the house.

"What if he doesn't buy it?" Nikki asked.

"He'll buy it if you do what we practised," J.T. promised.

They passed through the *Texas Chainsaw Massacre* dining room and ducked around the hulking Leatherface that darted towards them with a chainsaw held high.

They didn't slow down in the kitchen to let the bloody girl on the floor try to lure them in for a jump scare. Instead, they moved quickly down the hall to the first bedroom, where the masked killer had been last week. As they stepped into the room, they heard the tense music cycling in the background, and the lights flared.

It was a gimmick; the room was wired with motion sensors to trigger things whenever someone walked into the room. J.T. knew that the killer lay in wait just behind the old couch. Instead of moving further into the room to trigger the cue for the killer, he stayed near the door, and took the chain that he'd attached to a leather collar around Nikki's neck.

He noticed that another haunter stood still in the shadows in the back of the room. Nice. He'd get to freak out two of them.

"I'm not coming in any farther until I see you," J.T. called out. "I know you're waiting behind the couch. Stand up."

A black-gloved hand slipped fingers over the top of the couch back and then the black shine of a leather hood appeared. The figure stood, holding a long silver blade in its free hand. It began a silent walk towards them.

"Hold it right there," J.T. commanded.

The figure hesitated. J.T. laughed inside; he was sure the guy was not used to anyone ordering him around while in costume. Probably didn't know quite what to think right now. Which was exactly what he wanted at this moment. This scare was *his* to give.

J.T. suddenly yanked Nikki's chain and pulled her in close to him. He put one arm across her throat and pulled the switchblade out. Then he tripped the release and the blade shot out. He held it in front of her face.

"I want to see your face beneath that mask," J.T. said. "Take it off."

The figure did not comply. Instead, it began to move towards J.T. and Nikki.

"I'm serious," J.T. warned. "I want your mask. I've always wanted your mask. Give it to me. And your gloves too."

The figure hesitated, but then held its own knife out and took another step towards J.T.

"This is not a joke," J.T. warned. He held the blade of his knife above Nikki's left breast. "I'll kill her right here in front of you if you don't take off your hood and give it to me right now. This is not a joke."

The guy froze. He clearly didn't know which way to turn. He was pretending to be a psycho and scaring people, but here was a real possible psycho in the room with him. J.T. guessed the guy probably was shitting a brick right now wondering exactly what was going on here.

"That's it," J.T. said. "I gave you the chance, and you decided your mask was more important than this poor girl's life. Her blood is on your hands."

He lifted his knife away from Nikki's chest and the guy began to move towards him quickly.

"No, wait!" the guy yelled.

But J.T. just smiled and brought the switchblade down hard. He felt the haft smash into the thin plastic bag of blood just beneath Nikki's shirt, as the trick blade retracted.

Her shirt suddenly blossomed blood, as the hooded man reached out towards them.

Nikki screamed on cue.

"Back up, man," J.T. yelled.

He pulled the knife back, thumbing the mechanism to release the blade again so that to an onlooker it appeared as if he pulled a deadly blade back out of Nikki's chest. He held it up again as if he were going to stab her once more. Nikki screamed and thrashed in his grasp, just as they'd practised.

"No, no," the black-masked man cried. "Don't! I'll give you the mask."

The man dropped his blade on the floor and reached around to the back of his head and unzipped the leather so that he could slip it over his head. "Don't hurt her anymore."

The guy yanked the hood over his head to reveal a near-bald, black scalp and threw the mask on the floor in front of J.T.

"Let her go," the man said, as he began peeling off his gloves.

J.T. found it funny somehow that it was a black guy underneath the black leather mask. The whites of the man's eyes seemed to glow in the weird lighting of the room, and J.T. shook his head.

"Too late," he said, and slammed his knife down again, smashing another bag of fake blood which instantly soaked through Nikki's shirt.

She screamed and threw her head back as J.T. pulled his knife-hand back up and showed the unhooded man his knife.

"I wanted to do that with your hood," J.T. said. He let go of Nikki and she crumbled, falling to the floor. The chain clanked to the wood next to her. "But maybe I'll just have to wear it while I kill you!"

The man backed away from him, and put both hands in the air in front of his chest.

"No man, c'mon, I just work here. My name's Lenny. I'm not a real killer or anything. I'm just here to make it a good time for everyone, you know what I mean? This isn't even the normal room I work. I'm usually in the *Nightmare on Elm Street* room. Do you like Freddy Krueger?"

J.T. bent down and picked up the hood. He grinned as he felt the leather between his fingers. This was playing out exactly the way he'd hoped. The guy was eating it up.

"Get down on your knees," J.T. demanded.

The guy dropped to his knees instantly, and J.T. stifled a snort. This was too easy.

"Now put both of your hands on your chest."

The guy complied, and J.T. smiled. "I'm going to see how it feels to be you," he said, and pulled the other man's 'killer' hood quickly over his head. He adjusted it with one hand as he held the knife out towards the kneeling man to keep him still.

Nikki lay still on the floor, presumably dead.

"I wanted you to have a taste of your own medicine," J.T. said as he stepped closer to the man with his knife raised high in the air. The feeling of the hood over his face was energising. He felt as if he really could knife the guy and walk away untouched.

"Please just let me go," Lenny cried. He took his hands off his chest and J.T. shook his head. "Oh, no," he taunted. "I don't think so."

J.T. raised his knife high in the air, and Lenny cowered, shaking his head and leaning backwards.

And then suddenly Lenny's mouth gaped open.

His eyes bugged wide.

J.T. didn't know what he was doing at first, and then the man's frightened eyes looked down. J.T. followed the man's gaze.

A triangular barb of metal protruded from between Lenny's fingers. A splash of gore painted his knuckles.

"Oh, that just fucking figures," Lenny wheezed. "I told June the black guy always gets it."

J.T. looked up, confused at what had happened. The figure from the far end of the room moved towards them. She had some kind of arrow launcher in her arms.

He realised then that he'd been made.

What he had been doing to the 'hooded killer', she was doing to him. Only...she was using real weapons. Blood streamed across the kneeling man's knuckles and there was no way that it was fake. Lenny gasped one last time before toppling over to hit the ground.

J.T. looked up and met the eyes of the woman who held the weapon. Her face was blank, as if she didn't have a thought in her head other than to put a spear through his heart. "Get up, Nikki," he said through gritted teeth. Then he turned to leave the room.

Something clattered to the floor behind him and J.T. couldn't help but look back. It was a fatal distraction. The woman in the cowl had dropped her arrow launcher and now held a long silver knife in the air, not dissimilar to the fake one that J.T. had used to 'stab' Nikki. And she was almost on top of him.

"Wait," he begged, but the glint of metal was already in the air and moving. When it hit him in the chest, for a moment he barely felt a thing. It was as if the woman had tapped him.

And then the pain began. The heat spread down his ribs and his shirt suddenly felt heavy and wet.

"Why?" he asked. This wasn't fake. He'd hoped the guy with an arrow through his chest was somehow false, despite everything, but this...this was his own death.

J.T. sank to his knees, holding the wound in his heart. He knew that he wasn't getting out of this alive. Behind him, he heard Nikki finally moving. Finally realising that something had gone wrong.

"J.T.," she finally said. "What's the matter?"

He opened his mouth to tell her, but when he did, he choked instead, and something hot and thick suddenly slipped over his lips.

"Go," he whispered, and fell backwards then, landing on the floor next to her feet.

Nikki screamed.

J.T. felt something weird spreading across his chest. Not a cold feeling, but not hot either. It was the same and different, everything and nothing, and he knew that it meant only one thing.

The end.

"Run," he croaked with his last gasp of energy.

She bent over him for a second, her face a mask of horror and concern and fear.

"Please," he begged.

She got up then, finally realising that she was in danger. But it was too late.

J.T. saw the pale fat girl move towards Nikki, with the knife that was still red with his blood held over her head. She didn't say a word, but simply brought it down fast and hard.

Nikki's eyes went wide and she squealed for a second. It wasn't a yell or a shriek...just a thin sound of tortured surprise.

And then she fell to the ground next to J.T.

He tried to say her name, but nothing happened. No words would come out. And his arms wouldn't move.

J.T.'s last vision was of the killer wiping Nikki's blood off her blade with her fingers and walking away.

CHAPTER THIRTY-SEVEN

"How are things with Jeanie?" June asked.

Bong had crept out of his hiding spot for a few seconds between customers. Though he knew they didn't have much time. The groups were moving through the house fast tonight.

"She's still pissed off," he said. "I can't blame her, but I can't really prove to her that nothing was really happening either. At least she drove in with me tonight."

"That's something," she agreed. "I'm sorry if I got you in trouble."

Bong shook his head. "I got me in trouble, and I'm not completely sorry."

June raised her eyebrow.

"The best thing about doing this whole haunted house thing was meeting you. I'm not sorry about that."

June smiled. "I'm not sorry about that either. But I really like Jeanie. I didn't want to do anything to hurt her. She hasn't talked to me at all the last three nights."

Bong nodded. "She's stubborn. But she'll come around."

"Are you guys going to come to the after party tonight?" she asked.

"Are you going to throw your arms around me and kiss me there?" he asked.

June snorted. "Would you be happy if I did?"

"Not the right question," Bong said.

"Okay," she said. "Do you want me to?"

Bong shifted, suddenly looking uncomfortable. "Also, not the right question."

Something creaked on the wood planks outside, and Bong stepped back. "I think we have company."

A guy with a short blond goatee and a black shirt that had a ski mask design on it stepped into the room. He pulled a woman wearing a *Nightmare Before Christmas* sweatshirt into the room after him. Bong ducked back out of sight before they saw him. He hoped.

June played it perfectly. She faded back at first, and then, when the guy saw her, she lunged forward again, staggering and clutching at the gash in her neck. The *Nightmare* girl pulled back but her boyfriend laughed.

"Come on," he said. "She's just dead, she's not scary."

That was, more or less, Bong's cue.

He started out of the hidden passage on the floor, moving with an awkward crab crawl towards them. When the guy registered that something was coming at him on the floor, he looked down and then leapt a yard away from her.

"Shit," he complained.

His girlfriend jumped with him. But she didn't scream. She pointed at Bong and said, "It's just like that movie *The Ring*."

"Yeah, or *Tomie*," he agreed. "Nice one," he said, pointing at Bong. "You got me there."

Then he pulled his girlfriend around June and back out of the room to take the stairwell down. He didn't acknowledge June at all.

When they disappeared, Bong stood up and grinned. "Well, I guess I got them."

June pouted a little. "Yeah. Well...they didn't think I looked creepy at all."

Bong smiled. "Sure they did. They were just too afraid to say anything. I thought you were great."

June stepped closer to him and shook her head. "The gash isn't what's making them freak in this room," she said. "You're doing the work."

"Without your gash, I couldn't scare them," Bong said.

"That's so romantic of you," she said.

"You think that's romantic?"

"I take what I can get."

Bong suddenly felt nervous. He hadn't wanted to start something with June. And he'd been telling Jeanie that there wasn't anything, that the kiss a couple nights ago had been an accident. Just a crazy moment.

But now....

"What exactly do you want to take?" he asked.

"What exactly will you give?" she answered, moving closer. "I'd take a kiss again."

Bong felt his heart pounding suddenly. June had been totally cool the past couple nights, no flirtation. And he'd been both disappointed and thankful. Now…he was nervous. He didn't want to lose Jeanie. And he didn't want to say no to June. Classic love triangle disaster in the making.

"I guess a kiss couldn't hurt," he said. As he did, he looked at the doorway. Would not be good if Jeanie walked in again right at that moment.

Before he turned his head back, June's lips were touching his. He closed his eyes and savoured the touch. Forbidden and wrong. But he couldn't pretend she didn't feel good. He'd run their first kiss over and over again in his head like a film loop this week and he ultimately had to admit that he wasn't sorry for it. June was really amazing.

The problem was, he loved Jeanie.

The other problem was…he was really feeling like he liked June a lot too.

He returned the kiss.

When he looked up, there was a woman in the doorway.

His stomach leapt, as his first thought was that it was Jeanie.

But it wasn't.

It was a woman, but he hadn't seen her before. She filled the doorframe. And she held a knife in her hand.

"We have company," he whispered, pulling back from June's touch.

"Shit," June whispered and backed away. Starting a 'scare' with a kiss was not exactly optimum haunt behaviour.

Bong backed away from her, but he knew he couldn't 'disappear'. Instead, he tried to get in a position where he could at least be…less seen.

The woman walked into the room, and as she did, Bong quickly realised she wasn't a normal 'guest'. She didn't have the same hesitant step as a normal haunted house patron. She walked with a purpose. And she was walking directly towards them.

Bong raised his arms, and opened his mouth as if he were a vampiric ghost.

The woman raised her arms, and that's when he saw she held a knife.

A long, silver, very real-looking knife.

CHAPTER THIRTY-EIGHT

Jeanie was shambling through the front of the house when she saw Lon standing in the foyer. He ushered a group of five teenagers into the *Texas Chainsaw Massacre* room and then motioned her over.

"What's up?" she asked.

"I've gotten a half dozen different complaints tonight from people who've gotten their clothes ruined. Big red stains on them from somewhere. I don't know what you guys did different tonight with makeup, but we're going to end up with a bunch of dry cleaning bills."

"I didn't do anything different," Jeanie said. "Maybe someone spilled something. Did any of them say what room they got it in?"

Lon shook his head. "Nope. They haven't noticed it until they're outside and walking to their cars. And then they double back to complain to me or Andreas at the ticket stand."

Jeanie shrugged. "Well, I don't know what to tell you. I can keep a look out but I haven't seen anything messy so far tonight."

The house manager nodded. "Keep your eyes open. If you see anything…clean it up. I don't want to end the month on a big drag. They're rubbing up against something messy somewhere."

"I'll look," Jeanie said. "But if people are getting messed up, they must be banging into someone. It's not like we poured fake blood on the walls or props. That stuff's all dry."

Lon made a face. "Well somebody dumped some shit somewhere."

Jeanie shook her head. There was only one answer that was going to be acceptable, so she gave it. "On it."

"Good," Lon said, and ducked back out the front door. She stole a glimpse after him and saw the line still stretched down the gravel path and out of sight. She hoped Lon was cutting it off soon; it was already after ten p.m.

She decided to take a walk through the whole place from the start to see if she could spot any fake blood spills to make Lon happy. She couldn't imagine why there would be any though. Jeanie walked down the hall to the *Nightmare on Elm Street* room. When she looked inside, she saw someone disappear into the closet. She assumed it was whoever was wearing the Freddy suit tonight. Angie was hanging from the harness in the ceiling, the front of her nightshirt shredded and stained in red.

"How's it hanging?" she called into the room, but Angie didn't say a word. She just hung there, staring at Jeanie.

"Nice," she said. "Fine, stay in character."

She backed out of the door before a group trapped her in the room. Seconds later a couple slipped by her and entered the room. She heard the guy exclaim in awe, "Wicked!"

Jeanie moved down the hallway and decided to go upstairs to check on Bong and June.

The attic was strangely quiet. The last group must have just moved through and headed down the back stairs because nothing was moving here. Above her, hanging from the ceiling, was a new prop. She looked and grinned. It was super realistic. A woman with blue hair, a tight black t-shirt and bare feet hung from the rafters on a rope noose. That noose had been hanging dramatically empty for the month, but she appreciated that someone had finally filled it. A bit too little, too late, though. What was the point on the last night?

Jeanie walked beneath the figure and felt something wet splash on her face. When she touched a finger to her cheek, it came away shiny and red.

"What the fuck?" she said, and looked up at the figure again. She could see now that the woman had cut marks all down her arms and chest. And those marks appeared to be dripping with blood.

"So that's where the mess is coming from," she said. Jeanie looked at the floor beneath the figure and realised it was slick with red. "Stupid," she said. "No wonder people are getting their clothes fucked up."

She'd have to see if Mike could come up and cut it down quickly before anyone else got dripped on. What the hell did they hang it up there wet for? She shook her head and walked through the costume maze. Somehow, it seemed creepier tonight, probably because Bill and Tanya weren't jumping out at her. Speaking of which…where were they?

She frowned and walked over to the nursery. It was weird to have a nursery and no kids in the house, but Bong had been pretty effective in jumping out at people from his hidden vantage point. The room was scoring well with attendees, at least the ones they'd quizzed on the way out. Lon had been trying to gather some data from visitors on what they liked and what they didn't like over the past week as they left the place. He was already thinking about next year.

She ducked her head under the ragged overhang. The entry to the room was supposed to be reminiscent of the room in the climax of *House on Sorority Row*, though Jeanie doubted that anyone would ever place it. Especially since, though you walked into a room that was filled with a child's nursery items, instead of a kid or mutant childlike adult, you got a throat-slashed woman and a J-horror creeping adult. A little mix-and-match with the monsters.

Whatever. It had proven a solid room throughout the month, despite the mixed theme.

"Hey," she said, as she poked her head inside.

June was lying on the floor. Which wasn't usual. Ghosts didn't usually act like corpses. The weird thing was that she was covered in blood. Her whole gimmick had been a kind of zombie thing, with a throat slash. But tonight, she looked like someone had slashed her arms and legs and chest and…well…everything. She had cuts and blood spatter all over her.

Jeanie had to admit the effect was solid. But…she hadn't seen June do it. The last time she'd seen her, she just had the neck slash, as she had worn all month.

"Going all out tonight, huh?" she said. There was grudging admiration in her statement. At the same time, she looked at June and stifled a voice inside that said, *Too bad those aren't real, bitch.*

"Coast is clear for a second," she said with false buoyancy, and looked away from June. "Bong?"

There was no answer.

Jeanie walked over to the faux hallway where she knew he hid, ready to crabwalk out when new 'victims' entered the room.

Bong was there, on the floor, where he usually was.

Jeanie screamed.

Because Bong wasn't going to be crabwalking out of the corridor again tonight.

His fingers were reaching out to the floor behind him, while his toes hung down on the blood-smeared floor near his vacant face.

Someone had chopped off his arms and legs and left them lying on top of his torso…only in the reverse order of where they should be. The raw gristle of his thigh was propped on the meaty opening where his arm should emanate. And vice versa.

"Oh my God, oh my God, *oh my fucking God!*" Jeanie screamed.

She looked back at June and realised the makeup artist had not added fake blood to her ensemble tonight. She had been slashed to death.

The blood was not makeup.

Jeanie dropped to her knees and reached out to Bong…but her fingers stopped short of touching him. Because…his feet were pointed at her, rather than his arms.

"Why?" she cried, and touched her fingers to his bare, bloody leg.

Somebody in the outside attic room screamed. It didn't sound like the scream of someone scared. It sounded like someone being killed.

"What's going on?" she whispered. Her stomach was suddenly a hard, clenched ball of fear. It hadn't all really sunk in yet, but she knew that Bong was dead, and she was in danger.

Self-preservation took priority over her emotions for the moment. Jeanie walked to the doorway, and carefully peered around the jamb.

Another scream echoed from the attic area outside.

Jeanie could only see the shifting blue and purple light reflecting off an old hag costume on the rack in front of her. A man's voice suddenly cried out from the direction of the stairwell.

"Please just let me go, I won't tell anyone, I promise."

A moment later, she heard something like a wet punch. There was something else, another soft noise she couldn't place. And a soft thud.

Then the eerie synthesiser music took over.

Jeanie stood there for what seemed like forever, breathing as quietly as she could. She hugged the wall and stared at the vacant eyes of the old hag mask, crazy grey hair streaming out in all directions around the face.

At any moment, she expected it to jump off the rack at her.

But the hag stayed still.

Jeanie started walking slowly down the aisle, straining to see past the 'maze' of weird costumes and masks that separated the 'secret attic nursery' room from the entrance to the attic. The bass on the soundtrack playing overhead was throbbing in a steady, tense rhythm. For the first time all month, Jeanie really wasn't happy to have the soundtrack to a horror movie playing overhead. She loved horror movies…but she didn't want to be in a real-life one.

She moved down the wall, step by step, until the main area of the attic finally came into view. She saw the feet of the corpse hanging from the ceiling and it suddenly dawned on her that it wasn't a prop. It was a dead body, hanging from the rope.

Bleeding.

Underneath the hanging body's feet, two other bodies lay spread out on the floor. A woman lay there on her back, black hair splashed across the wood like an explosion. Her pink t-shirt was soaked in the centre with dark red colour.

A man was just a couple feet away. He was curled into a half-ball on the floor, as if trying to shield himself from something. His back faced the woman's corpse and his hands were pressed outward, as if trying to drive something back. Someone had taken more time with him; his shirt had been cut to shreds (without concern for the flesh beneath it) and his shorts had been sliced down the thigh, opening them to the private spaces within.

Those...had been removed.

"Jesus," Jeanie whispered, as she saw the glob of red flesh that lay against the corner of the far wall.

Part of her knew what organ the glob was, and part of her refused to acknowledge it, despite seeing the man's pants cut open, and the splash of blood that stained the half-shorts that remained around his waist, and the wooden floor beneath him.

Somebody in the house had slashed the throat and chest of this guy's girlfriend, and then cut off his 'nads. Jeanie was about to run for the stairs down, when someone began walking up.

She saw the black hair of a thin, weathered woman with her hair tied in a ponytail, along with another fatter, pale-looking woman in a black t-shirt, plastic glasses and a plaid skirt, ascend the stairs and step onto the floor of the attic.

She saw them look at the hanging woman, and then down at the floor where the butchered bodies lay. She saw them grimace and then grudgingly approve, through the shifting lines of their faces.

And then she saw the figure moving behind the old bureau that stood on the side of the stairwell up. It was another woman, she noted, with bare pale arms, and a hand holding a long silver blade above her head.

The two women who had just walked up the stairs gave a typical, low intensity shriek and began to move quickly towards the costume maze.

Only, the knife woman followed.

And she wasn't there simply to scare.

The blade came down and stabbed hard and fast into the ponytail woman's shoulder.

The woman looked confused and surprised and hurt all at the same time. It made for a strangely impactful expression on her face as the killer lifted and brought the blade down again and again. The woman crumpled under the stabbing blows, before her friend even realised what was happening.

When she finally turned and saw, the plaid woman screamed. Then she ran towards the stairs. But the woman with the knife moved surprisingly swiftly. She brought the blade around in a horizontal arc and caught the fleeing woman in the cheek. Even in the garish light of the attic, Jeanie could see the line of the cut open, expand and burn red.

Plaid woman screamed and stumbled, slapping one hand to her wounded face. When she lifted it, her hand came back completely covered in blood. Her eyes bugged as she realised how badly she was hurt.

All of this happened in a moment, and in that moment, the killer did not stop moving. She stepped in front of the bleeding woman, lifted the blade and brought it down. Plaid woman made the mistake of looking up, which turned out to be the last mistake she would ever make.

The silver point flashed through the air. Then it connected with her right eye, and slid easily inside her skull.

It all happened in a flash, but the woman dropped like a brick. Her head slid back off the knife, and the killer simply stood back and watched as the plaid woman's body spread out and shivered briefly on the floor. Her hands tremored and grasped towards the stairway, but her legs kicked once and crossed over each other. The rippling flesh of her thighs was exposed all the way to the pale wrinkles of her ass, as the plaid skirt flipped up in the wrong direction. And then she went still.

It was anything but an elegant death.

Jeanie held her breath until the killer moved again. Satisfied, apparently, that she had fully dispatched the woman, the killer turned and walked slowly to the stairs. Jeanie watched as foot by foot her body vanished down the exit until her hair dipped below the floor and disappeared. Then Jeanie crept out of her hiding place and took a deep breath. The air came in hitches, as she stifled her body from crying and yet still tried to catch her breath. She knelt down next to the body of the plaid woman and pulled her skirt down, giving her a modicum of decency in death. Something warm touched her hand, and she yanked her hand away instinctively. But it was just the growing river of Plaid's life leaking away. Blood was puddling around the woman's body fast.

Jeanie pushed back off the floor and forced herself towards the stairway. She wanted to go back to the farthest reach of the attic, crouch down and hide until daylight. But she knew in her head that she wouldn't be safe until she'd gotten out of the house. And neither would anybody else. Jeanie couldn't just curl up and hide as one by one the woman slashed and killed guest after guest. She had to find Lon and have all the houselights brought up. They had to evacuate the house. Her heart pounded so hard she could barely breathe as she leaned against the wall and crept down, stair by stair.

The house remained full of sound — creaks and moans and the tense tones of synthesisers that made each room feel like you were walking into a movie. And there were still the distant sounds of shrieks and laughter, the sounds of people enjoying a good scare.

But it all sounded smaller somehow, the guests far away. Jeanie knew how long the line was outside, and how fast they should have been cycling people through the house. But nobody had come upstairs in several minutes.

She could hear the chainsaw revving though, down in the dining room. It was a cycle. The motor would whine to life and then crescendo louder. It shook and screamed with deadly promise, usually corresponding to Brad holding it over his head and shaking it at the guests, who would screech and run into the next room.

But right now, while it sounded like Brad was scaring people with the tool, nobody was getting past the next couple of rooms and corridors to walk up the stairs.

Where were they going then?

CHAPTER THIRTY-NINE

The line stretched back to Midlothian Turnpike, and the buzz from the crowd was slowly growing louder as the night went on. Hidden flasks kept many people warm, and others had shown up already well-liquored. People laughed and yelled, and every little while a cop walked up and down the line, watching for…whatever warning signs cops watched for when they were on crowd control duty.

A woman with shock-red, kinked hair and a loose white suit full of multi-coloured polka dots nudged a fat man wearing white-face and old bum clothes covered in blood.

"Hey, Ted," she said.

The bum-zombie next to her grunted.

"How much longer do you think?" she asked.

"What difference does it make?"

"Because I'm worried they'll cut off the line if it gets much later."

He shrugged. "Then I guess we'll get a good night's sleep at home."

She elbowed him. "Lotta help you are," she said.

"Sorry, but this just feels like déjà vu. Only this time, we have stupid costumes."

"Mine isn't stupid," she said.

"Like there aren't a thousand evil clowns out on the street tonight," he said.

"That's how I fit in without being noticed," she said.

"Hmmm."

"You have to admit, this should keep us from being stopped at the ticket stand because someone recognises us."

"Nobody would have recognised us if we'd just come as ourselves," Ted said.

"That guy who called the cops on us last time would have," she answered quickly.

"Maybe. If he was here," Ted said. "But now, since you're in a clown suit, it's going to be really difficult to stay under the radar."

"O ye, of little faith," she said. "Just work with me here."

"The last time I did that, the cops came."

"This is different," she said. "It's the final night. And it's Halloween. If something happens here tonight, I don't think it's *us* that the police are going to be after."

The group ahead of them suddenly surged forward, and Jillie grabbed Ted's arm and squeezed. "There's something going on in there tonight," she said. "I can feel it."

"Indigestion," he said.

"I'm serious," she said. The crowd all around them filled the air with stories and voices, but Jillie still whispered. "I have this horrible, black feeling. Like I've never felt before. It's almost as if someone or something was sucking all of the life out of the sun."

"That's because it's eleven o'clock at night," Ted said. "And the sun went away a long time ago."

Jillie threw her head back to look up at the stars. The night sky was clear and cold. "You're impossible," she said. "Sometimes I don't understand why you do this at all."

"Mainly because of the beef sandwiches you buy me at Nicky's," he said.

"I'm not talking to you anymore."

They stood in silence for a couple minutes, and then surged forward again. There were only a handful of people between them and the ticket taker now. Behind them, there was a sudden wave of voices. They sounded angry. Someone yelled, "Fuck that shit," and another yelled, "Come on, we've been here...."

Ted looked back and then said, "Looks like they finally cut off the line."

Jillie nodded. "Figured that was coming soon. We're good though. We'll be in before midnight, which is all I really wanted."

"You know nothing is going to happen at the Witching Hour, right?" he asked. He looked up at her with black zombie eyes – God she hated those contacts – and raised an eyebrow.

"Maybe not then," she said. "But something *will* happen tonight. I feel like something is already going on in there."

"It's called having a good time," he said.

"Not the things I'm feeling. They don't feel good at all."

Ted had nothing to say to that.

The line moved forward again and suddenly they were standing at the two steps leading up to the porch of the house. "We'll take two," Ted said to the man sitting at the table with a cashbox. He pulled out his wallet to give the man thirty dollars.

"Buyer beware," the man said, and handed Ted their tickets.

"That's what I'm afraid of," Jillie whispered.

Ted didn't answer her, but led them forward towards the door. A man in a black suit with white-face makeup grinned at them through ruby-red lips. Inside Ted groaned at yet another clown outfit. But then the dark clown opened the door, and they stepped inside.

CHAPTER FORTY

Lon took his position in the den. He'd had to leave the ticket stand because for the third time tonight they were missing a haunter. First Lucio, then Brad and now Chris. He'd seen Mike was filling in for Brad when he walked past the dining room. It was too late now, but next year he had to put some strict things in place to stop this from happening. They couldn't run this place on the busiest night of the year with people abandoning posts. Maybe if you didn't show up, you got docked a week's pay?

He shrugged and took an appreciative look around the room. He had to admit, when it was empty, the den was pretty eerie. Between the music that was piped in, the red and blue and green spotlights that lent the room a surreal flavour and the stained glass (false) windows and dark shadows in every corner, the place was definitely prepped to scare.

Lon was prepped to scare too. He wore the grotesque rubber mask of a pustulating rotting corpse figure that looked surprisingly real, and he held a long dangerous-looking axe across his shoulder. Never mind that it was plastic, it *looked* good. If you were standing in front of him and it was pointed at you, you would not have blown it off. You would have backed away in fear.

He'd filled in at this position before, and virtually every time he jumped out from behind one of the alcoves of the room to hold the axe out at the patrons, somebody screamed.

Honestly, Lon hated the sweaty feel of the mask, but he loved the screams. It meant he was doing something right.

Tonight, he held his blade high. It was Halloween. If Argento wasn't here, he wanted to represent the guy well. This room, this costume, was Argento's creation. It's what the designer of this house had wanted.

Wherever Argento was, Lon wanted to make sure his vision was done right.

So he was ready when the door opened for his first 'victim.' He leapt out and stood at the ready with his axe.

The only problem was, the girl at the doorway did not appear in the least bit scared.

Instead, she stepped forward, with a long silver blade of her own cradled on one shoulder.

What is that about? he wondered.

All of his preparation suddenly fell to the floor. He was no longer the guy in place to scare…he was faced with a woman who was scaring *him*. Because…he was pretty sure her weapon was real. And he knew his was certainly not.

"Hey," he said. "Can I help you?"

It was the dumbest 'customer service' phrase he had ever spoken, but he had to say something. Why not ask it before he got cut into tiny scrubs. Why was she here? Who was she? And why was she threatening *him* in his own haunted house?

She didn't have the same kind of interest in communication.

The woman lifted her blade and ran towards him. Suddenly he realised that there wasn't any communication that was going to occur here. There was only victim and killer. And he was on the wrong side of the equation at the moment.

"Wait a minute," he demanded, dropping his fake weapon and frantically looking around for something to hide behind. Some way to avoid her blade. He ducked behind the couch, forcing her to choose which side she'd come after him on. When she hesitated, he ran to the bookcase and frantically toggled the lever to open the secret door.

It opened and he slipped through just as the crack of a blade fractured the shelf his fingers had just touched.

Lon stumbled into the secret room that led to the back stairs into the basement. The star within a circle symbol that had been etched into the centre of the floor still remained from whatever Satan worshippers had put it there decades ago.

Argento and his team had played off that, and painted the walls with a series of symbols of witchcraft and the occult.

Lon ran for the stairwell, but the woman swung the long knife at him like a bat. The flat of the blade caught him in the hip hard, knocking him to the floor. He scuttled backwards as the blade came down again, the business end this time, catching for a second in the floor before she pulled it up again and readied to strike.

He pulled himself up but there was nowhere to go. Lon stood face to face with the girl, and realised that he was really up shit creek here. This was not a prank. This girl was deadly serious. Her dark brown eyes never seemed to blink. Her jaw was clenched with fatal determination. She stepped relentlessly forward, one foot at a time, forcing him to the wall. A giant Ouija board was painted on the wall behind him and out of the corner of his eye he could see the arc of its letters. His face was next to the K.

"You don't want to hurt me, I work here," he said. "I'm helping to haunt this haunted house."

She shook her head, and pinned him against the back wall with her body. Then she held the blade to his neck.

"You can't haunt a house until you're dead," she said. "But I can help there."

She stepped back and with one fast motion brought the heavy blade up and then down, whispering one word as it connected with his face.

"Goodbye."

CHAPTER FORTY-ONE

Jeanie put her foot down on the plank floor that Mike had laid at the bottom of the stairs, and felt her heel slide forward. She lost her balance, but grabbed for the banister and saved herself from falling on her ass. When she righted herself, she looked down to see what she'd slipped on.

"Oh fuck," she whispered.

The floor was a river of red.

She looked to the left, and three bodies lay there in a row, their throats cut from ear to ear. When she looked to the right, the scene was worse. One by one she counted the bodies. Seventeen. Counting the ones on the right, there were twenty people dead in this hallway.

"Why?" she whispered as tears slid down her cheeks. She knew her makeup was running down to her chin, and for once in her life, it didn't matter.

Jeanie pursed her lips and forced herself to step forward, ignoring the fact that she was walking through pools of blood. She had to get to the front of the house, and find out if anybody was still alive. The chainsaw still whirred, so that said someone was still up front.

She resisted the urge to tiptoe, and instead walked flatfooted down the slippery hallway. The last thing she wanted to do was slip and find herself coated in the death of twenty people.

As she passed the Argento room, she looked inside and saw a man and a woman lying on the floor. And then she stifled a cry as she saw the dark face of Lenny lying equally still nearby. Her stomach clenched and she balled up a fist to wipe her eyes.

This really wasn't a dream.

She walked to the end of the hall to peer into the *Nightmare on Elm Street* room, and saw Angie hanging in her invisible harness from the ceiling, as she did every night. What was not the same as every night was the blood, which was literally raining down on the bed below. Jeanie restrained the urge to barf. This was not an effect. Angie was dead and bleeding as she hung upside down from the ceiling.

She refused to look again and turned back to the hall.

Jeanie stepped carefully past the dead bodies, worried that at any minute the killer would return around the corner. But the hallway remained empty of life. Step by step, she made her way to the end. When she reached the corner, she peered around to the right, and could see the black glass of a window at the front of the house looking out onto Bachelor's Grove.

The LED lights tucked into the corners of the hallway flared red and purple in the sidewell of her vision as she peered into the back entrance to the dining room.

The screams of the house seemed to have diminished now, and all she really heard were the tense notes of the Goblin soundtrack playing nearby and the buzz of an angry saw.

"Where is everyone?" she whispered, and hugged the wall closer.

She couldn't believe that nobody had tracked her down already.

Somebody screamed in the room ahead, and she didn't fade back. Instead, she stepped around the corner and into the room. She stood in the back quarter of the dining room that represented the *Texas Chainsaw Massacre* movie. The room was shaped like an L so she couldn't see the main attraction yet. Just around the corner she got a glimpse of Brad hefting the chainsaw. He was playing his part well; the blade of the tool rose into the air frequently and she could hear the patrons screaming in answer. But she couldn't see who he was threatening with it. Or what they did when he made the blades whine.

Jeanie crept forward, trying to see what was going on in the room ahead without anyone actually seeing her. She peered around the corner of the L finally and stifled a gasp.

There was a hole in the floor next to the 'cannibal' table. A big open rectangle cut through the floorboards that had not been there before. It was right in the path that people were supposed to take to walk through the *Texas Chainsaw Massacre* room. She crouched down, so that her head wouldn't be seen above the table, and slipped along the wall to position herself on the far side of the table. Even though the killer seemed to have left Brad alone, she instinctively didn't want to be seen. The killer could be lurking right around the corner.

But what the hell was with the hole in the floor?

As she reached the front corner of the room, its meaning became clear.

A group of four turned the corner. Two couples in their mid-twenties stepped into the room; they all looked as if they were well on their way to a hangover. One man with shaggy black hair took his arm off his thin, hawk-nosed girlfriend and threw it in the air in a fist. "Groovy!" he yelled.

"Wrong movie, asshat!" the other man said. "It's more like, 'You wanna have dinner with us? My brother makes great head cheese.' Get it?" he pointed at the head on the dining room table. "Head cheese?"

Brad/Leatherface had secreted himself against the back wall until the group was fully in the room, and then he revved the chainsaw and jumped forward behind them. The only way for them to go was forward...only, there was a big hole in the floor there.

"Nice," the 'Groovy' guy said. But almost immediately, his girlfriend screamed as the chainsaw clipped her on the arm. A gouge of red appeared instantly.

"Holy shit," the boyfriend said. "That thing's real!"

He turned to face down Leatherface.

"What the fuck man, you just hurt her for real! What do you think you're doing?"

Leatherface didn't say a thing. Instead, he simply revved the engine and jabbed forward with the chainsaw on full speed. It caught the complainer in the gut and suddenly the air of the room was filled with a red-hot mist. And the sounds of a hideous scream.

Leatherface pushed the chainsaw forward until the whirring blade came out the other side, next to the spine of the complainer. Then he pulled back the tool and let the body fall backwards, into and through the hole in the floor. He held up the tool as the other three stood on the edge of the hole, screaming. Then he brought it down fast, catching the arm of the girl he'd already wounded.

But this time, it was more than a wound.

Shirt and skin and blood sprayed into the air and the girl's arm suddenly fell free. The knuckles of her lost hand hit the floor first, but then the arm toppled over, disappearing into the black space behind.

The girl grabbed for her shoulder, now spraying blood like a tiny hose, and seconds later, fell backwards to join her lost arm.

That left the other couple, who teetered on the edge.

"Over the table," the guy screamed, and dove between the manikin figures towards the bloody props displayed on platters. But Leatherface didn't miss a beat. He brought the chainsaw down and severed the man's right hand. The fingers were still clutching for the tablecloth when the guy pulled back and screamed, blood spraying from the stump below his wrist. His girlfriend or wife echoed his scream and grabbed for his torso, but then turned her head away in disgust when she was suddenly sprayed in his blood.

Leatherface waved the chainsaw behind and in front of them. They twisted and turned, their feet just barely on the edge of the hole. And then the man lost his balance and toppled into the chasm. The woman grabbed for him, but all she managed to do was lose her own balance in the process of trying to save him. They disappeared into the hole, and a second later, the air filled with a sharp, horrible shriek. And then the only sound in the room was the background music soundtrack, and the idling groan of the chainsaw.

That wasn't Brad wearing the Leatherface mask.

Jeanie crept slowly along the floor out of sight behind the table. Maybe she could get on the other side of the madman and make a break for the front door before he turned from the hole.

But then she put her hand down on something soft.

Jeanie's whole body went stiff. Her hand had touched someone's arm. She looked down and saw Brad's stubbled jaw just a couple feet away.

But that was all she could see of Brad's head. Because the top half had been sawn off at the eyes.

Jeanie wanted to throw up. But she knew if she made a move of any kind, she'd be chopped up just like the foursome now at the bottom of the hole. She pressed herself tight against the corner of the room, trying to remain unseen in the shadow. Just a prop, not someone to be sawn up.

Leatherface returned to his own position standing back against the wall, awaiting the next group to appear.

No wonder nobody had been getting upstairs, Jeanie thought. They were all at the bottom of a hole, chainsawed into pieces. Everyone had to pass through this room before reaching the stairs.

Something tickled her nose. Maybe it was the smell of the blue smoke from the chainsaw. The room was thick with ghostly clouds that hung like demons in the air. She wrinkled her nostrils and breathed through her mouth, trying to hold the feeling down. Still, that tickle in the back of her nose grew and grew until her eyes began to water.

And then it couldn't be denied and came out, all in a loud, angry sneeze.

Leatherface turned and the eyes behind the mask glinted in the low red light.

She didn't move, but Jeanie knew he saw her. And then it suddenly dawned on her who the man behind the mask had to be. She knew his build, and his work shoes. He wore the same blue-checked flannel shirt she'd seen for weeks working around the house before showtime.

"Mike?" she whispered.

He revved the chainsaw and began walking towards her. Jeanie darted back the way she'd entered, but instead, Leatherface turned back and ran out of the room towards the front door. Jeanie hesitated, not sure why he was running away from her. But as she turned the corner of the L to leave the room out the back hallway, she understood.

Just as she reached the door, the chainsaw revved, and swung towards her.

Jeanie stumbled backwards and he kept coming, waving the whirring silver teeth of the blade at her chest and head.

Jeanie turned the corner back into the dining room and started to run towards the front door. Only, she took the short way around the cannibal table, her habitual route for the past few weeks when walking through this room.

And a second later found herself standing on the edge of the big black hole.

She looked down and the garish lights of the basement played over a pile of body parts. There were heads, arms and torsos all glistening in a gory heap directly below. At the highest part of the mound of corpses, it was dark, but at the edges of the heap of bodies, she could see the tips of long, tall spikes.

She knew right where they were, in terms of the basement. The Vlad the Impaler exhibit was just below. Dozens of five-foot-high sharp metal spikes, all reaching for the ceiling.

Oh shit.

The chainsaw was in the air buzzing closer and closer behind her head. Jeanie had no options.

She jumped, aiming for the darkest part of the stack of bodies.

Her landing was soft, though something bit at her left calf. Above her, she heard the chainsaw connect with the floor where she had been standing a second before. Then the machine whine faded away, as Leatherface pulled it back and returned to his position at the front of the room to wait for new guests to enter the house.

Jeanie was safe for a moment.

Now she just had to get off the pile of bodies and back to the floor of the basement without impaling herself in the process.

She turned her head and found herself looking directly into the blood-splattered face of the 'Groovy' guy. His eyes were open in terror. Jeanie couldn't help it. She let out a short scream.

Then she tore her gaze away from that bit of horror and took in the rest of her situation. She felt wetness seeping into her clothes. And as she looked down the length of her body, she could easily see why. Her knee rested inside the crimson cavern the chainsaw had ripped into someone's gut. The gristle of the shoulder end of a woman's arm was shoved up against her chest. Something hard pressed against her groin, and as she shifted slightly, she saw what it was. The decapitated head of a man. He had a five-day growth of beard, but he was bald on top. His eyes were also open, staring sightlessly at Jeanie's crotch. She shivered and looked away, towards the hallway that led past this grisly exhibit. There were three rows of silver spikes between the edge of the pile of bodies and her escape.

Above her, the chainsaw let out an angry war cry as a woman screamed in true terror. Jeanie now realised that there was a difference between the screams that they'd elicited in patrons from an unexpected scare versus those in a true deadly situation. The cries of true horror sounded different. It wasn't something she could have explained, but you could hear it.

Something hit her in the back, and she gasped. It was heavy. She turned to see what it was and choked.

It was half of a woman.

Intestines slid over Jeanie's ribcage as they exited the shredded cavity of the victim. They looked like bloody snakes and she shrieked at the sight. But a second later, her scream was cut off when another weight hit her. The other half of the victim. The woman's pink gym shoe landed on top of the face of the dead woman beneath her. Before Jeanie could react, another body fell from above. She caught the blur of a heavyset man with glasses, and then heard the most horrible scream she had ever heard as he belly-flopped onto a handful of steel spikes next to the stack of corpses. His scream stopped abruptly as the spikes jutted through his back in three places. Another had caught him in the side of the head, and stuck fast in his skull. While his body slid down the spikes a couple feet, his head pinned him to the top of the spike.

"Jesus," Jeanie whispered. She resisted the urge to panic. While there was death all around her, she had escaped the chainsaw...now she just had to escape the spikes. The tops of the pointed spikes were all stained red, with bodies and body parts hanging on many of them halfway to the floor – like toothpicks with human olives. Argento had never imagined an impaling zone this cruel when he'd set it up with a handful of fake bodies streaming fake guts.

Jeanie grabbed at the dead woman's hand that hung over her, and pulled the woman forward. If she was going to get to the edge of the rows of spikes without being impaled herself, she needed to build a bridge. She rolled the ragged rib cage over to rest on the edge of a spike, but as soon as she pressed down on the woman's jacket, the spike slid through the bones, and the upper half of the woman began to slide down the spike. The next corpse was lodged at least three feet down.

No, she thought. *They can't slide. They need to wedge.*

She grabbed at the woman's long blond hair and held her from slipping down the spike. And then she had an idea, thanks to the fat man nearby.

Jeanie pulled the head by the hair and positioned the woman's mouth over the tip of an impaler. Grimacing but not giving in, she pressed the spike through the glossy lips of the dead woman. The head sunk, but caught.

That was the ticket.

If she could use a handful of heads to create the base, stopping the soft flesh of the bodies from slipping down the spikes, she could then layer the tops of those heads – anchors – with a couple other bodies. A gruesome human suspension bridge.

Another scream from above, and two more bodies fell through the opening. One landed on Jeanie's legs, the other impaled itself a couple feet away. Not where she needed it to be.

She took a breath, and smelled the strong scent of iron. And something far more pungent and foul. The bowels of dozens of people had opened beneath her.

Rather than throw up, she grabbed at the denim jacket of a man who now lolled across her legs, and dragged him forward and over the woman whose head she'd impaled. Jeanie could think of only one thing.

She was getting out of here.

A hot rinse of blood soaked into her shirt as she dragged his corpse, but she ignored it, focusing only on getting the man's mouth in the place she needed it to be. Fellating a silver spike.

As the bodies continued to fall in a grotesque rain of screams and blood spray, she grabbed and moved them, layering pelvises over skulls on the spikes. She layered their limp, heavy bodies across each other, crisscrossing the corpses in a Lincoln Log style. Her hands and arms were slick with blood, but she hardly noticed now. She shrugged off the fake guts that were strapped around her waist so that she could move easier, and slapped them across a spike. More building material.

A man's voice screamed from above her, and the chainsaw whirred again. An arm suddenly fell through the hole, and bounced off the corpse pile to fall to the floor a couple feet away. The rest of the man came through the hole a second later, screaming without stop. He missed the centre of the bodies and a spike suddenly poked through his thighs. His chest, however, rested on the edge of the island of bodies and he reached out his hands to Jeanie.

"Oh God, fuck," he cried. "Please help me."

He struggled, but all that did was make his legs slip farther down the spikes. He was pinned like a butterfly. As his legs slid down, he let out a series of sharp guttural cries. Jeanie turned towards him and took his hand.

"Stop moving," she said. "You're making it worse."

And then another body fell from above. Another man. The guy landed on top of the pinned man's waist, and she saw his eyes suddenly bulge.

The force of the new body pushed his stomach down hard on a spike that had been buried in the chest of another pinned corpse. A rain of blood splattered on the floor and the man didn't scream or beg anymore. Jeanie let go of his hand, but took the hand of the body that had killed him. It had avoided getting wedged, so she dragged it behind her across the corpse bridge and laid it across the head of a woman.

That did it. She had wedged a bridge of ripped and bleeding bodies right up to the edge of the spikes.

She crawled across their still-warm flesh slowly, spreading her weight out as much as possible. Beneath her, she felt flesh shifting, sinking.

"Please, please, please," she whispered as slowly, carefully, she crawled across the dead. And then she had her hand on the back of the skull that rested on the final stake between her and the open ground below. She pulled herself forward, as the bodies beneath her shifted and moved. Something sharp poked at her thigh. Was it a spike or someone's broken bone?

She didn't want to find out. Jeanie pushed against the skull beneath her hand and felt it sink. The spike below was working its way through the skull of the corpse. But now Jeanie could look over the tower of spikes and see the open floor four feet below.

"Now or never," she whispered, and closed her eyes for a second, steeling her nerve. Then she rolled across the bodies, not stopping when she reached the edge. She flipped right over the edge as one of the bodies behind her gave way, sliding two feet down a stake that she'd been resting on. It didn't matter. For a second she was in the air, and then she landed hard on the ground.

Jeanie cried out as her thigh slammed the wood, but she kept rolling and staggered to her feet in a heartbeat.

She looked down at herself and grimaced. Her jeans and t-shirt were absolutely sodden with blood. Shreds of someone else's flesh stuck to her pants like lint. Jeanie looked up as another body came through the hole in the ceiling above to smack down on top of the pile.

She forgot about the gore and turned away towards the exit of the basement. She could be out of the house in seconds and then could finally find Lon and get him to turn the house lights on and stop sending people inside.

Her leg hurt from where she'd landed, but Jeanie limped towards the cellar stairway out.

She could see the Exit sign just ahead, with the white sign above it disputing the light. Argento had painted 'NO' in bright red letters above 'EXIT'.

Jeanie moved towards it, safe at last.

Someone moved out of the corridor ahead of her and took a position directly in front of the stairs leading out.

A figure with a long silver knife.

Jeanie began to cry.

The killer from the attic blocked her way out.

CHAPTER FORTY-TWO

Jillie tugged on Ted's arm as they stepped into the foyer. "See, I told you this would get us in okay."

"Yeah, but now you stand out like…a woman in a clown suit," he said.

The chainsaw whirred in the room to their right and Jillie pointed straight ahead. The arrows on the floor told them to turn right. 'This Way To Your Doom', the words next to them encouraged. The hallway ahead had police tape across it. Most of it had been knocked down already, but a couple strips still barred the way a foot above the floor.

"Let's go this way," she said.

"And get us thrown out for going the wrong way?" he said.

"I think this leads straight to the stairway to the attic," she said. "Come on."

She stepped over the tape and ducked into the hallway beyond. Ted followed, shaking his head. Screams erupted with the whir of the chainsaw behind them, and Jillie motioned Ted forward. When they reached the kitchen, Jillie stopped and crouched down.

"What is it?" Ted whispered.

She pointed at the puddle of blood surrounding the woman on the floor.

"That's real blood," she said.

"That's what they want you to think," he said. "Don't you remember, she's going to jump up any second and give you a heart attack."

Jillie shook her head. "Not this time," she said. She pushed the body over, and despite knowing that the woman was dead, she jumped back when she saw the ravaged torso. The woman's neck had been slashed ear to ear, and the blood was obviously real, when you saw it next to the makeup blood. Someone had slashed down the centre of her shirt, severing both the cotton of her tee and the strap of her bra. It had also dug deep into the line of her sternum, ending in a foot-long hole in her belly. Wet red and yellow chunks of flesh hung out of the wound, and Jillie dropped the body back to the ground.

"It's happening," she said. "I knew it from the start."

She stood up and went to the sink. A blackened face with poached eyes glared back at her. The man was very, very dead. A spotlight lay in the water next to his face. It was still plugged in to the wall socket, but it no longer was giving out any light.

"So now that we know it's happening, how do we stop it?"

"Stop *her*," Jillie corrected. "This is all part of a ritual," she said. "We have to stop it before anyone else is sacrificed for it."

"Yes, but how?" he said.

"We have to find her heart," Jillie said. "And put a stake in it."

"But she's already dead," Ted said.

Jillie shook her head. "If this is part of a reincarnation spell, I don't think so. Not anymore. There have been too many sacrifices already."

Ted looked confused, but Jillie grabbed him by the arm and pulled. "Come on," she said. "She'll be in the basement. That's where all of the other events in this house have been. They found animal bones down there, and magic ritual symbols in the past. All in the same spot. All dead centre of the structure. The house's heart. It's where she pushed me. It's where she's held on all these years, waiting."

Together they ran down the hallway past the strobing lights and howling music. When they turned the corner, they found the bodies.

"Oh my God," Ted said. "Is it too late?"

"I don't think so," she said. "It's not quite midnight yet. That's always the hour of change. The weakest moment in the fabric between today and tomorrow, natural and supernatural. Come on."

Carefully they threaded their way through the corpses blocking the hall until they reached the stairs down. Jillie didn't slow, but immediately launched down them.

"Wait," Ted called in a loud whisper. "Be careful," he warned. "Whoever did this is still here."

"I'm counting on it," Jillie said on the fourth step. Then she took the next three and in a second stood on the plank floor of the basement.

"What are we looking for?" Ted whispered.

She shrugged. "We'll know it when we see it. I don't know how all the sacrifices work, but her centre is down here. That way," she said, pointing to the right.

Ted nodded, but didn't move. "Okay," he said. "Lead on."

Jillie shook her head. "Chivalry is dead."

Ted shrugged. "This is your party and I don't want to *be* dead."

Jillie rolled her eyes and began leading the way down the aisle. "We'll all be dead eventually," she said.

"Yeah, but we don't have to die tonight," he said from behind her.

"We're not going to die," she said. "We just have to avoid getting stabbed."

"Someone should have told that to him," Ted murmured, and pointed.

They were passing a display that was clearly an homage to *The Exorcist*; there was a bed and nightstand in the centre, and a girl with a green-tinged face and glowing eyes sitting up in the centre of the bed. Her hair was wild and the soundtrack overhead kept repeating two lines in the midst of a nerve-racking soundtrack: "The power of Christ compels you!" one voice cried and shortly thereafter, a demonic growl declared, "Your mother sucks cocks in hell!"

But the bed and the soundtrack and the flaring lights weren't what Ted was talking about. There was a man lying in front of the bed. He could have been part of the set, but a closer look made it clear he wasn't. The man wore jeans and a black shirt with a cartoon on it that boasted 'Fast zombies miss the brains'.

Jammed into his mouth was a long wooden pole; a crucifix was mounted on the opposite end. It had probably been a setpiece for *The Exorcist* room, but now it was a murder weapon. Blood pooled around the back of the man's head, where the end of the pole had plunged through his neck to gouge its way into the floor.

"I wonder who he pissed off," Ted said.

"I don't think he had to piss off anyone," Jillie said. "She wants the blood of everyone standing in that line outside spilled in here."

"But why?" Ted said.

"She needs their life to return," Jillie said. "She needs gallons of blood. This isn't just vengeance. There's a purpose."

"A method to the madness?"

She nodded. "Yeah, I just don't know what the method is. Or rather, what the last act is. I just hope we're not too late to stop it."

They walked past another display, this one an homage to *Hellraiser*. And like in the movie, a man had been mounted on a cross in the centre of the space, with chains liberally covered in hooks attached to the body. The man's arms and legs and cheeks and abdomen were all gouged and pulled tight by hooks, his flesh stretched like yellowed taffy off his bones and pinched towards the walls.

But like the last display, the star of this torture scene was not a dummy. There was no makeup here.

The puddle on the floor beneath his legs was the result of a bladder voided, and the blood spatter rained on the floor was real blood, the trickle of life that had dripped from the holes of the hooks. The man had been bled dry as he hung helpless in the air.

Jillie walked into the set and reached up to put her fingers on the man's chest.

"What are you doing?" Ted whispered. His voice was sharp.

"Just trying to tap in," she said.

Jillie rested her head and stood there for a minute, not speaking. When she finally pulled back, Ted asked, "What did you feel?"

"Nothing," Jillie said. "I saw him die. And I felt nothing at all."

She looked perplexed, and Ted pulled her arm. "Come on," he said.

She nodded and stepped away from the body. Her face was troubled, but she walked back into the aisle and only paused briefly as they passed the next display. There was a woman's torso there, propped upright on a church altar, with her vacant eyes staring towards the aisle. Her waist and legs were missing, and a stream of blood leaked over the edge of the altar to drip down and spread on the floor.

Jillie only shook her head. "This is not good," she whispered.

"Ya think?" Ted said. "Should we be recording anything?"

"Sure," Jillie said absently. "If you want. But this is different. This isn't a haunting situation."

"What would you call it?"

"A ritual. A massacre."

Jillie walked further down the aisle, and the lighting changed. Ted reached into his backpack and pulled out an EMF reader. Maybe Jillie didn't care right now about documenting all of this, but later, she'd be asking what he'd been doing in here with her the whole night.

There were times she could be really unfair…and unforgiving.

The meters on the tracker were alive.

Ted held the tool out towards the aisle behind them and slowly moved it forward, watching the readings. The LED meters shivered and moved; nothing drastic, but they weren't still either.

"There's activity here," Ted announced, looking around the spotlit dark. "But nothing focused."

"That's all of the victims," Jillie said. "Not the main event."

He followed her around the corner and they began a new row of grotesque sets as they walked towards the exit. Having done this once before, Ted understood how it flowed, even if he didn't remember the 'kill' scenes exactly.

Ted reached out to grab Jillie's shirt. She slowed, and he pointed down the long aisle in front of her before whispering, "Who is that?"

There was a woman standing at the edge of the aisle. And she was clearly a woman, not some prop. Her face moved, and she looked both left and right as she studied the room. But when Ted trained the EMF reader on her, the dial did nothing.

"Jillie," he called. "Look."

He held the reader out in front of him, and she glanced at the dial.

"She's alive," Jillie said. "But there's no way that this is simply the work of one disturbed woman. Let's see what's really going on."

Jillie kept walking forward, towards the girl at the end of the aisle. She had unruly brown hair, kinked and curled in a wild way across her shoulders. She stared straight ahead though, her gaze focused on something down the other aisle, as she held a long silver blade into the air.

Ted followed behind, holding the EMF reader out in front of him. The needles looked nervous, but really didn't move. On either side of the walkway were sets depicting scenes from horror films, but Ted didn't look at most of them seriously enough to try to guess what they were. When he did look, he saw people bleeding from a wide variety of wounds. He didn't want to see those; instead he tried to focus on his EMF meter rather than the death that was clearly in evidence all around him.

"Who is behind all of this?" he asked.

"Someone with a plan," Jillie said. She strode forward then and held up her hand, gesturing for the woman to stop whatever she was doing. They were close, and she saw the opportunity to intervene.

The woman didn't see her right away, and instead lifted her knife higher to threaten somebody in the aisle ahead. Jillie and Ted couldn't see who, but they began to run forward.

"Stop!" Jillie screamed.

The woman paused, surprised by the interruption. She turned to face Jillie and changed the focus of the knife blade. At the same time, she kept her gaze divided, watching whoever she had been threatening. Without warning, she suddenly darted down the side aisle away from them.

Jillie ran to follow and Ted was right behind. When they reached the aisle, they finally saw who the woman was really after.

A girl stood just a few feet down the passageway from the killer. She was covered in blood, head to toe. She could have been representing Sissy Spacek from the pig blood scene in the movie *Carrie*. The woman with the knife suddenly ignored Jillie and Ted and moved toward the girl like a storm.

"Stop!" Jillie cried again.

But this time it was Ted who didn't hold back. He elbowed past Jillie and ran the five yards down the aisle to catch the woman.

"Leave her alone!" he yelled, as he drew closer to the woman.

The woman with the knife stopped midway down the aisle and turned towards him with the blade raised.

"Stop!" he screamed.

The woman's answer was to swing the blade like a scythe as she turned towards him.

Ted slowed his approach, but it was too late. The woman moved fast.

Ted gasped as the steel of the knife slipped easily through the cotton of his shirt and into his chest.

"*Noooo!*" Jillie screamed, but she could do nothing to save him.

Ted gasped and choked.

The knife moved fast through the soft flesh of Ted's belly. There was a pinch at his heart. It felt like it should have been more painful, really, but Ted didn't have the chance to say that to anyone. Instead he groaned and collapsed like a house of cards to the floor.

The killer only gazed at him for a moment, however, before turning her attention back towards the other woman waiting at the end of the passageway.

Jillie dropped to her knees, grabbing for Ted's hand. His shirt bloomed with blood and her fingers were almost instantly warm with his life.

"Hold on," she whispered to him. "I'll get an ambulance."

Ted grimaced and slowly shook his head. "I don't think so," he said. "Just don't let her get to you."

"You're going to be okay," Jillie promised. But she knew as she said it that he wasn't. His chest was like a well of blood, and his breath came in wet wheezes.

"You can have my fries," he gasped. His mouth twisted in a pained scowl, and then went still.

"Ted?" Jillie whispered. She repeated his name louder, but he didn't move.

His eyelids didn't blink.

Her eyes filled with tears, but then self-preservation forced her to look up from her friend. She knew the killer had to be just a few feet away, maybe already coming for her. But when she looked up, through her bleary gaze, she realised that the knife woman was gone. And so was her intended victim.

Jillie felt a small relief at that, since it allowed her to release her grief and hold Ted.

She put her arms around him, ignoring the wet blood that covered his chest.

"I'm so sorry I dragged you into this," she whispered, and laid her cheek on the stubble of his. "So, so sorry," she whispered, as her tears slipped down to pool on his bloody shirt.

CHAPTER FORTY-THREE

The nails hurt his back.

Mike screwed up his eyes and moaned as he rolled over on Emery's dangerous bed. How long had he been asleep there? he wondered.

He rolled his feet over the side and pushed himself up to a sitting position.

That's when he realised that he was covered in blood. He looked down his arm and saw his sleeve was dark with it. His other arm was the same.

He hadn't lain down in the bed that way. And he didn't feel injured. Had he gouged himself badly on a nail? He ran a hand up and down one arm and shook his head. The sleeve was damp with sticky blood. Only, nothing on his arm hurt. He didn't think he was hurt. He just felt a little…woozy.

So then…how had he gotten all bloodied?

Mike stood up, and tried to survey his body in the dim light of Emery's room. There was just a single candle, and Emery and Katie were nowhere to be seen. His sleeves were sodden with blood, and his chest and belly and crotch were all damp with it as well.

What the hell?

Mike started to walk towards the stairway when his foot connected with something on the floor.

He looked down and saw a chainsaw lying there.

A familiar Leatherface mask lay on the floor nearby.

"What did you do?" he whispered. Then he climbed up the stairs to reach the attic.

The eerie music played, but nobody was there. Mike descended the stairwell to the main floor and realised the house there also seemed empty. It was as if he had slept until after closing time. All the lights were on, but nobody was home.

Mike walked around the corner and abruptly stopped.

It might not be so much that nobody was home, but rather, that everyone who was home was dead.

The corridor was filled with bodies. And clearly these were not props, but real, bloodied, murdered bodies.

"What the fuck?" Mike whispered.

He stepped between the corpses until he reached the hallway that led to the kitchen and the front foyer. People were lying on the floor everywhere. His stomach contracted to a tiny ball of ice. The world had turned dangerous and strange in a way he had never imagined in his worst nightmares.

Mike walked towards the front of the house, intending to find Lon. But when he reached the foyer, he looked outside and saw that the deck was empty. The ticket-taker booth was untenanted, and the long line of people to get in to the haunted house…was gone.

How long had he slept?

And why was he covered in blood?

Mike stepped back from the door and looked instead towards the *Texas Chainsaw Massacre* room. The walls seemed painted in blood. He walked inside and looked around. The 'cannibal' table had blood spatter everywhere. The tablecloth was drenched. The 'props' that Argento had made were no longer creepy unto themselves – their fake blood was dripping with the real thing.

He looked at the plank floor and saw the oblong hole that had been carved into the basement. Why had anyone cut a hole in the floor?

Mike shook his head and stepped back to the main hall. He had to find Katie, and he knew where she probably was. He headed back through the hallway of bodies towards the stairway down. While the sounds of Goblin and John Carpenter still echoed through the air from the various rooms, otherwise, the house was quiet.

He stepped down the stairs into the basement and found it equally deserted. But then, as he walked down the aisle towards the secret room, he realised that it wasn't completely empty. While there didn't seem to be any living patrons roaming the halls in search of a good scare, there did seem to be plenty of dead patrons.

Each of the display rooms that made up the basement Aisle of Atrocities was now filled with dead people.

Some were chainsawed and some were stabbed…but all of the bodies he saw appeared very dead, no matter what 'set' they were in.

Mike felt frightened beyond anything he had ever been. Something terrible had happened here tonight, while he had been asleep. But what? And why?

He reached into the recessed opening and pulled open the door to the room where Katie's bones lay.

And almost instantly, he heard the first voice to break the silence since he'd awoken.

"There you are," Katie said. "We've been waiting for you!"

CHAPTER FORTY-FOUR

She had escaped the psycho who had cut off Bong's arms and legs, managed to slip past the maniac with the chainsaw, build a bridge of human bodies to avoid being impaled and land bloody but basically unharmed on the ground just yards from the exit to this slaughterhouse.

And after all that, she was going to die anyway. It wasn't fair.

Those were Jeanie's first thoughts as she confronted the girl from the attic with the bloody knife.

She stood in a faceoff with the girl, who barely seemed there at all. The killer's eyes seemed to stare right through Jeanie. But Jeanie didn't trust that blankness; she'd seen the damage this monster had done with her knife. The evidence lay bleeding on every floor of this house.

Jeanie feinted to the right, and the knife followed her. The woman's body did not. Her feet stayed planted in place, blocking the aisle. Jeanie could turn and run back the way she'd come, but then she'd have the knife at her back. She needed more distance between her and the killer before she could chance turning around.

Jeanie edged a step backwards, and then another.

The girl with the knife stepped forward, maintaining the distance.

Fuck. What the hell was she going to do? She didn't have a weapon, and this girl was twice her size and held a knife that she clearly was not afraid to use.

She was going to have to turn and run and pray that she could put a couple steps between them before the killer reacted.

The knife suddenly raised in the air as the killer prepared to attack.

Jeanie steeled herself to go, when someone yelled from just around the corner.

"Stop!" a woman's voice cried.

The girl looked at the source of the voice, and as she did, Jeanie stepped backwards a step. And then another. And another.

"Leave her alone," a man's voice cried.

And then the killer took off and Jeanie seized the opportunity. She turned and ran.

Behind her, she heard the steps of the killer, and the voices of the couple. She couldn't pause to look back, but when she turned the corner she realised quickly that there were no longer any footsteps at her back. She slowed her pace enough to glance behind, but didn't stop.

She was no longer being followed at the moment.

And then the basement echoed with a scream.

Jeanie swore beneath her breath. She knew the knife meant for her had just found at least one of the people who had given her the opportunity to escape. And if the killer had taken care of those two, that knife would be coming for her again any second.

Jeanie rounded the corner to the left, and then stopped before the pathway turned left again. The stairway out of this hellhole was at the end of this corridor. But was the way clear?

She hugged the false wall of one of the exhibits and peered around the corner. Spotlights showed blue and red and green against the walls and floor, and a strobe flickered in one of the exhibits near the end of the corridor. There were a couple bodies lying on the floor but otherwise, nothing moved.

Jeanie took a breath and stepped around the corner. But just as she did, something crashed in the hallway she'd just left.

She ducked into the exhibit to the left to get out of sight.

It was supposed to be some kind of dungeon; there were chains hanging from all of the walls, and a woman was locked in a wooden rack. The device had never been functional; Jeanie knew, because she'd helped Argento assemble part of it.

But it looked impressive, with its big wooden wagon wheels and plank backing boards. And iron manacles.

Somebody had made it look more real than it was. There had been a bloody manikin chained to the device, but now there was a real woman there. Her wrists and ankles were pulled tight to the opposite ends of the rack, which made what had happened to her midsection more dramatic.

She was broken open like a piñata, her groin and ribs yanked far apart to allow her intestines to cascade like bloody vines over the edge of the wood.

Jeanie grimaced and looked away. She slipped behind the Iron Maiden that Lucio had designed in his garage and crouched down on the floor. She should be able to stay safely out of sight here for a while.

She could just see the corridor from there. Jeanie let out a breath and then forced herself to take in another, trying to still the pounding in her chest. In the distance, she thought she could still hear the sounds of talking, or sobbing. But it could have been part of the soundtrack too; the whole basement had distinct zones of eerie sounds and synthesised throbbing all designed to make the walk through its exhibits more intense.

Something dripped on Jeanie's head.

And again.

She reached up to wipe it and her fingers came away dark.

Jeanie looked up and saw the source. A man in ripped jeans hung from chains attached to the rafters. His shirt had been removed. His throat was a red circle of slashed flesh that had dripped and drooled in a dozen different rivers down the hair of his chest and belly. His face hung down, and she could see the sightless whites of his eyes in the dark.

Without thinking, she started to rise, to get away from the blood, but just as she did, she saw feet in the corridor.

Jeanie froze in a half crouch. She didn't dare breathe.

Another drop of blood hit her forehead, and ran down to her nose. She screwed up her face in disgust but still managed to hold her breath. She would *not* let the killer know she was here.

Drip.

The white soles of tennis shoes moved a step farther down the corridor. And then slowly, another.

Drip.

Jeanie was dying to wipe her face, but she didn't dare move a muscle.

The feet turned then, and began to slowly walk back the way they'd come. The way she had come.

Jeanie slowly took a breath, and let it out. And breathed again. She raised one hand in slow motion and brushed it across her forehead, nose and cheek to clear the blood away. She wiped it off on her jeans, which were already heavy with other people's blood. She refused to think about that, and forced herself to stay focused on the corridor.

Nothing moved.

Slowly she relaxed a little, and settled down to wait. The seconds passed like hours, and she forced herself to count to one hundred.

From somewhere in the distance, she heard voices.

She rose, and forced her feet to step past the Iron Maiden and rack to the edge of the exhibit.

Jeanie looked to the left and right, and saw only spotlights and dry-ice fog.

Now or never.

She stepped into the corridor and walked towards the exit, her feet moving faster and faster the closer she got to the stairs that led up and out of the back of the house.

Something was dripping all over her face now; she didn't want to know what. Jeanie wiped it off her cheeks with the back of her hand. The red arrow on the floor directed her out of the basement and through the red-painted door. The cement stairs beyond looked like a life raft.

Jeanie vaulted up them and emerged outside behind the haunted house, beneath the dark of the midnight sky. She hurried around the side of the house and saw the pathway to the turnpike. It was completely clear. There was nobody standing in line to get into the house.

Because they were all dead, she thought.

There was nobody at the ticket-taker booth. It was weirdly empty and quiet. She could hear the light breeze riffle the leaves that still clung to the oaks that barricaded the house.

The moon shone icy bright through the tips of the trees on the edge of the clearing nearby, and Jeanie wiped at her face once again, looking down to see water glistening on the back of her bloodstained hand.

The drips on her face were tears.

When she realised that she was crying, the tears only intensified. She started sobbing and couldn't contain the noises that came from her chest and throat.

Jeanie shook her head and began to run down the gravel path towards the deserted turnpike.

She was all alone.

CHAPTER FORTY-FIVE

Katie stood near the coffin that held her bones, though they were no longer simply bones. When Mike looked inside it, he saw Katie. Or her doppelganger. Katie's double lay silent and naked in the coffin; her body now appeared fully formed, from the small creamy nubs of her toes to the dark thatch of hair at her crotch to the soft, round breasts that he longed to suckle again. Only her face remained slightly incomplete; her lips still didn't quite connect right…there was too much scarlet at the edges; he could see the white of her teeth with the front of her lips closed. Emery held a knife in her hand; she raised it in the air as she began to walk towards Mike. He backed away.

"Don't worry," Katie said. "Emery won't hurt you, I promise you that."

"Yeah, okay maybe," he said. "But who *will* she hurt? This place is a slaughterhouse. What the hell happened while I was asleep?"

"Just what had to be," Katie said. "You want me to be alive again, right? In the flesh, so you can actually touch and feel me?"

"Yes, of course," Mike said.

"Well, that's what we've been working on," she said. "We've been doing what we need to do to make that happen. Because, I want to be with you finally, too."

"But why so much blood?" he said. His voice rose with incredulity and anger. He waved a hand towards the coffin. "When this all started, you said we wouldn't have to kill anyone. You just needed a little blood each night. I was okay with that," he said. "But not this. This place was supposed to be a fun haunted house, not a death trap."

"There was only one way for me to return," Katie said. "I'm sorry it had to be this way but…you want me to be with you again, right?"

Mike nodded. "But why," he said. "Why did all those people have to die?"

"Power," she said. "On the night of the becoming, I needed all of their energy."

Emery stepped towards him.

"Emery, give Mike the knife," Katie said.

Katie's quiet but very bloody accomplice lifted the blade, and offered it easily into Mike's hands. He took the weapon, but frowned.

"What am I supposed to do with this?" he asked.

Katie stood just in front of her coffin and bowed her head as she answered.

"I need you to kill her," she said. "Her blood will complete my return to life."

Katie reached out a hand to touch Emery's shoulder. Without protest, the girl knelt, and offered her chest for Mike to address. He made a face and looked back at Katie.

"What are you saying?" he said. "She's been your best friend!"

Katie nodded. "I love her, I do. But…a witch can have only one familiar. And Emery has been mine for more than fifty years. She began the process of my return…and now she must give the final energy to complete it."

"But what about *her*?" Mike asked, pointing at the chunky girl who knelt and stared at his feet without looking up. "Doesn't *she* deserve something for her service to you? Something more than death?"

Katie shook her head. "Yes," she said. "She deserves to finally be set free. It is time for a new person to join me. Emery has helped me for many years but…she's been with me since I died in 1963. It's because of her that I'm here today. But now… I need someone who understands the world today. Someone who can help me not only survive, but thrive. Someone who can be my lover, as well as my familiar."

Katie looked at Mike with eyes that sucked out his soul. "I need *you*."

CHAPTER FORTY-SIX

Jillie wiped the tears from her eyes and rose from the floor. She couldn't bear to look at Ted's body anymore. She couldn't imagine life without him near, but what made it worse was the guilt of his blood that was on her hands. His death was her fault. She should never have dragged him into this. Her throat was thick with grief but everywhere she turned her head, it got worse.

There were mutilated people everywhere. Men held the red ropes of their guts between their fingers with the mask of surprise and sudden, unexpected death painted on their faces. Women hung from rusty meat hooks from the low ceiling. Bodies lay in gory piles on the floor and bled out from where they were pinned to the walls by nails and stakes. Nearby in a tableau that looked like an old barn with bales of hay and a rustic horse stall, a teenage boy wearing a Camp Crystal Lake shirt was staked to the wall with the tines of an old pitchfork. The decapitated head of a girl lay on the floor just beyond his feet. The girl's body rested nearby on a bale of hay, her open throat still dripping a slow trickle of blood on the floor below.

"This has to stop," Jillie whispered.

She walked over the bloody floor to an exhibit meant to look like an old crypt. Maybe it was supposed to reference *The Mummy*, she wasn't sure. The false walls were painted to look like roughhewn stone 'bricks'. In the centre of the room, two stone sarcophagi sat with lids half removed. A hand gripped the edges of one, as if a figure were about to rise from the tomb.

On the floor between the stone coffins, a man lay with a long, silver blade jutting out of his middle. Jillie forced herself to walk over, grip the haft of the blade and…pull. She needed a weapon if she was going to track down the witch.

The blade slid out of the dead man easily, and she quickly turned away from the corpse.

The woman who had killed Ted had walked away from them towards the end of the basement, and that's the direction that Jillie headed. The haunted house theme music was still playing through speakers hidden in the ceiling, with groans and sighs and occasional screams adding tension to the already spooky rhythms. But above the soundtrack, she could hear voices.

Someone else was still alive down here.

Jillie moved towards the voices, passing body after broken body along the path. She stepped carefully, quietly. She couldn't tell where the voices were coming from; the Aisle of Atrocities hit a wall just a few yards away and nobody was alive in any of the macabre 'sets' on the right or left side of the walkway. But as she reached the end of the aisle, she saw an opening between the sets to a dark access corridor behind the fake walls of the horror 'exhibits'. And there was a crack of yellow light in the shape of a doorway just a few feet away.

So.

Jillie stepped over a dead girl and wound her way around a wooden post to emerge in the narrow corridor behind the sets.

"I never wanted anything like this," a man's voice was saying inside. He sounded upset.

"It's too late for that," another voice answered. A woman. The killer? Jillie wondered.

She took a deep breath and put her hand into the wooden inset that served as a handle for the door. The door opened inward as soon as she touched it. No turning back now.

Jillie stepped into a small room lit by a single bare bulb screwed into a fixture on the ceiling. On the right side of the room, an old coffin sat on the floor near the wall, its lid removed.

A beautiful young woman stood in front of it. She was slim with long dark hair that draped across her shoulders in easy curls. Her eyes were dark pools, her lips heavy and filled with a secret humour. Her hands were on her denim-hugged hips.

She was looking at another woman, a stocky girl with mouse-brown hair who knelt at the feet of a man. Jillie could only see the woman's back, but she could tell that her head was bowed down, as if awaiting execution.

Jillie wanted to rush forward instantly once she looked at the man. He was dressed in work boots, jeans, a t-shirt and a denim overshirt. All of his clothes, from bootlaces to collar, were spattered and dark with blood. There was a bloody handprint on his back.

The man held a knife. From his clothes, it was clear that he'd used the weapon, repeatedly. And from the stocky girl's position on her knees in front of him, he was about to use it again.

"You must," the pretty girl said. She was speaking to the man and didn't seem to have noticed Jillie's entry. "It's the only way. And the time is now."

"No!" Jillie ran forward, raising her own knife. She had to stop him. She aimed at the centre of the man's back and brought her arm down as hard as she could. But the man moved at the last second, twisting away as she brought the knife down. Instead of his back, she caught the side of his arm. He yelled as the knife bit through his shirt sleeve and carved a channel in his flesh. A fresh bloom of red joined the sodden cloth all around it.

The man grabbed at his wound and staggered to the left. The kneeling girl came to life then and grabbed at Jillie's legs. But Jillie turned and twisted, throwing herself away from the girl and towards the coffin.

"Get rid of her," the pretty girl commanded, and the other woman rose from the floor. When she turned, Jillie realised in a flash that this was, in fact, the woman who had killed Ted.

Jillie retreated until her back hit the edge of the coffin. The touch of the wood startled her. Jillie glanced behind her and saw the body lying between the short wooden walls of the old coffin. The first thing she noticed about the body was that it looked fresh. Not rotten like the wood it lay within. That and its nakedness. And then she recognised the face. It had the same high cheekbones, narrow nose and black hair as the woman standing just a few feet away. A dead twin.

Jillie looked away from the body and held the knife out in front of her, threatening the thickset woman who was coming at her with both hands outstretched. The other woman didn't move, but seemed to be in charge. She directed the man.

"Help Emery get rid of her. Hurry, it's time."

"Can we use *her* blood on the body to finish it?" the man asked. He walked towards Emery holding his wounded arm.

The pretty girl shook her head. "Emery's blood began to raise me. Only Emery's blood can complete the spell and bring me back in my new skin. The hour is now. The power is thick in the house at this moment but it'll quickly drain away. Hurry. I want to be reborn for you."

The woman stepped closer to the coffin and put her hands on the feet of the body within, gently touching the ankles and calves of her twin as if marvelling at their soft beauty.

It all hit Jillie in a flash. This woman was the witch of Bachelor's Grove. The girl who hundreds had reported walking half-dressed and chilled along the turnpike. The girl who consistently disappeared as soon as a driver picked her up and tried to take her home. The witch who had been trying to find a way back into the world for decades.

On a hunch, she took one hand off the knife. While she kept the blade trained on Emery to hold the woman at bay, with her other hand she grasped at the witch's arm.

Her fingers passed right through the woman's skin. As she'd expected.

"Your name is Katarina," Jillie said.

The girl looked up in surprise. And smiled. "Very good," she said. "Have we met?"

Jillie shook her head. "No," she said. "But I've felt your energy in this cemetery for years. And I've stood at your grave."

Katie nodded. "I see," she said. "Well, perhaps you can lie down in it. After tonight I won't be needing it anymore. Mike?"

The witch pointed at Jillie, and Mike began to walk forward with the knife in hand. Jillie did not understand exactly how Katie's body in the coffin had been reborn, but she understood that this night was all about reuniting the spirit of the witch with this flesh. The incarnation had not happened yet. But it was about to. And she knew how to stop that from happening.

Ghosts were fleeting, but flesh could be killed.

Jillie turned her back to Emery and raised the knife. She didn't know much, but she knew that whatever happened, she could not let the witch of a half century of legend return to the living. She brought the knife down.

Emery dove forward at the same moment.

Jillie's blade bit into something soft before lodging with a wrenching finality in bone. Blood sprayed, drops raining warm against her face. And then her arm yanked to the side, as the knife and the flesh it skewered moved.

The body she had stabbed was not the vacant vessel of the witch. The blade had stabbed deep into the chest of Emery. She had flung herself over Katie's unraised body at the last second.

The girl's eyes bugged out as she gasped and coughed while still trying to shield Katie's body from further attack.

The sudden cold bite of metal in her back took Jillie by surprise. It stabbed down from beneath her shoulder and in seconds she felt her chest fill with fire.

She cried out and struggled to turn as the man pulled a dripping knife out of her back. His face was twisted in anger and fear and horror and he screamed out a single word.

"Stop!"

Then he brought the blade down again. Jillie reached out with both hands, but the knife only sliced past them with an icy kiss that blossomed instantly into hideous fire. And then something hit her neck. Even as she felt her skin open, she heard the knife clatter to the floor and the man turned away to reach for Emery. He had abandoned his attack on her to lean over the coffin.

"How bad is it?" he asked.

"Bad enough," the witch answered.

Jillie felt the world ending. She opened her mouth to speak but only blood came out. Her legs suddenly gave out and she collapsed backwards to slam her head on the floor.

The last thing she saw was the witch's ghost climbing into the coffin.

CHAPTER FORTY-SEVEN

"Hold her over my body," Katie instructed. With one hand, the witch gently stroked Emery's forehead as Mike cradled the dying girl's upper body in his arms, supporting her spasming form a couple feet above the vessel below. The back of Emery's thighs rested against the coffin.

"You have always been mine," Katie whispered, her lips just inches from Emery's choking mouth. Blood oozed steadily from the place where the knife had been buried near Emery's collarbone.

"There are no words that I can say," Katie said, bending low to kiss the girl's crimson lips. Emery's eyes stared wide and fearful, looking back and forth between Katie and Mike as the end crept closer.

"It's been a long road to tonight and you always walked it bravely," Katie said. "Go now into the night and finally be free. Free of earth. Free of me and my demands. I'll always treasure you."

Tears streamed from the corners of Mike's eyes as he held the body aloft. He let the blood drip across Katie's body's face and neck and chest. He painted the waiting flesh with Emery's blood as Katie's ghost looked on and said nothing.

When Emery's eyes glazed over and her lips stopped gasping, Mike lifted her body up and away from Katie's flesh. He laid her down gently on the floor next to the coffin. Then he knelt next to her and with his finger, closed her vacant eyes.

Katie stripped off her ephemeral clothes, letting each article drop to the floor. As they hit the earth, they disappeared. Figments of truth, no longer needed. When she stood completely nude, Katie pulled herself up and over the walls of the coffin. With a faint smile, she turned to sit on the coffin's edge, and then laid her back down on the chest of the blood-smeared body within.

"What should I do?" Mike asked. Katie didn't respond. Instead, she closed her eyes and then seemed to...sink ...into the flesh beneath her.

For one strange second, there were two Katies visible. She looked like a double exposure, her two noses and chins at first an inch and then a centimetre apart.

And then there was only one.

A naked, bloody body that now displayed perfect butterfly lips.

As Mike watched, the tip of a moist pink tongue slid through those lips and licked the blood away.

Katie's eyes opened.

A smile crept across her lips and she turned her head to meet Mike's eyes.

"At last," she whispered.

She raised one arm and flexed her fingers above her face. Then she did the same with the other, her grin growing as she twisted her arms and fingers one by one. Then she put her arms back down and used them to push herself upright.

"Take off the locket," Katie said. Mike did, and set it into her outstretched hand. Katie dropped it into the coffin and then held that same hand out to Mike.

"Touch me," she said.

He took her hand, and she squeezed. "You can feel me, can't you?"

He nodded.

"And you're not wearing the locket," she said.

He nodded again.

"Because I'm real, not a ghost anymore," Katie said. "I'm alive again."

Mike shook his head.

"You don't know how long I've waited for this moment," she said. "All of the minutes and days and months and years stuck here in this house, doomed to wait and wait and wait until the time was right."

"All of the rumours were really true," Mike said. "You've been haunting this place all these years."

"I've been here," she said. "I've been waiting."

"And Emery?" Mike asked, pointing to the dead girl on the floor.

"She performed the ritual that started it all," Katie said. "After my husband killed me, she brought me back, using her own blood. At first, even she couldn't really see me. I screamed with all my might and she would squint, as if she maybe heard some faint sound in the distance. She didn't know that those sounds were me, trying to reach her. But she never gave up. She started performing other rituals. Blood rituals. And with every sacrifice, she gave me new energy. Made me stronger. Until she could actually see me and we could finally talk again."

"And your reward was to kill her," he said.

"That was always the price," Katie said. "She knew that on the very first night that she cut her wrist and dripped her blood on my corpse. She could shed the blood of others to give her spell more power – give me more power – but in the end, only the blood of she who woke me could fully raise me."

"Then why did it take so long for her to do it?"

"Because there was never enough blood," Katie said. She lifted one leg over the coffin and Mike reached out a hand instinctively, to help her step down to the floor.

"You know how many people had to bleed in order for my bones to grow their flesh back," she said. "Until you opened this house again, we saw one person in the cemetery every couple months. And almost none of them ever made their way into the house. There were never enough people to form a critical mass until you came. When I found out what you were doing, I knew that the time had finally come. I knew that you were here to save me."

Katie took Mike's face in her hands.

"Emery kept me from slipping away," Katie said. "But you made it possible for me to come back."

"Not just me," Mike whispered, pointing at the door that opened on the rest of the basement. "Dozens of people out there are dead."

"It takes an enormous amount of power to accomplish what we did tonight," Katie said. "But we can't look back now. The only way is forward."

Katie stared into Mike's eyes as she ran her fingers through the hair on the back of his head. "Will you move forward with me?"

Mike looked into her eyes and felt the power there. He tried to blot out the images of the blood in the hallways. He tried to forget the fact that two women lay dead on the floor on either side of them. He tried to remember sitting on the porch just a couple months ago in August with Katie, listening to her stories, living for the light lilt of her laughter.

"I want to," he said. "But I don't know."

"Come with me," she said, taking his hand.

Katie led him out of the basement and up the stairs to the main floor and then the attic. When he opened the trap door in the attic to finally descend into Emery's room, Katie reached up to the door in the ceiling and pulled a bolt shut. They were locked into the hidden room. There were still candles lit along the walls, just enough to allow Mike to see the nails of the bed and the naked woman who approached him now from the stairwell.

She moved like a ghost, gliding along the floor in her bare feet. But she was a ghost no longer. When her hands touched Mike's arms, she drew her hands up and under his sleeves, touching him and kneading his muscles with the tips of her fingers. Then she brought her hands down to his waist and drew them up under his shirt, ratcheting it up until he lifted his arms and allowed her to bring the blood-drenched, sticky cotton up and over his shoulders.

She threw the ruined shirt into the corner and then unbuckled his belt. As his jeans slipped down to the floor, Mike gasped.

"I don't know," he said. "I really don't know if I can do this now. After tonight...."

"I'm here," Katie whispered, her lips just centimetres from his. He could feel her breath. "I'll always be here for you," she said.

Then her mouth moved down his throat to his chest and belly and below.

Mike closed his eyes. And instantly he saw images of carnage. The reflections of the night had embedded themselves on the back of his eyes.

"I think...I think I'd like to go home for tonight," he said, despite the warmth that engulfed his erection.

Katie raised her head from his crotch and smiled sweetly. "This is your home now," she said.

Mike frowned. "No," he said. "I mean my real home. I could take you there. It has a real bed, with a real mattress."

Katie smiled thinly, but shook her head no.

"You can never go home again," she said. "Not after you killed all of these people. They'll be waiting for you."

"What are you talking about?" he said. "Emery killed those people, not me."

"You did your part," Katie said. "Emery used the knife, but you used the chainsaw."

Mike shook his head. "No," he said.

"Yes. While you were sleeping, your body let me in. And together, we cut through the hearts of dozens of people tonight. Your strength. My need. Together we swung the chainsaw back and forth and the people fell in pieces one after the other to the basement below."

"I don't believe it," Mike said, though, even as he said it, he could smell the ghost of engine oil in his nose and see the spray of blood as a whirring blade bit through tendons and muscle and bone. "And even if it was true, nobody would know it was me," he said. "Nobody is left alive!"

"There is one," Katie said. "She's probably reached the police by now. And even if she hasn't…your prints are all over that chainsaw. And you're the only other person running the house who isn't dead. But you're missing. Who do you think they'll blame?"

Mike felt his stomach and throat squeezing shut. "I have to go," he said. He pushed her aside and pulled up his jeans, fumbling to buckle them. He ignored the bloody shirt on the floor and headed straight towards the stairs back to the attic.

"If you leave me, they'll put you in jail for the rest of your life," she said. "Or give you the electric chair."

"Not if I get out of here now," he said. "I can wash my prints off the chainsaw, and go to the police myself."

"Too late," Katie said. She sat on the edge of the bed with her arms crossed. "Jeanie saw you doing it, and she's already gone for help. And who do you think they'll believe? A frightened girl who just escaped from a slaughterhouse…or the drunk that she says killed everyone?"

Mike hesitated. In the distance, a police siren began to whine.

"What do I do?" he whispered.

"You serve me," Katie said. "Just as Emery did."

She patted the bed beside her. "Come here. They won't find us here."

"I just want to go home," Mike whispered. Tears of frustration and fear rolled down his face.

Katie stood up and walked across the room. The red and white plastic cooler from Mike's truck was there. When she returned, she sat down again next to him and popped the tab on a Pabst Blue Ribbon and held it out to him. Cold drops slid down the can as a cocoon of foam arched out of the opening.

"Your home is with me now," she said. When he took the can and slugged back a long gulp, she brushed the hair away from his eyes. "Don't ever forget that."

When he finished the beer, she kissed the tears from his face, and pushed him down to the bed. Mike didn't protest too much. He really didn't know what to do at this point. He was overwhelmed. Lost.

And then her lips were on his, and his mouth filled with the heat and need of her tongue. For a few seconds, he forgot about the horror of the night and lost himself in the promise of her. The girl he had fallen in love with so many weeks ago. The girl who until tonight had seemed sweet and playful and innocent. The girl who had really been a ghost. The ghost of a witch who was anything but innocent.

He kissed her back with growing passion and then felt the wetness of her need upon him. And then he thought about nothing but filling her for what seemed like hours.

It wasn't hours.

But when he lay back, spent and gasping for breath, Katie rested herself half on, half off of him. She kissed him gently on the mouth and the cheek.

"Give me your hand," Katie said.

He didn't question her, but offered his left hand.

She took it and squeezed it in hers. "You are mine now," she said. "In heart and soul and body."

She lifted a knife in her free hand and he flinched.

But Katie only kissed him and lifted her hand from his clutch to the air above them. She pressed the blade into the centre and drew it down. A red mouth opened in her palm.

She took his hand next, and touched the blade to it.

"My blood in yours, and your blood in mine," she said. "Forever and always."

She said other things then, words he didn't recognise. But he didn't pull his hand away as the cold steel threatened his skin. "You won't ever leave me?" he whispered.

Katie shook her head. And then she drew the knife down until droplets of red splattered Mike's chest. She tossed the knife away and gripped his wounded hand with her own. Their fingers entwined and locked.

"My life is yours," she whispered.

"And mine is yours," he answered. It seemed like the right thing to say. For better or worse, it was true.

She smiled and pressed her body against his, holding their bleeding hands up above their heads. She kissed him deeply, and he responded. He realised that he was already 'ready' to consummate their new bond. And she didn't hesitate to guide him inside.

He was lost in the smell and heat and feeling of her when he realised that there were sirens now just outside. And the tread of boots and steps overhead.

Katie's eyes drew him in, and she nodded. She heard them. She kissed him and pulled him close. Mike accepted her embrace and didn't pull out from her until they were both nearly asleep.

Voices and radio calls and yells and commands echoed from the attic above and the main level below.

Mike only barely heard them. He pulled Katie close and the whole world simply went away.

They fell asleep in each other's arms, hidden in the secret heart of the house, as just a few yards away, police officers and ambulance drivers began to lift body after body onto stretchers to move them to the many trucks with flashing red and blue lights that gathered outside.

EPILOGUE

A pickup truck rolled past the ribbons of broken yellow police tape that still fluttered loosely in the faint winter breeze. The truck bounced down the ruts of the old gravel road that led from the Midlothian Turnpike around the small pond that bordered Bachelor's Grove Cemetery. Its tyres left darkened tracks in the hardened crust of snow that covered the ground in a blanket of white.

A pretty girl in an unseasonably short skirt and a half-buttoned yellow blouse stepped from the cab to the ground, her dark hair bouncing across her slim shoulders. Then the driver's door opened and a big man in a long black wool coat and blue jeans quickly got out to join her.

She took his hand in front of the truck and led him up the wood steps to the front door of the old grey house hidden deep in the shelter of the forest. A faint plume of smoke rose from the chimney on its roof above. When they stepped through the creaking door inside, the woman leaned up to kiss the man, and then drew him down the hall into the house towards the bedrooms.

When they reached the bathroom next to the master bedroom, she pulled him inside.

"I have a surprise for you," she promised.

But when the man stepped within the white-tiled room, the door behind him suddenly swung shut and an arm wrapped around his chest from behind. The steel of a cold blade slid firm against his neck.

The man struggled and kicked as the thick arm of the unseen man held him fast. But the knife only locked down harder, biting deep into his skin, and the man was forced to stop moving.

"You've been gone a while," the unseen man said from behind.

The girl shrugged. "Slow night. But I picked you up a twelve-pack of PBR. It's in the bed of the truck. Don't forget to get it out before you drive away the evidence."

"Small favours," he said, as the girl unbuttoned her shirt and then slid out of her skirt in front of them. Her bra quickly joined the clothes on the tile floor, and she scooped down her panties to step into a white porcelain tub.

"Brrrr!" she complained, as she sat down on its cold surface.

"This will make it better," said the man holding the knife. "Your weekly bath."

He pushed the man forward until they stood at the very edge of the tub, looking over the girl who lay within. The man gasped and renewed his efforts to punch and knee at his captor, but he couldn't seem to break free. Not with a knife at his neck anyway.

And then without ceremony, the knife wasn't simply *at* his neck...but *in* it. The blade dug across his throat and bit down hard. The captive man thrashed in desperation then, but couldn't escape the iron grasp of the other man. It was too late anyway even if he had; the knife sawed away at his soft flesh and in seconds his need to escape dissolved in a shower of blood. His life sprayed in a crimson mist across the tile, and the naked woman below closed her eyes and licked her lips as it rained down to cover her.

"Nothing takes away the chill of winter better than blood," she sighed.

The man holding the knife frowned but said nothing. Instead, he pulled the hair of the victim, yanking the head back to open the wound further. He aimed the open gash of the victim's throat carefully, working to ensure that every drop cascaded down the flawless white skin of the woman in the tub. Nothing wasted.

She reclined and arched her back, luxuriating in the warm spray of life that covered her. She may have returned from the dead, but she still needed the transfusion of life to keep her here.

*　　*　　*

Katie rubbed her hands across her belly and thighs and breasts, smearing herself in crimson.

A tear slid from the corner of Mike's eye as he drained the last weak spurts of blood from the man's dying heart, but he said nothing. He shook the tear away, and made sure that every last drop landed on Katie's thirsty flesh before he dragged the body back outside to add to the pile in the unmarked, hidden mass grave out back.